WHEREABOUTS UNKNOWN

A COLLEEN HAYES MYSTERY

MAX TOMLINSON

SENDERO
PRESS

Whereabouts Unknown is the prequel to the Colleen Hayes mysteries set in 1970s San Francisco. Published by Oceanview Press, the Colleen Hayes books, in order, are:

Vanishing in the Haight
Tie Die
Bad Scene
Line of Darkness
Night Candy

See Oceanview Press for more:
www.oceanviewpub.com/authors/max-tomlinson
Max Tomlinson's site: maxtomlinson.wordpress.com
Copyright: Max Tomlinson, 2024
Sendero Press
Republished 6/26/2024

All fights go to the ground.

CHAPTER 1

1977, *Santa Cruz, California*

"Remember what I said about this window, Justine."

Sitting in bed, five-year-old Justine watched her mother pull the yellowing blind down on the window facing the Bad Boys house next door.

"No peeking at the Bad Boys," Justine said.

"Correct." Mom came over to Justine's bed to sit next to her. She stroked Justine's hair. Most days, Mom looked like one of *Charlie's Angels*, with her thick brown hair cut just above her shoulders and her firm smile. But tonight, she looked tired. The green in her eyes was lost in the soft light seeping from the small bedside lamp. Daddy had been gone for a while.

"That's right," Mom said. "No peeking at the Bad Boys."

The Bad Boys were the motorcycle men who lived next door. Then there was the Bird Lady, who lived with them, with her long red hair and earrings, earrings that looked like silver birds. Justine worried about her. She wasn't safe.

"Mom?"

"Sweetie?"

"When is Daddy coming home?"

"I don't know, Juss." Mom pulled the covers up and gave Justine's forehead a kiss. "I don't know." Mom got up, went to the door, clicked the light off. "Sleep tight. Remember what I said."

"No peeking."

"Good girl." Mom left the door ajar.

Justine fell asleep and dreamt of water. Waves rose and fell with her breathing.

Until the motorcycles pulling into the driveway next door woke her up.

The engines shut down. There were two of them tonight.

Justine shivered, hearing the skinny one, the one they called the Spider. He had a face like a skeleton. Mom said he took stuff that made him look that way.

Then the front door next door squealed open, and Justine heard the Bird Lady come out on the porch.

"Did you guys take care of it?" she said in her late at night voice, slurry.

"Tomorrow," Spider said.

"What the hell happened?"

"None of your damn business, Eva," Spider said. "Now get back in the motherfucking house."

Mom said the Bird Lady was just a confused teenager, and that Eva wasn't even her real name, just a name she picked when she came to stay with the Bad Boys.

"I am not some animal you can keep in a damn cage!" the Bird Lady said to the Spider.

"Don't give me any lip, Eva."

More boots shuffled and Justine knew all three of them were in the driveway now: the Spider, the Bird Lady, and the big one, the one they called Fridge. Or was it Dredge? Justine could picture him standing there, by the stack of tires, watching while the Bird Lady staggered around, and the Spider clenched his fists. Justine could almost see the big one, Fridge or Dredge, the one Mom said had a problem, standing there in his leathers with his hands in his back pockets, like a big little boy, staring at the Bird Lady, his big ball of fuzzy hair blowing in the breeze.

Then he started talking, the big one, quietly, telling the Bird Lady to shush, and asking the Spider to calm down. Spider, he said, let's just go inside, get a beer, *man*. Leave Eva be. We're all wasted. *Man*.

Then the Spider told the big one to shut the fudge up unless he wanted to be a cripple. Then he yelled at the Bird Lady and Justine wondered if she better look out the window in case something might happen to her.

But Mom had told her *no*.

Justine remembered the first time she saw the Bird Lady, back when Daddy was still around: it was daytime, and the Bird Lady came over to Justine's window and said: *Aren't you just the cutest little thing?* Justine remembered her sad red smile and her bird earrings twinkling, catching the light through the trees on the street. Justine thought it meant she should fly away from here.

Then Justine could hear their boots clopping onto the creaky wood porch of the house next door.

"Inside, Eva," the Spider said.

The door screeched shut and their voices faded.

Justine felt a twist of relief. She hadn't gone near the window. And the Bird Lady seemed to be OK for now.

CHAPTER 2

Dredge thought Spider said they were going to buy the kilo from the Mexicans.

Not pull a fast one.

The rumble of Dredge's chopper echoed through the late-night valley as he steered his new '77 Electra Glide into the secluded lot overlooking the summit. The fog was rolling up from Santa Cruz, wafting across the ground like watery smoke.

The other Dead Boys were already there, in their denim and leathers, motorcycles parked in a sprawl. Spider was leaning on his oily bike, the Rat. His long greasy blond hair was tugged back behind his ears. He drank from a tall green can of Rainier Ale.

Dredge shut Pearl down, tilted her gently onto her stand. He climbed off carefully, a big awkward boy in studded leather, so as not to scratch the Fat Bob gas tank. Pearl was something, with her raked front end and chrome sissy bar. She should be. She cost him most of Gramma's inheritance. He pulled off his helmet. He was the only Dead Boy to wear one. A cold breeze blew through his hair, which was puffed up in an electric frizz ball.

"You're late," Spider said.

"Pana's crew aren't even here yet," Dredge said.

The other Dead Boys watched him silently: Sawney with his permanent leer, Beano with his vacant stare, Fritter, a curtain of hair around his bald pate. Drinking tall beers. Cigarettes glowed in the fog.

"We thought you might not show up, Dredgie," Spider said.

A rumble with the Mexicans was the last thing on Dredge's wish list. But Spider had the goods on him.

"Well, here I am, Spider," he said.

Beano, the English one—who claimed he used to be with Hell's Angels UK—made little squawking noises. The others snickered.

"You bring the money?" Spider said.

Dredge patted his back pocket.

Spider drank. "And how'd you leave Eva?"

"Asleep in front of *Don Kirshner's Rock Concert*. Alice Cooper was on. She was passed out."

"As long as she ain't going anywhere."

"She won't." Dredge wished Eva would. For her sake. He'd go with her. If she asked.

And pigs might fly.

It was cold in the night wind. He crossed his big arms and sat back on the saddle of his bike.

The growl of a V8 engine broke his thoughts. Car. Coming into the lot.

A '64 Impala low-rider, up high on raised shocks, navigating the uneven ground. Lights in the wheel wells, illuminating the thing like a spaceship in the darkness.

Three shadows in the car, along with the driver. Four guys total. Doo-wop playing on the 8-track. "Earth Angel." For some reason that spooked Dredge. More than he already was.

He turned to Spider. "I thought Pana wasn't bringing the whole crew."

"Wasn't supposed to," Spider said, drinking beer, his Adam's apple bouncing. "But it won't make any difference."

The car turned and bounced. With a release of air, it sunk down into the long, wet grass. The engine died but the headlights stayed, flickering through drizzle. The car door opened, and Pana stepped out, "Earth Angel" drifting out behind him. *Earth angel, earth angel.* Pana went and stood in front of a headlight, a small light-skinned cholo with a net over his sculpted hair. Wearing a tight white sleeveless T-shirt, even in the cold, his sinewed arms were muscled.

Three car lengths away he stood and faced Spider.

Spider said something to him in Spanish.

Pana returned a smirk, shrugged. Said something back to Spider, before switching to English. "They're just my homies, Spider. Along for the ride. You know? And I see you got all your boys here, too, huh?"

"Good thing," Spider said. "You remember to bring the methane?"

"'Course I brought your speed, man," Pana said. "I even gave you over a key, just to show no hard feelings. And you *did* remember to bring my bread, right?"

Spider drained his beer, crumpled the can, tossed it in the grass.

"Dredgie did," Spider said. "At least I *hope* he did. He does tend to miss things now and again."

"I hope he did, too." Pana said, eyeing Dredge. "Let's see the dough, Dredg-ee." He made the name sound a little musical—and a little bit comical.

Dredge stood up, dug the last of Gramma's inheritance out of the back pocket of his baggy leather pants. The wad had a thick rubber band around it. He held up the stack. Bills fluttered in the rising cold breeze.

From thirty feet away, Pana put his hand out lazily, fingers tickling the air like he might be scratching a dog's chin. "Bring it on over."

Dredge started to head over to Pana, but Spider's raised arm stopped him.

"I'll take it from here, Dredge."

Dredge found himself handing over the last of his money to Spider, before he realized how far this shit had gone. And in such a short period of time. Gramma would have had a few things to say.

Spider dropped the cash in the back pocket of his leathers. Then he spoke to Pana. "Let's see the mumpy."

"What the fuck, Spider?" Pana said, throwing another tight shrug. "Don't you trust me, bro?"

Pana and Spider stood still, staring at each other.

"All right, all right." Pana turned to the car, waved for someone to come on out.

The back door opened and a big fat *vato*, bigger than Dredge, got out, hard gut bulging in a red Santana T-shirt. Had a big plastic baggie full of something white in his hand. The crystal. It seemed to glow through the fog. He held the bag in front of him in both hands, like it was his lunch.

"See?" Pana said to Spider. "We're good to our word, bro."

But just as Pana was turning back around, Spider pushed himself off the Rat and took long strides across the grass. On the back of his motorcycle jacket the skull with the burning reefer in its teeth shimmered over the words DEAD BOYS SC. And just underneath that, sticking out of his leather waistband, Dredge saw the handle of Spider's Charter Arms Pit Bull. It didn't stay there long because Spider reached behind in one easy motion while he walked and drew the gun.

And stuck it in Pana's face.

Spider stood there with the gun and a grin while Pana babbled something frantic in Spanish.

But before he could finish, the Pit Bull went off. Point blank.

And then Pana wasn't saying anything.

Just lying flat on the ground now, one boot twitching in the head-lit grass. The echo of the shot thudded around the valley in the fog soup.

A car door squealed open.

Dredge flinched and ducked behind his bike. The other Dead Boys moved forward. Fritter had a sawed-off shotgun out.

Dredge's heart was pounding like a hammer about to break. He saw Spider, calm as could be, taking aim at a figure in the passenger seat as the figure started to duck down. Spider moved up to the front of the car, past Pana's dead body, to target the man trying to hide. The shot exploded and punched a hole in the windshield. Something dark splattered the inside of the glass.

The other rear door opened.

Fritter strode over, long blonde hair trailing off his bald crown, his shotgun up, as a Mexican guy climbed out, a pistol shaking in his hand.

"Drop the gun," Fritter barked.

The kid let the gun go, but when he saw the shotgun still on him, he screamed, turned, leaned into a run.

Fritter nailed him with the big bore, the kid's back arching. Then he fell like a bag of sand off a truck. More thunder bounced.

It was all over so fast.

The big *vato* with the baggie of meth was still standing by the other side of the Impala, mouth open.

Spider swung the Pit Bull on him.

The other Dead Boys stood silent.

To his credit, the big guy didn't run, didn't raise his arms.

"What you goin' do, now?" he said to Spider in a low voice.

"What's your name, hombre?"

"Felix."

"Well, Felix, what should I do? Bearing in mind that you motherfuckers are trying—well, *tried*—to take over my business. Tried to sell squawk to *me*, at more than the going rate?"

"Well..."

"*I* run this burg." Spider pounded his skinny chest once with the side of his fist. "The Dead Boys *own* Santa Cruz. Like a bitch."

The Dead Boys voiced their approval with hoots and cheers.

Felix held the bag up. "You want it? For free?"

"No, I want you to eat it."

"*Eat* it?"

Spider put his free hand up to his ear. "Is there an echo?"

"I can't eat a kilo of speed, man. No one can."

"See how far you can get," Spider said.

CHAPTER 3

"Prisoner Hayes?" the female Parole Hearing Examiner said, adjusting her black-rimmed glasses as she read from a document.

Colleen Hayes stood and said *Yes, Madam Board Member,* the way she had been instructed to. The woman she addressed was heavyset, sitting between two male Parole Board members at a Formica table in the front of the makeshift courtroom outside the Denver Women's Correctional Facility. The air conditioner couldn't keep up, the Colorado summer cooking the tar on the roof of the bungalow.

Colleen felt unnatural in the same form-fitting two-piece skirt suit she had worn at her sentencing nine years earlier and at every subsequent request for parole since. The outfit was woefully out of date for 1977 and had been let out to accommodate a slightly more muscular Colleen who had been working out in the weight-room since her incarceration. But it helped set the expectation of freedom compared to the baggy orange jumpsuit, white socks and flip flops she'd worn for most of the decade. Colleen had been a smaller woman to begin with. Now she was a hardened one. It was part of the process, a natural physical defense mechanism, but it was also an evolution of what she had done and what she had seen. Rachel, the guard Colleen had befriended, had cut Colleen's dark brown hair into a feather cut that was current. It also softened the face prison had given her, the creases that had been etched either side of her unyielding mouth.

The female board member eyed Colleen over the top of her glasses. "This is your ... fourth petition for parole?"

"Yes, ma'am." Colleen cleared her throat. The first request had come just shy of six years into her fourteen-year sentence, thirty-eight percent of her time served. The minimum. She hadn't been too surprised when that was turned down. But she thought she had a chance after that, even though her ex's family always protested an early release whenever Colleen came up for review. Colleen saw her ex-husband's brother now, a year on, a year heavier, a year angrier, sitting across the hearing room, wearing an alcoholic scowl. He wasn't allowed to speak, but he could be there. And he could file an objection. And he always did.

But eventually they would have to let her out.

She just hoped it was sooner rather than later. For Pamela's sake. Pamela, her daughter.

Pamela's time was running out, out in California. Hanging out with scum, taking drugs, whatever she was up to.

A male board member, with a glistening bald dome, was next to speak. "And why should we consider your request now, Hayes? You've barely served two-thirds of your sentence."

"I believe I'm ready for parole, sir," Colleen said, doing her best to keep her voice reasonable, calm.

He gave what might have been a smirk. "Really? You killed your husband. With a screwdriver."

"I did it to protect my daughter."

"You did it with intent."

Colleen looked down. It seemed things might go the way the other three requests had, despite the fact that there had been extenuating circumstances and she was due for automatic parole in another year anyway. But the governor could always overrule that. "I have a statement I'd like to read," she said. Her hands vibrated slightly as she held several sheets of well-marked, yellow-lined paper.

"Make it quick," the third board member said. His hair was blow-dried and touched a trendy, striped collar. He sported a wide paisley tie with a big loose knot. Colleen tried to size him up. Some guy who owned car dealerships and donated to the governor's campaign? He certainly didn't look simpatico. Parole board members could come from anywhere. Some had worked in law enforcement, but all were appointed to a four-year term, usually as a political favor. And many had opinions on women behind bars.

Colleen didn't need the paper statement for anything more than to keep her hands from visibly shaking; she knew the speech by heart. She had recited it silently in her bunk at nights, in front of the mirror, in front of Rachel, in the guard's office when the other guards were on rounds. Colleen spoke about her Bible study, her volunteer work with the other inmates, the associate degree in English earned while incarcerated. As she read, she heard someone cough and wondered if the board members were growing impatient. When she was finished, Colleen looked up at the three faces staring blankly at her. She could feel her ex-brother-in-law across the room, glaring. Her own face was warm. She hoped it didn't show.

"We'll take a five-minute recess," the female board member said. The fluorescent light flashed across her lenses as she rose, giving her an distant quality.

The three board members left the room.

If Colleen had to go another year without seeing Pamela, she would have to, of course, but she wasn't sure how. Her daughter was into her late teens and heading towards personal destruction in San Francisco, or thereabouts, if her last postcard was any indication. Always drawn to the dark side, dark people. Colleen braced herself as a familiar sadness began to take hold again. She remembered the magpie earrings she had given Pamela when she turned thirteen. Pamela's face had softened for the first time in a long time as she gazed at the silver birds in the palm of her hand.

But Colleen hadn't given any thought to how her eight-year-old daughter would fare when Colleen killed Pamela's father ten years back. Now she regretted that act every single day—for Pamela's sake more than anything.

The parole board was gone fourteen minutes. During that time, Colleen mapped out her next year inside Denver Women's Correctional Facility: how many classes were left to take, how many more uniforms could be stitched for the state's male prisoners, how many letters could be written to the State Parole Board.

But how much more time did Pamela have? Another year seemed generous. She was eighteen now. The last time Colleen had seen her, her daughter's long red hair hung lank and unwashed, and her eyes were puffy and red. Pam had lost a good fifteen pounds. She didn't have that many to lose.

The board members returned, the floor scraping as they took their chairs.

The light bounced off the woman member's glasses.

Colleen stood and took a breath.

"Your request for parole has been granted."

Colleen blinked in astonishment, and she felt herself sway. Excited chatter popped around the room. The case had been headlines in 1967. The blow-dried guy on the parole board asked for silence.

"This is all pending the governor's approval, of course," he said to Colleen. From his tone, it seemed that he might have struggled with the decision.

"Thank you," Colleen said in a voice that seemed to echo in her head. "You don't know what this means."

Almost a decade inside was coming to an end.

"I promise not to disappoint you." She felt like a fraud. Because if Pamela came to any harm, *someone* was going to regret it.

But a lie was small thing in the scheme of things.

"Be careful out there, Hayes," the female member said. "Things have changed since 1967."

Wasn't that the truth? When they put Colleen away, demonstrators were protesting the war in Viet Nam, hair was long, and love was free. But since then, the Day-Glo paint had peeled off the walls. The hippies were shooting speed. It was all going to hell.

Especially where Pamela was concerned.

So being careful was the least of Colleen's worries.

CHAPTER 4

DREDGE LAY on Gramma's bed, watching the picture of JFK vibrating in the moonlight. As the wall thumped with the rhythm of Spider and Eva going at it in the room next door. Dredge turned his eyes back up to the darkened ceiling, trying to make out the twisting shadows up there, trying not to listen. Curling around they were, the shapes, the speed in his brain turning them into laughing faces.

He'd been up since ... since the Mexicans. One day? Two? He wasn't sure now.

JFK rattled on the wall.

Sounded like Spider was passing a damn kidney stone.

At least he couldn't hear Eva respond to Spider's onslaught.

Eva couldn't be into it. Could she?

Maybe it was Dredge. Dredge not wanting Eva to give in to Spider. Wanting Eva to be more than just another cycle tramp.

Dredge threw off Gramma's orange chintz bedspread, rolled his sizable frame over, dug through the vinyl albums scattered sleeveless on the floor next to the bed. Picking one at random, he sat up, making the sagging bed creak as he flicked on the amplifier on the bay window ledge behind the bed. Red dials took form in the dark. He slapped the album on the turntable, lifted the tone arm, let it down with a little *vip* in between tracks. The record sounded crackly, like someone frying bacon.

Dredge sank back into Gramma's bed, his ravaged head screaming. Wished he had a joint to smoke, take the edge off all the speed.

And the dead men up at the summit.

A cow bell clanked out a lonely four-four intro, then a drum, then a guitar, sounding almost eastern.

The Chambers Brothers started singing about *time*.

The bed next door knocked against the wall.

Dredge reached over his head, found the volume knob, cranked it.

Time!

Then Gramma started hobbling around in Dredge's brain, giving him hell. *Those friends of yours. You weak fish. You let those animals in my house. You weak, weak fish ...*

God damn it, Gramma!

Dredge leapt out of bed, snapping an album with his big bare foot. Pulling on his baggy leather pants from a pile, he saw beer cans like mushrooms, growing while Gramma yammered, could see her in the shadows, bumbling around on her aluminum walker, accusing him of drinking and taking drugs again. Well, maybe he had.

Damn speed. He was seeing things, hearing things. Beer. He needed beer.

Lumbering like a frightened bear down the hall into the kitchen stacked with bags of trash needed taking out, Dredge shut the door, so he didn't have to listen to Spider anymore. Into the slimy fridge for a can of King Cobra. Then, sitting in the semi-darkness, staring at a cereal box on the counter, just able to make out Tony the Tiger in the kitchen night-light. Tony turned into the Maharishi. Then the Maharishi turned into Adolf, little mustache trembling, followed by the sounds of screaming Nazis wisping into Dredge's ears.

Come on, man, he said to no one.

The light hurt his eyes. Dredge got up, pulled the night-light from its socket, laid it ever so gently on the kitchen counter. Oh, his head. Popping the tab on the can, the beer fizz screamed at him.

What were normal people doing right now?

Gulp that beer.

That foxy mom chick next door, with her weird little kid, always staring out the window—what was Mom doing? Sleeping? Alone? Dredge drank stinky malt liquor and wondered how you landed one like Mom next door. Slim with a nice straight nose, and she could surely do better than that punk husband who took off on her and her kid. Maybe they were all like that, like Eva was with Spider, went for the guys that treated them like the bottom of a bird cage.

Half the beer gone, Dredge played with the hairs on his big belly in the dark.

Gramma came shambling back.

I found those magazines under your bed...

Gramma, kindly shut the fuck up. Please.

Don't you dare talk to me that way, you foul-mouthed, witless, witless little boy!

Gramma, how would you like that walker wrapped around your wrinkled pencil neck?

You're going straight to hell for what you did!

Yow!

Dredge found himself standing up all of a sudden, in the kitchen, howling in his mind at an old dead woman. His heart raced.

Gulp that beer.

Time for another. He got two cans out this time.

Another can open, hand to his head, and all he could hear down the hall was *bam-bam-bam*, the wall banging over the music.

Then silence, meaning just the Chambers Brothers.

Jesus Christ in a hammock.

Dredge sat back down with his beer.

Spider had Eva. Dredge had a stack of mags. Under *your* bed now, Gramma, by the way.

Halfway through another beer, sitting in the dark, Dredge heard Spider snoring. Like a vacuum cleaner sucking up a marble.

Then light footfalls in the hallway. Up to the kitchen door.

The door opened, the blackness breaking open with a rim of muted light.

And Dredge saw her standing there, in her skimpy black undies and sleeveless black T-shirt, little shoulder straps. Boots in one hand, jeans, studded leather jacket in the other. Her thin white body, nipples poking through.

Like a vision, she radiated.

"Eva," he said, his voice a little out of control now that he was using it for the first time in a long time and a lot of speed and other things had passed since then. "Have a beer with me?"

Eva put a finger up to her lips.

"Quiet, Dredgie," she whispered. "What're you doing up?"

"Couldn't sleep."

"Why so dark in here?"

"My eyes hurt."

Eva shut the door behind her quietly and Dredge could feel her presence in the black room, see her silhouette as she sat down on the dinette chair opposite. He could smell her as she lifted her derriere off the kitchen chair and pulled her snug jeans over the fine skinny butt. Smelled her sweet scent, a girl and a woman, strawberry, sex and whatever else. He tried not to smell what Spider might have done to her.

"Going somewhere, Eva? It's late."

"Shush," Eva said. "Yep, I'm getting out of here, Dredgie—once and for all."

Dredge took a gulp of brew. "Not this again."

"Yeah, I know. But this time, I mean it, Dredge. Really mean it."

"Spider's only gonna get pissed, he hears you."

"Spider's passed out." Eva pulled a boot on her bare foot, and he wished he was the zipper going up along her calf.

He thought about being younger, a kid, when it looked like his whole life was still ahead of him, even as fucked up as it was, living with Gramma, but he'd thought he was going to make it, despite everything. Back in the great never-never...

The beer can slid from his fingers and *panged* the floor. Beer sloshed him back awake.

"Dredge!" Eva whispered hoarsely. "Will you *puh*-lease be quiet?" Pulling her other boot on, zipping it, standing up, she put her arms in her leather jacket. With each movement, the vision of her came at him.

"You can't leave now, Eva," Dredge said, picking up the wet can, almost empty. "Wait until morning."

Down the hall in his room, the song ended.

And then there was silence, or something close. He could hear the wind blowing, up over the ridge to the golf course across the way.

"Did you hear something?" Eva whispered.

"Is Spider awake?"

Then they could hear Spider snoring again.

"Dredge, he told me about the Mexicans."

Funny but Dredge almost forgot about them. No, that wasn't true. He was just trying to blot them out. They were there, all the time, *all the time,* looking at him as their bodies rolled down the hill.

"Spider *told* you?" Somehow Dredge was standing up again, drinking an empty beer.

"He was bragging about it." Eva's silhouette shook its head. "What the hell happened? Spider used to be cool. Now look. I can't believe things got so bad so fast. It's the speed, Dredge. That shit is burning holes in all of you."

"I wasn't really part of it, Eva."

"So, you'd like to think. You were *there, hombre.* It's called *being an accessory.* And Spider's in your house. Shee-it, Dredgie. You're sleeping with the grim reaper. You need to get out of here, too."

"But it's my house."

"It's not like you can kick Spider's ass out."

They both knew how likely that was. Dredge ran his big hand through his wild frizzy hair.

"What do I fucking do, Eva? What do I do?"

"Go back to bed, Dredge. That way, when Spider wakes up, you never saw me leave." She kissed two fingers and pressed them to his lips. "Then, when you come down from the crank, get your butt out of here too. Do it."

"Yeah." Dredge sat down, head spinning. "Yeah."

Eva opened the door. The light from the hallway lit her up. Then she became a blur and was gone. He heard her pad down the hall. The front door opened, soft, then shut.

Something made Dredge's eyes wet.

He stood up, his head whirling; the booze, the crank, the misery, all of it.

"Wait, Eva. I'll come with you."

But the floor seemed to fall away, with nothing to support him. Dredge's sizable frame tumbled into a sack of empty cans. Clanging everywhere. Rolling in the darkness. The dead cholos were staring at him.

———

Dredge was dreaming of running through syrup when something cold and wet hit him in the face.

"Wake the fuck up," Spider said. "You almost let Eva walk off."

Cold and sticky. It was beer. Spider had thrown a damn beer on him. Dredge rolled in the clutter of cans.

"How long have I been passed out?" he said.

"About thirty seconds," Eva said through her teeth.

She was standing next to Spider, Spider in just his leather pants, thin and spindly feet sticking out. His toenails looked like talons.

Dredge sat up, the liquor and speed rushing up to his skull like a bullet headed to his brain. He must've crashed, literally, woke Spider up. "Yeah, I know," Dredge said, stabbing his eyes to focus, climbing up off the floor with effort.

"What do you mean: *Yeah, you know*?" Spider

squinted. "You mean you were just going to let Eva walk the fuck out of here?"

"No..." Dredge rubbed the back of his aching head. "We were going down to the liquor store. I was just getting the car keys. I guess I fell. I'm a little tired. Sorry, Eva," he said.

"You're sorry all right, Dredge," she said.

"Dredge," Spider said. "You watch Eva. I mean *watch*."

Spider turned, stormed off toward the garage, out the kitchen door. The door slammed.

"Eva—you OK?"

"Bathroom," Eva said. "I think I'm gonna be sick."

Dredge led Eva down the hall to the bathroom. He stood by the open door while she splashed some water on her face, stumbled to the toilet, peeling her jeans down her thighs. She sat down on the pot, looking defeated.

"Dredge, do you mind closing the damn door while I pee?"

"Sorry," Dredge whispered. "You know how Spider gets."

"Yeah," Eva said. "I know how he gets." She raised her eyebrows. "Door?"

Dredge pulled the bathroom door shut, stepped back. Half a minute later, Spider came in the kitchen door with a lit cigarette in the corner of his mouth and a two-foot length of chain, the one he locked the Rat up with, and a pair of handcuffs.

"Where's Eva?" Spider said.

"Taking a whiz."

Spider's washed-out eyes turned indigo. "Say what?"

A squeal came from the bathroom.

"She's climbing out the damn window!" Spider dropped the cuffs, snapped the length of chain, turned, headed for the front door, presumably to cut Eva off.

Dredge followed, his head bursting with every step.

Then the front door was open, Spider outside, saying: "Hey, Eva. Where do you think you're going? Come on back."

"Fat chance, Spider," Eva said, walking away in brisk strides. "I hope you like getting your ass reamed in Soledad." She picked up her heels and took off.

"Eva!" Spider growled. "Get back here!"

Justine was asleep when the voice came, like an animal crying. In her mind she could see the Bird Lady's hair, stringy and wet, hanging around her face.

Then the Bird Lady screamed, and Justine was awake, heart pumping.

"You get your bastard hands off me, Spider!"

Bodies slammed into metal—the hood of the old dead lady's station wagon next door.

Justine was already at her bedroom window, finger in the ring hook of the blind, sliding it up just above the window frame. She pressed her chin onto the sill where she hoped the Bad Boys wouldn't see her. Shivering in her blue flannel nightgown, she crossed one big toe over the other, staring.

There was the Bird Lady in her tight jeans and high boots, bent back over the hood. The Spider held her down with something around her throat. A chain. He didn't have a shirt on, and his body was white where it wasn't tattoos. Holding the Bird Lady down with the chain, he puffed on a cigarette in his mouth.

By the doorway, in a hint of streetlight, was the big one, Fridge, the one Mom said had a problem.

"Hey Spider," he said. "Go easy on Eva, man."

The Spider had the Bird Lady pinned down. "You want to leave now, Eva?"

"No, Spider," the Bird Lady croaked.

Justine stood paralyzed at the window. The big one, who used to live in the house with his grandma until she went to heaven and the Bad Boys moved in with him, stood there next to the stack of tires, his hands in the back pockets of his baggy leather pants, watching the Bird Lady on the hood, her legs flailing. Just watching. He wasn't doing anything.

The Spider pulled the chain tighter. The Bird Lady flapped her arms.

The big one came out of the shadows. "Hey Spider, man, now come on." And: "Spider—ease up—please." He touched the Spider's shoulder. "Hey, come on, man. We're all a little wasted. Eva didn't mean a thing. Did you, Eva?"

Her neck free, the Bird Lady gurgled. Her heels scraped the car grill as she slid off the hood and landed on her butt in the gravel. "I didn't, Spider."

The muscles in the Spider's upper arms relaxed as he let the chain go slack by his side. He even smiled if you could call it a smile. He looked like a skull grinning.

"Hey, I know you didn't, Eva."

The big one had his hands in his back pockets again. Justine could see him biting his lip.

The Spider said to the Bird Lady, "No more talking the Mexicans, Eva. Got that?"

The Bird Lady climbed to her feet, shaking her head up and down, but she was having problems talking.

"You got it, Spider," she squawked, holding her throat.

"Now that's more like it," the Spider said.

"Now what say we all go inside, get ourselves a can of

something cold?" the big one said. "Now how does that sound?"

And then, all of a sudden, Justine felt eyes upon her. The Spider was looking straight at her.

Taking the cigarette out of his mouth, he tossed it in the gravel. "What the hell," he muttered.

Justine's feet wanted to move but they were nailed down in his stare.

Then the Bird Lady said to her, "Will you please just get away from that window, sweetheart?"

Justine's feet reacted. She spun, was off, until she literally ran into the bedroom door and slammed it shut by accident. Her hands were shaking as she tried to pull it open. She heard the Bird Lady calling the Spider a bad name. Then the Bad Boys crunched back into their house. Finally Justine fumbled the door open.

And plowed into a pair of long bare legs in the doorway. Thigh level was Mom's shortie nightie and up there was Mom. Mom's hair was tousled from sleep. Justine felt sick to her stomach as she pushed herself against Mom's legs.

Mom broke away and stormed over to the window as she fastened her robe. She pulled the blind down so hard it tore. She whirled back around.

"*What* did I say about this window?"

Tears ran down Justine's face. "He was hurting her, Mom. He had a chain."

Mom came over. Justine thought Mom was going to be angry, but she just placed her hand on top of Justine's head. "Did they say anything to you, Juss?"

"No. Are you going to call the police?"

There was a long silence.

"In the morning." Mom stroked the top of her head. It felt comforting. "In the meantime, this room is off-limits.

You and I are going to be roommates. Come on." Mom led her to her bedroom where they climbed into the warmth of Mom's bed and cuddled. Justine buried her head under the pillow.

Justine didn't understand. Mom went to college but mumbled in her sleep and ran to the phone whenever it rang. Justine clung to her, but she still saw the Spider, staring at the window.

CHAPTER 5

THROUGH THE WINDOW of the Greyhound pulling into San Francisco, Colleen watched the indigent shuffle along Mission Street. This was the combat zone.

California wine country.

Not the wine country in Northern California, where they'd give you a little glass to try, but a different kind, where the bottles had twist-off caps and were kept cold in dairy cases in corner stores. Where people drank it from a bag.

One man dragged himself along the street, the sun bright this morning, showing San Francisco for all it wasn't—the kind of place you came to with flowers in your hair.

The Greyhound nosed into the terminal on Seventh, the driver stomping the brakes at a docking bay, throwing those passengers who had stood up around. Colleen waited, stole one more glance at the pictures she'd had in her hand since Oakland.

Pictures were said to be worth a thousand words but the first one left as many unsaid: a postcard from Pamela, her one and only, dated last December, addressed to her at the

Denver Women's Correctional Facility. On one side was a black warehouse bar called The Hornet Lounge; the other side was slanted with Pam's black scrawl:

I've made so many mistakes in so few years. I've used up my quota. I've found an answer to my problems. One that is final. Please understand.

She hoped Colleen would understand.

Colleen took a breath and found herself holding it in. Every time she read those words, they never failed to deliver a chill. What if she was too late? Suicide was painless, the song went, but not for those who were left behind.

The other picture was of Pamela Hayes herself, and it was one Colleen had to hold at an angle, adjusting it over the one in her memories. In her mind Pamela was still pretty, sassy, full of spirit, wearing the silver magpie earrings Colleen'd given her for her thirteenth birthday when she visited her in prison with her grandma. In the photo, however, taken last year, Pamela was a bitter seventeen-year-old, slit-eyed, looking past the camera, hair flat and matted, dyed black as coal, with that hard look Colleen had seen on faces inside Dever Correctional.

She wondered what Pam looked like now.

But at least in the photo she was still wearing the bird earrings.

Paroled, Colleen had gone to her mother's—Pam's grandma—in Denver. Contacted Missing Persons when she learned Pamela hadn't been heard from in months. Called the FBI. But Pam had just turned eighteen—a free woman. There was only so much they could do.

So, Colleen watched it snow while her mother drank 7 and 7 in the other room, the TV braying, and said between drinks that Pam'd have to make her own mistakes. That was just the way it was.

Going to prison was Colleen's doing. Pam wasn't going to pay for it.

Her mother watched Colleen pack her bag, with a freshened-up drink in her hand.

In SF now, on Seventh Street, the last of the herd pushed their way off the Greyhound. Colleen put her postcard and photo away, stood up and hefted her seabag from the overhead rack. She wondered if Pam still had the earrings.

▭

After checking into a flop hotel south of Market, Colleen headed out to find any trace of Pam. Down by Third Street, drab and industrial, she could hear The Hornet Lounge before she saw it. A live band was speeding through a number with guitars that could cut glass. Music had gotten harder, edgier.

Outside an old warehouse painted matte-black sat a string of bikes, well-bred to greasy, all lined up like big toys. Off to one side, a couple of characters in black leather were making some sort of deal. They eyed Colleen as she pushed open one of the bar's windowless doors and went in.

The band was on the attack with an ear-piercing thrash. The singer, a young woman with a bright orange crewcut, snarled into the mike. The guitarists stood in a low-slung, spread-legged stance, grinding out chords in front of a bunch of leather kids jumping up and down and bashing into each other.

It took Colleen's eyes and ears a moment to adjust. The bar was dark. The rest of the clientele were the denim-and-leather crowd, with an assortment of headbands and tattoos. There were women, one a rough and weathered biker mama, with a bleached-blonde beehive and satin hot pants tipping cigarette ash into an empty beer bottle. Colleen fit right in with her bomber jacket, worn jeans and two-day bus sheen.

The band finished their song, slamming it into a brick wall.

Colleen ordered her first beer in nine years while her ears settled, drank it straight from the bottle. Gassy and weak, it didn't taste the way she remembered and she realized she had outgrown something. When she showed the ponytailed barman Pam's photo, the man shook his head and went back to serving other customers.

Colleen showed the photo to anyone who would look at it. To no avail.

She asked for the manager. He wasn't there.

The band came back on stage, picked up their instruments. Pounded into a fresh assault.

Colleen left her half-finished beer on the bar and went back to her hotel.

But she came back the next night. She had nothing else to go on. There *had* to be some kind of a connection here. Pam had sent that postcard.

Colleen ordered another fizzy beer, sat on a stool, waited. Listened to a band playing what they called Punk, noisy music for angry kids with spiky hair.

A skinny guy with a bushy Turk mustache appeared next to her. He was a human rail, forty going on sixty, the years hard lived. His dark hair was touched with gray, slicked back, thinning and he sported not just one earring, which she had seen on men in Denver the other day, but three, all on one lobe, in a row. He wore black leather and looked sick, like he might be on something.

"I heard you're looking for Pamela Hayes," he said.

Colleen felt a flash of optimism. "Do you *know* Pamela? Any idea where she might be?"

"I was going to ask *you*." He laughed sarcastically. "She owes me three hundred bucks."

Colleen felt a stab of encouragement. "Help me find her and I'll see what I can do."

"Right." He shook his head, turned to the barman. "Hey, Gus—who do you have to suck to get a drink around here?"

The barman with the ponytail came over, leaned on his hands.

"The fuck you think you're doing, Leon, coming in here again?"

"Still trying to get my last check. Where's Maurice?"

"Take a word of advice, man—get out of here before he sees you."

"I need that check."

Gus gave a hard sigh. "You really want me to get him?"

"Yeah, I really do."

Gus nodded once, went to the cash register, picked up a phone.

"You used to work here?" Colleen said.

"Sad, isn't it?"

"With Pamela?"

"That's not what she called herself when she worked here."

"No? What *did* she call herself?"

"Eva."

Eva? "Why *Eva?*"

"It's a long story."

"I got time."

"Well, I don't. I need my check."

"Why won't this guy pay you?"

"Ask Eva. *Pam*. Whatever you call her. She disappeared —along with the bar's take for the shift, not to mention my three bills. That's why Maurice won't pay me. Fucking fired me on top of it. Because I got her the job. Like it was my damn fault some teenybopper ripped him off. Hey, she ripped me off too."

Colleen took a sip of beer, shook off the thought that her daughter was apparently a thief. Her mother was a murderer. Pam was still her daughter. "Maybe I can help you get your check."

Leon gave Colleen the once-over. "I hate to be the one to tell you this, but how big are you: five-six? Hundred and twenty pounds? Have you *seen* the people who work for Maurice?"

"Maybe I'm the power-packed concentrate."

"I'll give you that." Leon nodded. "I've seen more fat on a greasy potato chip. You work out."

"Now and then." Colleen shrugged. "So, it's a deal? I help you get your check, you help me find Pam?"

"You don't know what the hell you're talking about. But go for it." Leon turned back to the bar.

The back door flew open, and a thickset man stormed in, wearing a red polyester lounge suit and white shoes with gold buckles. He had Vegas-phase Elvis hair and sideburns. He was followed by a young muscle-builder with a crewcut wearing a tight yellow smiley-face T-shirt.

The man in the red suit saw Leon.

"You," he said in a raspy voice. "Out."

"I have just one question, Maurice: Where's my fucking check?"

"Up your ass, sweetheart. I hear there's plenty of room."

Half a dozen regulars thought that was funny.

Leon glowered. "You really want me to call the drug squad?"

"That's it," Maurice said, thundering over. "Get him, Jimmy."

The crewcut kid nodded and came over, flexing his fists.

"I think you best watch out, Leon," Colleen said, then drained her beer. She felt her muscles tensing up.

The kid grabbed Leon by the collar of his leather jacket, hauled him off his stool, and tossed him toward the door. Leon flew like a stringless puppet and did an involuntary somersault. The kid followed, aimed a kick at Leon's ribs. There was an audible crunch, Leon howled, all of which seemed to hold the bar's attention.

Without thinking, Colleen flipped the longneck bottle, caught it by the neck, smacked the butt off on the bar rail with a tinkle of glass. She held the jagged weapon down by her side. In her mind she saw her ex looking at her with a screwdriver sticking out of his neck. Everything seemed to go back to that day. Her vision began to shimmer at the edges.

"You want your money, fag?" Maurice said. "I'll give you your money. Hold him down, Jimmy." Leon tried to coil up but was pinned down under Jimmy's shoe.

Colleen jumped behind Maurice, who was swinging his leg back for a kick, and grabbed his hair. Maurice shouted in surprise as she shoved the broken bottle directly under his chin, jabbing a spike of green glass into soft flesh. She yanked his head back, pressed the broken tip into skin. A glob of blood collected around the tine of glass. Maurice winced.

"Tell Jimmy to back off," she growled. "Now."

There was a pause while silence seeped in around the bar.

"Let him go, Jimmy," Maurice said between his teeth.

Jimmy removed his foot from Leon's chest, stood back. Moaning, Leon climbed to his feet. Out of the corner of her eye Colleen saw him listing to one side, holding his ribs.

"How much do they owe you?" Colleen said to Leon, holding Maurice's head tight, the glass blade steady.

"Two hundred, eighty-seven dollars."

"Pay him," Colleen said.

Maurice blinked. "Pay him, Gus."

The ding of the cash register was followed by the shuffling of bills in the otherwise silent bar. A slap hit the counter.

"Money's on the counter," Gus said.

"Get your money, Leon." Colleen kept the green spike firmly in place while Leon scrambled around her, crablike. "Make sure it's all there." She could hear him leafing through the bills.

"It's here," Leon said.

"Now get out of here." Colleen continued to hold Maurice's head up as he gave her the red stare. Leon walked around them in an arc.

"What about you?" Leon said to Colleen.

"Just leave." Jimmy was hovering on the periphery of her vision.

Leon left. The door swung shut behind him.

"Who the fuck do you think you are?" Maurice said to Colleen. He was doing a pretty good job of staying cool despite the broken bottle under his chin.

"Pamela Hayes's mother," she said. "They called her Eva. Where is she?"

"If I knew that, I'd go get the money back she stole from me. Now take that fucking thing away from my face. I did what you asked."

Colleen released the pressure of the bottle and let go of Maurice's hair. She stood back, realizing how she had lost it without realizing. She was on parole. She needed to remember that.

The clientele and barman watched her warily. The only good thing was that people in a bar like this were probably the last people to call the police.

"You and me, babe," Maurice said, shaking himself loose, then wiping the blood away, examining the smear of it on his hand before looking back at her. "We're going to tussle."

"Especially if you had something to do with my daughter getting into trouble." Colleen backed away to the double doors.

"Back there you called her *Eva*," Colleen said, steadying Leon as he hunched over outside the bar, clutching his ribs. "You said it was a name she used."

"*Eva Braun*," Leon gasped. "Christ, but that hurts."

"*Eva Braun?* Are you serious?"

"It's a punk thing," Leon said, trying to straighten up.

"I don't get it."

"Some thing from England," Leon said. "Johnny Rotten. Sex Pistols. Sid Vicious?"

"I've been away," Colleen said. "Why on earth would you lend a teenage girl who calls herself *Eva Braun* three hundred bucks?"

"She lived in my building at the time. Over on Divisadero. Said she wanted to get straight." Colleen guided Leon past an Indian motorcycle. "Ryan, my partner, died and Eva—well, she helped me look after him. She didn't have opinions about Ryan and me."

"Thanks," Colleen said as they stumbled along. "I needed to hear something good about her." She turned to see if anyone was following. She saw Jimmy, standing outside the black doors to the bar, hands on his hips, watching them in his Smiley face T-shirt. "What was Pam into? Smoking dope? Pills?"

"Things have gotten a teensy bit heavier since you *went away*. Where were you anyhow?" He gave her a squint. "Prison?"

"Is it that obvious?"

"Kind of. What did you do?"

"Pam never told you?"

"There was a lot she never talked about."

"I killed him," Colleen said. "Her father."

Leon nodded, as if taking it in. "When?"

She felt a need to talk about it, get it out. "Almost ten years ago now."

"Did you mean to?"

Colleen mulled that over for about the millionth time. "I did at the time."

Leon grimaced. "Where?"

Colleen was cast back, one more time, to that day when she'd come home from work, found Roger in the kitchen, cooking eggs, shirttails out. He'd been working on the faucet. His bucket of tools were on the linoleum floor. The shit-eating grin on his face told her something was up. She heard Pam upstairs, weeping, very softly. Colleen went up, found Pam sitting on her bedroom floor, hugging her knees, rocking back and forth. One knee was scabbed; Pam was at that age when one of them always seemed to be, but she'd been picking at this one and it was bleeding. The crust glistened. Pam looked up at Colleen like a frightened puppy— like what had happened might have been her own fault.

Colleen went back downstairs. Roger was shaking salt on his eggs, too much salt—pretending to focus on it.

She said to Leon now, not quite realizing she was actually speaking out loud, "I saw the tool bucket on the floor, the yellow screwdriver handle poking out—one of those new Posidriv ones?—with the cross-tip so the screw doesn't come loose from the head? It was poking out, waiting to be grabbed. Just waiting."

And then, somehow, the screwdriver was in her fist. She could feel the groove of the handle in her palm. Things started to flicker.

Then the screwdriver was sticking out of his neck.

Roger fell to the floor clutching his neck. After he stopped moving, she turned the flame off under the pan. There was blood in the eggs. "It was bubbling. I remember the smell."

There was a long pause. A boat horn blasted out on the bay.

"Jesus Christ," Leon said.

"Second-degree murder but it got kicked down to manslaughter."

"How much time did you do?"

"Nine years out of fourteen." Colleen lowered her voice. "I just got out. So Pam never told you."

Leon shook his head.

"She was ashamed of both of us," Colleen said. "Her father *and* me. Even worse? Stuck with her drunken grandma all those years, and me locked up."

Leon gave Colleen a wary glance. "Kind of like that bottle thing in the bar back there."

Leon had a point. But Pam came first, just like she did all those years ago. "You got your money back, didn't you? And now I need to find Pam. I'm hoping you can help."

They got to an old beater car, a white '65 Cutlass Supreme full of dents. A rusted gash lined the rear window. Leon dug out keys. "You drive."

Colleen led him around to the passenger side, helped him in. "We need to get you to a hospital."

"With what? I got no medical insurance."

"We'll figure something out."

"I can tell you where she used to live," Leon said.

"That's a start."

There was a pause.

"Eva was into speed," he said. "She picked up habits from a biker. Some guy by the name of Spider."

"Spider?" Colleen went back around to the driver's side of the car, got in, adjusted the rearview mirror. "Sounds like another punk thing."

"He's the leader of the Dead Boys. A Santa Cruz biker gang."

"Where can I find this Spider?"

"It's not going to do you any good."

"I'm guessing you've never been a parent," Colleen said.

"And you have? With your penchant for screwdrivers and broken bottles?"

"Is there a connection between Spider and Maurice?"

Leon winced as he shifted in the passenger seat. "Maurice owns three bars: one up here, in SF, which you now know about, and a couple down the coast, one in East Palo Alto, one more in Santa Cruz. He's got the white triangle sewn up."

"White triangle?"

"Speed—the kind you snort, smoke or shoot. Meth. Chemistry students at UC cook it up and the Dead Boys deal it. For Maurice. People can age thirty years in a few months."

"And you've seen Pam—Eva—use that garbage?"

Leon gave a sad nod.

Colleen started up the V8. The muffler had a hole in it. It sounded like a train.

They lurched out into traffic.

"You don't know what you're getting yourself into," Leon said.

CHAPTER 6

IGGY & The Stooges were blasting out of Gramma's Sears Silverstone hi-fi when the Santa Cruz black-and-white pulled up outside Dredge's house. Dredge was peering through the lace curtain of the peek-a-boo window. His heart rate shot up. Higher than it already was.

"Spider!" he yelled over Iggy growling that he wanted to be someone's dog. "Police!"

Spider, boots splayed out on the coffee table full of beer cans, barely opened his swollen eyes. He rubbed his scrawny face. "What fucking time is it?"

Heart palpitating, Dredge hopped over to the stereo, dialed it down. The TV was on, silent, dancers in platform heels and flares discoing away on *Soul Train*.

"Spider," he gasped. "Didn't you hear what I said? The cops are here." He looked over at Eva, sulking in the La-Z-Boy chair. She was reading a paperback, her bare feet pulled up under her tight cutoffs. Even with the cops outside, Dredge noticed that. If the world was coming to an end, he'd notice Eva.

And he'd worry about her too.

"Nice going, Eva," Spider said. "This is all because of last night."

Eva didn't look up from her book as she brushed a long strand of red hair out of her face. "Then maybe you shouldn't chase people around with your little chain." She turned a page. "And frighten little kids. Asswipe."

Spider gave Dredge a *what-the-fuck* shrug.

"Forget that," Dredge said in a shaky voice. "What about the pigs?"

"Stay calm," Spider said. There was loose skunkweed on the Stooges album cover, next to a baggie of same, a pack of rolling papers, not to mention healthy dustings of crank, a cut straw, and a bag of white powder from the other night's melee. "Stash the dope," he said to Dredge. "They need a warrant to search the place. Hey Eva, help clean up here."

"Clean it up yourself, douchebag."

Dredge grabbed the baggies, hightailed it out to the kitchen, skidded across the floor littered with cans from last night's tumble, and on out the back door to the garage where he stashed the weed and crystal in his toolbox. Locking up the garage, Dredge craned his neck around the corner of the house, peering at the black-and-white chugging away behind Gramma's Country Squire in the driveway. Then back into the house, scanning the kitchen for roaches, a set of works, anything bustable.

Gramma would turn in her granny grave if she could see what he had let the house become.

At the entrance to the living room, Dredge stood in front of the hall closet. The faint crackle of a police radio drifted in from out front.

Spider was sitting on the ratty green sofa, watching the silent dancers coming down the line in pairs. Drinking from a green can of beer.

Then Dredge realized.

"Spider—where's Eva?"

"Where she won't get us busted."

A muffled groan came from the closet in the hall just off the living room.

Dredge hoisted up his leather pants. "I hope that isn't what I think it is, Spider."

"Will you calm the fuck down?" Silent TV flashes ran across Spider's bony face. "You stash everything?"

"I think so."

Spider took a slug from the can. "They'll ask some questions about Eva, then leave. Anything else, they need a warrant. Ten to one they ain't got one. Not this soon."

Dredge heard the closet moan again. "You could have at least put Eva in the bedroom."

Spider stared at the TV. "You ever notice how it's always white chicks dancing with Black dudes and never the other way round?" He blipped the big remote, changing channels.

Bam-bam-bam.

Thumping from the closet door, Eva kicking it.

Outside, the engine shut off. Car doors slammed. Dredge's heart pounded. He lumbered over to the side window, gazed through the dirty lace curtain Gramma had put up when he was a kid. Two uniforms, one short and wide, the other tall and slender.

"Two of 'em, Spider."

"They tend to travel in pairs."

The closet door-kicking resumed.

Spider got up from the sofa, sauntered over to the hall closet, crouched down, said, "Those cops come in here, Eva, I don't want to hear jack shit. Not one sound. You dig? You kick that door again, I'll kick your skinny ass up and down the street."

Silence.

"Good girl," Spider said, standing up. "That fucking little kid next door. She snitched on us."

A heavy hand pounded on the front door. A lot of pounding, not helping Dredge's mental equilibrium.

Spider went back over to the sofa, dumped his butt down, picked up the remote.

"Police! Open up."

"Well, Dredgie," Spider said. "What are you waiting for?"

Dredge took a deep breath before he went over, pulled the front door open.

"Why, hello!" he said, sounding like a complete doorknob.

Two uniforms, belts, guns, the whole deal. A short man who looked like an ugly woman with a buzzcut. The tall officer smelled of mouthwash and had a combover.

Dredge felt like he needed to pee.

The short one spoke. "Someone was seen restraining a woman in your driveway last night." He stared up into Dredge's face. "You know anything about that?"

"Well," Dredge said, holding the doorknob too tight, starting to get sweaty. "There was a little commotion out there. It actually woke me up. Some people walking by decided to settle whatever was bothering them in my driveway." He shook his head. "What can you do? Terrible. Just terrible."

"Is that right?"

"Yes."

"Well," the tall cop said. "How about we come in and you can tell us all about it?"

Dredge looked over at Spider on the sofa. Spider shook his head *no* and mouthed the words Dredge was to say.

"Got a warrant?" Dredge said sheepishly.

"Don't need a warrant for domestic abuse." The tall cop blinked. "So basically, you can let us come in or we come in anyway."

"Domestic abuse?" Dredge said. "What's that?"

"Some new bullshit," Spider said, biting a nail.

The shorter cop shoved the door into Dredge, knocking him aside. The two entered the living room, the short one waving away the air in front of his nose. "Jesus." He stopped when he saw Spider. "You. You're the one."

Spider said to Dredge: "The fuck is *she* talking about?"

"We have a witness." The tall cop consulted a notebook. "Says a redheaded woman was seen being held down on the hood of a car by a skinny guy in leathers with blond hair. Last night." He looked up. "Sounds like you. Apparently had a chain or something around her neck."

"Who are we talking about, now?" Spider said, staring at the TV.

"Turn that damn thing off," the short cop said.

Spider looked at him, popped the remote. The screen faded into a pinpoint and died.

"Where is she?" the tall cop said.

"Where is who?"

"I'm gonna ask once more," the short officer said. "And then you're coming downtown. And I hope I don't accidentally smack your head getting you in the back of the car."

The tall cop frowned.

"Oh—you're talking about Eva?" Spider said. "I believe she went out for cigarettes. Didn't she, Dredgie?"

"Yeah," Dredge said. "I think so."

"You *think* so?" The tall cop turned to Dredge. "OK with you if we look around?"

"Well..." Dredge said.

"Got a warrant?" Spider said. "Because without one, all you can do is look for my old lady. In plain sight. And I just told you she went out."

"What are you doing, hanging out with this guy?" the tall cop said to Dredge. "He doesn't care about you. Just tell us where the girl is and when we're satisfied she's unharmed and not under any threat, we'll leave."

"Look," Dredge said. "Eva *did* go out—to cool off. They *did* have an argument last night—but it wasn't anything. No one got hurt. I don't know where you heard otherwise. Nothing happened and it won't happen again."

The shorter uniform went over and stood with his back to the closet door. He crossed his arms over his chest.

"No warrant," Spider said, drinking beer.

The tall cop said to Dredge, "OK if we look around now? If you cooperate, it looks better if we have to pull you and your buddy in."

"*When* we pull you in," the short cop said.

"Suit yourself," Dredge said, not sure what to do now.

Spider interrupted: "But it don't mean shit, if you ain't got a warrant. Anything you might find ... Don't. Mean. Jack." Spider threw a shrug.

The tall cop leafed through his notebook, said to Dredge: "Ran a check on you. Henry Beaumont. Thirty days for a lewd-and-lascivious. Do you realize that if this guy gets pinned for hitting the girl and you help him hide that, you get nailed too? That's two charges against you."

"Who says I hit anyone?" Spider said, drinking beer.

"We got a witness said you were holding her down, threatening her."

"That little kid from next door?" Spider laughed. "You got a 'witness' who watches *Sesame Street*."

All of a sudden, there was the *boom-boom-boom* of Eva kicking the closet door.

Dredge jumped.

The short officer burst into a smile as he turned to the hall closet. "Well, hey. What do we have here?"

"Won't do you any good," Spider said. "I got a lawyer who'll say this is illegal."

The short cop looked at the tall one. "Probable cause, plain and simple."

"I would have to agree," the tall cop said, closing his notebook.

"Go ahead," Spider said. "Check it out—while I call my fucking lawyer."

The short officer went to the closet. "They locked her in." He turned the key in the closet door, pulled it open.

"Jesus Christ," he said.

He helped Eva out. Steadied her, hand on her elbow. He turned to give Spider a grin. "Looks like you're busted, lollipop."

"I don't know how she wound up in there," Spider said. "She said she was going out. She's been loaded to the gills since last night when she went off on me. Ask her." Spider stared at Eva. His eyes were hard and threatening. "Ask Eva if anything happened. She's gonna tell you she stumbled into the closet because she was loaded. Because no one did shit. Did they, Eva?"

"And she locked herself in? from the outside?"

"You'll have to ask Dredge about that," Spider said. "It's his house."

"Tell us what he did," the tall cop said to Eva. "And we take him away."

Eva looked down. "Spider didn't do anything."

The short cop let out a low whistle. "I knew it."

"Knew what?" Eva said, looking up at him.

"That you'd back out," the short cop said. "That's all your type ever does."

Eva's eyes turned dark. "And what type is that?"

"Let's go," the short cop said to his partner. "She's just wasting our time."

The tall cop spoke to Eva: "He's only going to do it again. You owe it to yourself, and others, to press charges."

There was a pause while Eva's head shook. She glared at Spider. "He put a chain around my neck. I thought I was going to die. And now he thinks he can threaten the little girl from next door."

So that's what started Eva into kicking the door. Spider mentioning the weird kid who had been watching last night.

"And she's a lying sack of shit," Spider said.

"He killed those Mexicans on the summit. Him and the rest of the Dead Boys. He was bragging about it."

"No shit, Sherlock," the short one said.

"Now that does sound interesting," the tall cop said.

Dredge's heart was a hammer.

"Not Dredge, though," Eva said. "He was with me, watching TV, while they were up there. *Don Kirshner's Rock Concert*. Huh, Dredgie? Alice Cooper was on."

"Yes," Dredge said, his voice cracking with nerves. "Alice Cooper."

"Pure shit," Spider said. "Talking out her ass."

"You're coming with us," the tall cop said to Spider, reaching for his handcuffs.

The short officer grinned at Spider and rubbed the handle of the baton on his belt. "Please put up some resistance."

The tall cop said to Spider: "Stand up, turn around, put your hands behind your back."

"I need to call my lawyer."

"When you get to the station."

"Fuck that shit."

"Say that again." The short cop pulled his baton. "Nothing would give me more pleasure."

"That's enough," the tall cop said to him. "Come on," he said to Spider.

Spider spit on the rug, stood up, turned around, put his hands behind his back.

The short cop said to Eva: "Way to go, girl."

Spider turned his head, giving Eva slit eyes. "Yeah, Eva —way to go."

CHAPTER 7

WAS her parole officer *ever* going to show?

The plan had been to get an early start, check in with SF County Parole, then go look for a biker by the name of Spider. But it was close to 11 a.m. already and Colleen was still waiting. Since she'd moved, her parole required verification of living arrangements within forty-eight hours.

She wondered how verifiable The Falcon Hotel on Sixth Street, San Francisco, was. The flop house rented by the day, week, month, the kind of place where you slept in your clothes on top of grimy covers.

Downstairs, in a drunken monologue, a woman was berating someone for forgetting ice.

Colleen lit up a Winston, brushing her shoulder length hair back with her fingers, blowing two smoke rings, one after another, watching them drift across the small unlit room, along with the minutes that had turned into hours.

Pam—Eva—had borrowed money from Leon, apparently helped herself to more from the cash register at the Hornet. Never came back to work. She told Leon she needed to get straight. Well, that was better than saying she needed to end it all. But what was the truth? The last Leon had seen of Eva she had been hanging around a biker gang from Santa Cruz.

Colleen ended up waiting most of the day, called the parole office from the pay phone downstairs in the hall. No one could locate her parole officer. She was to stand by.

Stand by while time slipped by. Her frustration was growing.

Back upstairs, she lit another Winston and went over to the window, pulling it open to reduce some of the Lysol reek.

California, she thought, sucking smoke into her lungs. No palm trees here. And Pam ended up where? Some hole like this? With bikers? Colleen tossed the unfinished cigarette out the window.

Forget the damn parole officer. She had Leon's car for a couple of days while he recuperated. She'd head over to where Leon said Pam used to live. See if there was any trace of her there before she headed down the peninsula.

<hr>

Santa Cruz Police still had Spider in the holding cell, lying on a bench fixed to the wall. His hands were behind his head, completely still. The cell smelled of fresh cement. Spider didn't smell of anything fresh. Two Mexican illegals sat on the floor, eyes down. They'd been sitting on the bench when Spider was admitted but had been convinced to move.

Boots came plodding down the hall, up to the cell, the guard's thick cough accompanied by the opening of a door.

"I don't know how you did it," he said to Spider. "But you're getting out of here."

Spider sat up. "About fucking time," he said.

They wouldn't let Spider use the pay phone in the station, so he went outside, strutting down Center Street, Santa Cruz looking like a sleepy suburb in the middle of a beach town, and Spider out of place in his Dead Boy leathers. Headed for a pay phone, and a ride back to Dredge's.

A car pulled up alongside, an unmarked Ford LTD, with a telltale chrome spotlight on the door. Crawling along. The passenger window rolled down.

The driver, a Santa Cruz detective named Grisset, leaned over to glare at Spider through aviator-style sunglasses. Grisset was tanned, big and fit for his forty-odd years, like an ex-football player, with a head of thick sandy blond hair cut into a trendy shag, just this side of regulation.

He stopped the car.

"Get in."

Spider did. Grisset put the car into Drive, motored slowly along.

"That was dumb," he said to Spider. "Giving them my name."

Spider looked over with that near-death grin, a skeleton kept alive by all the shit running through his veins. Like electricity through bare wires, ready to catch fire.

"Got me out, didn't it?" Spider turned to the window, scratching his face.

"What are you trying to do? Get me busted? I've told you: I'm not with San Jose anymore. I'm not with Narcotics anymore. Those days are long gone."

"Yeah, I know," Spider said. "You're with Santa Cruz now. So you got even more influence as far as I'm concerned."

"Do you know what kind of risk I took, getting you out?

Trying to convince the desk sergeant your girlfriend was just talking out of her head?"

"I know how much fucking bread you been paid over the years."

"The Mexicans," Grisset said, turning to squint at Spider through his shades.

"Which ones?" Spider said. "There's a lot of Mexicans in California."

"You know what I'm talking about. The four found off the summit. Three shot, two with a .44 caliber, one with a shotgun. One guy looks like he OD'd, was force-fed meth. All members of Barrio Cruz. On the news? Any of this ringing a bell?"

"Drugs are terrible. Is that what you're saying? Yeah, I would have to agree. Drugs suck."

"Why did you tell your girlfriend—or whatever she is— you and the Dead Boys aced them?"

"I was a little out of my head. She'll be cool."

"She better. I did what I could to put the notion to rest. But if Detective Moran gets wind, he'll put two and two together."

"So take care of it."

"I'm the new guy. The Mexicans are Moran's case."

"Wetbacks should stick to picking lettuce." Spider spit out the car window. "Not selling speed for the Chinese. And the chinks should stay out of Santa Cruz. Immigrants taking our jobs."

"I keep telling you, all of that is behind me."

"Maybe you'd like to think so," Spider said. "How much did you pull down, looking the other way all those years when we were moving shit through San Jose?"

Grisset pressed the dash with his finger. "Nothing to do with me anymore. I'm out."

"There's only one way out."

Grisset shook his head. "I got a call from Maurice."

"Speaking of Mexicans."

"Another guy I don't need calling me anymore. Maurice says you better deal with that old lady of yours. *Eva* or whatever her name is."

"And what the fuck does Eva have to do with Maurice now? She quit that job."

"Some woman was nosing around the Hornet in San Francisco. Looking for her daughter—a girl named Pamela Hayes. Seems that's Eva's real name."

Spider turned and looked at Grisset. "So?"

"Colleen Hayes caused one hell of a fuss, threatened Maurice with a broken bottle."

"I like her already." Spider grinned with old man's teeth. "What does she look like? Pretty hot? Some of those older broads can be, you know?"

"You need to listen up."

"Can I file a restraining order if she molests me?"

"You think it's funny. Maurice doesn't. Maurice doesn't think the Mexicans are funny either. He thinks you're a bunch of cowboys. But the truth is, you're worse."

Spider lost his smile. "So Maurice wants the Mexicans and Lum and his Tong to take over the business? He should fucking thank me for protecting our turf. Meanwhile you're not doing a damn thing."

"Because I'm not involved."

Spider gave a wan smile. "Then what am I doing in your car?"

Grisset pursed his lips. "This is 1977. You scooter types are going to be a thing of the past if you don't learn a little finesse. That shit you guys're on..." Grisset shook his head. "It's gotten bad. Really bad. You guys are losing it."

"Not like you. With your blow-dried hair."

"Have you looked in a mirror lately, friend? You are decomposing right in front of my eyes." Grisset fought a sigh of exasperation. "Get rid of her. Eva. If you own a .44 that might have been used up at the summit, get rid of that too. Ditto with a shotgun."

"Did you just say 'get rid of Eva'?"

"I mean: send her on her way."

"And here I thought you might have meant something else."

"It better not come to that. If Moran finds out someone tattled on you about the Mexicans, you'll have a whole slew of problems. Problems we—you—don't want to deal with."

"You're Homicide now, too, right? So tell this moron to go pound sand."

"You just don't get it. I'm the new kid. Moran is the lead. Yeah, he's a lush but he's got an uncanny knack for catching people—especially sloppy people."

"So manage him, Grisset." Spider wiped his mouth with the back of his hand. "*Mi casa* and *su casa*. My business is your business. Got that?"

Grisset gripped the steering wheel, let a tight breath escape his lips. "Send Eva on her way. That means get her out of town. Tell your Dead Boys to lay low. Stay away from Lum and his people. And move out of that funhouse you're living in. That clown—what do you call him?"

"Dredge."

"Dredge? Really? That's a name? Like *Spider*? Jesus." Grisset laughed. "Well, Dredge has a bullshit prior, and the cops have been there before, and thanks to you and your girlfriend fighting, now they know where to find you. Fortunately, Moran is drying out so he shouldn't be an issue but if he does decide to look into things, well, you don't want to be caught with your pants down. Not unless you and your buddies all want to go to prison. Or worse."

"You don't want me to get busted," Spider said.

"Why do you think I'm telling you all this?" Grisset said, pulling over. He stomped the brakes and the car lurched to a stop.

Spider got out, slammed the door, ducked down to peer into the window. The sun behind made him look like a scarecrow in black leather. "Let me tell you something, Grisset: Like it or not, you owe me. You'll always owe me."

▭

"Let's go already," Dredge shouted from the living room.

Gramma's Country Squire rumbled in the driveway, ready to go.

Eva was still on the phone, out in the hall.

Dredge heard her say "thanks," then hang up.

Eva came out with a bulging denim bag hanging on her shoulder. She was wearing a black leather jacket, cutoffs and sneaks. Her eyes were pink and watery, and she looked more than a little delicate today. Life was hard all the way round, especially of late. And she probably needed a hit of something.

He sure did.

"You know," Eva said. "I've been thinking, Dredgie."

"I hope it's about getting on that Greyhound out of town."

"Chill out. The next bus to L.A. doesn't leave until four."

"I guess I'd feel a whole lot better if you were just out of *here*, Eva."

"Trying to get rid of me?" Eva gave Dredge a sly smile

that softened his big stupid heart. "You know what I'd like, Dredge? A pizza. When was the last time we had anything to eat?"

The way she said it. *Pizza.* She was adorable. He couldn't stand it. But she wasn't safe. "Let's go out for some. Before we go to the bus station."

"Yeah," she said. "And some beers. And just chilling out. *Here.*" Her winsome look almost dissolved the rest of his insides. But he was bunking with the angel of death by sticking around Granny's house with Eva.

He might be dumb. But he wasn't stupid.

"That sounds cool, Eva." And it did, having her all to himself. "But if you don't leave soon, maybe you won't ever, and, as much as I like having you around, you really need to split. You said so yourself, the other night. When Spider caught you."

"Now you're just being dramatic. Spider's not going anywhere. You heard those cops."

"You know what? You've got some kind of death wish."

"And you don't? Hanging around with Spider?"

Eva came up, ran a slender finger along his chin. "You're got some kind of a self-destructive thing going on, too, Dredge. That's why we get along so famously. We both like to walk on the wire."

He let out a deep sigh, taking in Eva, Eva in shorts and whatever else. She was looking thin, too thin, freak thin, but she'd look good to him in a burlap sack.

"I'm worried about you, Eva."

"Your damn grannie messed you up, Dredge. But she's gone now. And so is Spider. I thought you liked it out on the edge. You wanna be boring? Plenty of time for that when we're old. Why don't you come out here—on the edge—with me?"

He was a worrier, to be sure.

But Spider was gone.

He had Eva all to himself.

If he was man enough.

Life was short.

Outside, the bucket chugged away, waiting, punctuating his thoughts of being with Eva a little longer.

"What do you say, Dredgie? Hmmm? Pizza?"

He just loved the way she said it. And his name.

"Let's go *out* for pizza," he said.

"I'm still beat from the other night," she said. "I need a nap before I head off. I need a hit of something. You got any of that kinky-poo joy powder?"

"For medicinal purposes."

"Do I have to beg? Like a dog? Is that what you want?"

"A quick toot—then we leave."

She gave him that wink.

He pulled the snuff rocket from his pocket. A glass bullet-shaped bottle of high-speed chicken feed. He twisted the little clear plastic screw, shook a hit of white crystal into the head, turned the screw back to separate it off, held the bullet up to Eva's cute nose.

"Boss." She pressed a nostril shut, sucked in the gack like a mini-Hoover, reared back, gave a little gasp, shuddered with crystal voltage rattling her skinny frame. "Better get the other side while you're at it, Dredgie boy."

"Then we leave, right?"

"Then we leave. I know when I'm not wanted."

Dredge shook out another dose, a fat one, and it disappeared.

"*Ay, caramba,*" Eva shouted, rolling her shoulders, jumping around, eyes flaring.

"Normally I don't approve of drug use," Dredge said.

"But I won't be antisocial." He jiggled out a solid measure for himself, banged it up the right side of Mr. Nose.

KaBang. Brains smeared into sweet mush.

And another hit into the other nostril. The nose knows, boys.

Woo woo. I'm a fire engine.

Eva started dancing to no music whatsoever, a flickering sweet skeleton in front of his vibrating eyeballs. "Your damn grannie, Dredgie." She scooted over to the hi-fi, flipped on the radio. "Messed you up. But I'm here."

Stayin' alive! Stayin' alive!

"Shoot me now," Dredge said. "Not those guys."

"Disco sucks," Eva said, spinning the dial. She stopped on Styx. *Just sail away.* Overproduced progressive candy-ass bullshit.

"Holy crap," Dredge said. "What's happening to music?"

"That is just plain bad. I don't know how else to say it."

"610," Dredge said, pointing at the hi-fi with a trembling finger, eyes glued to Eva's skinny butt as she writhed. "Do it now."

Eva laughed and dialed in Dr. Don Rose on KFRC. The Big 610. Dr. Don blathering about his dog Roscoe eating his lunch, which he followed up with a squeeze horn and honking noises.

And the hits just keep coming...

Paul Revere and the Raiders came on, grinding organ, the *chop-chop* of guitars.

"Ow! I love this old stuff!" Eva dropped her bag to the floor, cranked the volume. She kicked off her white laceless Keds, little pink toes curling into the rug as she started doing the Hitch Hiker, pulling off her leather jacket while she moved, arms here, there, thumbs up and out. Smiling.

Winking. Jerking. "Come on, Dredgie. The wicked witch is dead!" She tugged Dredge toward her, and he stumbled, laughing. He fell into it, yeah, who couldn't? And every time he caught up with her, dancing like an idiot in his big baggie leathers, she'd change steps on him.

The Monkey. Swim. Pony. Mashed Potato. Boogaloo. Twist. Of course, the Twist.

Then he did his own dance. *Goat Dance.* Gramma had never thought much of it. And told him as much. Amongst other things she didn't think much of. He had to keep the Goat Dance to the confines of his bedroom.

Until now.

Goat Dance!

"Not too shabby, Dredgie." Eva oozed around him in a snake-armed Egyptian as the Raiders broke into a scorching guitar solo. "Not too shab-beh."

Maybe Eva could leave first thing in the morning.

Dual guitars twanged off into the fadeout.

The two of them were left standing there, gasping and grinning at each other like fools.

Then, outside, the rumbling of the Country Squire stopped. The air rang with silence.

Eva stared at Dredge with buggy eyes.

"Damn," Dredge said with a quiver in his voice, going over to turn the volume down. "I forgot I left the bucket running. It died."

Eva came up to him. "Dredge?" She rubbed his cheek with a soft fingertip. "Maybe you should think about getting out of here, too. Until Spider gets put away for good."

He felt that urge he couldn't control. He had never thought he would say something like this, not to someone like her. But he wanted to tell her how he felt.

"You know what, Eva ...?"

Eva started, eyes popping like a rabbit's.

"What the hell was that?" she said, dropping her voice.

The slow footfalls of familiar boots. Stepping up onto Gramma's porch. Scraping the wood.

Dredge's stomach dropped.

The front door opened.

There stood Spider with the keys to the Country Squire in his hand. He held them up.

"That is en-vi-ro-men-tal-ly very fucked up, Dredgie. Wasting precious fossil fuels like that, especially since that fucking thing don't get more than six to the gallon. Didn't you hear what President Carter said?" Spider looked at Eva, her full shoulder bag on the floor. "Going somewhere, Eva?"

"Not really," Eva said, staring at the rug.

"Damn right," Spider said.

CHAPTER 8

THE SECOND LINE of speed stung Dredge's left nostril more than the first one did the right. Like bathroom cleanser on his sinuses. He came up off the mirror, head spinning, and not in a good way. Totally wired. But the only way out was up. He needed Dutch courage to get him and Eva far, far away from this scene with Spider.

"We got to go meet Lum," Spider said, looking for a vein, perched on the shiny green textured sofa Gramma had bought when Dredge was a kid. Tugging at the plastic tube with his teeth, making his rocky arm bulge with blood, Spider held the needle as he tapped the crook of his elbow with a dirty fingernail. Eva was zonked out in an armchair on the shot Spider'd given her, some sticky brown rock powder in tinfoil. Eva couldn't say no to Mexican black tar. And Spider wouldn't take no for an answer anyway. Wanting to shut her down. In her cutoffs and slinky black top, mouth open and eyes shut, Eva looked more vulnerable than anything right now.

"Lum?" Dredge said. It just kept getting worse. Lum was the head of the triad trying to muscle its way into Santa

Cruz. Pana and Barrio Cruz had been Lum's biggest customers—until Pana and his compadres had met with the Dead Boys the other night.

It occurred to Dredge that he could possibly turn State's evidence on Spider. Or simply disappear, save his own rotten ass. But that would leave Eva with Spider.

Spider tapped the vein here and there, looking for a good place to hit it. "Guess Eva didn't figure I'd be released so soon," he said, as if reading Dredge's mind. "Guess Eva figured I'd be in the pokey for a while, huh, ratting me out to the cops?" He looked up, squinting.

"She didn't mean anything," Dredge said, heart thumping away, and not just from the speed. As if listening in, Eva murmured something in her stupor, and her leg slipped off the chair. Foot sideways on the floor now, head titled back, a speckle of drool collected in the corner of her mouth. "She just was not real happy with what happened in the driveway, you know, Spider? I'll make sure she won't take off while you go meet Lum."

"You'd like that, wouldn't you, Dredgie?" Spider touched the bulging vein with his fingernail. There were already several bruises on his arm. "Maybe try to take her to the boneyard while I'm out? Well, you're too late. I already ruined her for any other man."

Dredge felt his face redden. "I'm just saying…"

"Come on, Dredgie," Spider looked up, grinning. "I'm just fucking with you, man. Why are you always so dang nervous?"

"Something to do with shooting Mexicans? You getting pulled in by the cops? Ounces of stolen crystal in my garage? Half of it flowing through my veins?"

"You and me, Dredgie. We're Dead Boys. Brothers."

"Are we?"

"And we're gonna go meet Lum together. Eva too. Make this a family outing. We'll talk to Lum, then I'm gonna head over to Sky Londa. Grannie's place is just too hot right now. I need to get away from Grannie's pad for a while."

Spider wanted to meet with Lum so the Dead Boys could move in where Pana had left off. Take over distribution. That's why they wasted Pana's crew. Lum's outfit was next.

"Are the rest of the Dead Boys gonna be there?" Dredge asked.

"You bet. But you're my right-hand man."

Dredge wondered. "So why're we taking Eva too?"

"I can't have Eva go wandering off. Don't worry. She can wait in the car while we make the deal."

Dredge took four deep breaths, thinking it over, his body filling the matching shiny green armchair. If Spider thought he was his main man, then that gave him time to get Eva away from all this. And time was what he needed. Just like the song said.

"I'll get Eva ready," Spider said. "You go rev up Grannie's Go-Kart one more time."

Christ. Take Eva. Take Gramma too. Dig her up.

Dredge watched Spider as he finally caught the vein, digging the needle under the skin, working it in. Pushing the plunger, grunting, eyes bulging like they might pop. Then he slipped the works out and undid the hose, exhaling like he was expiring. The needle tipped with blood. Spider tossed the items on the coffee table next to the big bag of white powder they'd taken from Pana. A bent spoon fell off the table.

Then he stared at Dredge with pupils like dinner plates, like Dredge might be a fish in a giant bowl. It was unsettling.

"You ready, Dredgie?"

"Yeah, sure." It came out as one tight word, *yehsure*. Dredge got up, found the keys to the Country Squire on the window ledge. Through the dirty lace curtain, across the driveway, he could see the little girl next door sitting in her mom's dinged-up green Pinto with the gray-primered fender. Mom was just coming out of the house.

Mom was looking fine, as per usual, although Dredge wasn't quite seeing her so much that way in his jumped-up state. Her dark hair was all swooped over and she was getting into her car in her flared jeans tight in the thighs and butt, starting up the car, making sure the kid had the seatbelt on. Backing out, not looking Dredge's way, on purpose of course. Going to a class or something, up at UC-Santa Cruz, take the kid to the babysitter's first. Dredge had stood outside Mom's window, listened to her on the phone. OK, so he shouldn't do that.

Her little girl Justine was watching Dredge through the hair hanging in her face. That kid watched everything. Dredge let the lace curtain fall back into place, feeling like a rat in church. He waited until they left, went out to the Country Squire, started it up, gunning the pedal to keep it alive. Black smoke blew out into the street, wafting over to the ridge to the municipal golf course in the rearview mirror.

Once he got Eva away, things would be better. They sure couldn't get any worse.

After a few minutes breathing fumes, Spider finally came out in his leathers, all zipped up even though they weren't taking the bikes. Eva stumbled alongside. Spider put his arm around Eva, holding her, going, "Think you wanna be sociable now, Eva?"

Dredge started when he saw Eva's hands together in front of her in handcuffs.

He leaned out the window. "Jesus Christ on a pogo stick, Spider. Tell me you're not serious."

Spider ignored him, and Eva and Spider got in the car, Eva in the back, blinking in confusion, looking out the window, eyes sliding down her face. Spider got in front, turned around in the torn bench seat, played with Eva's red hair.

Maybe Dredge should just drive down to the police station.

But that would have required courage.

"What the fuck we waiting for, Dredgie?"

"Take 'em off, Spider," Dredge said, clearing his throat, sounding meeker than he intended.

Spider stopped with Eva's hair. "What did you just say to me?"

"I am *not* driving around with her in those cuffs."

"I told you I can't let her take off on me. Not when we're talking to Lum. Now, lighten up."

Dredge opened the car door with a squeak, got out.

"Fuck it, Spider. Fuck it to death. I'm not gonna do it. I'm not."

There was a pause while Dredge waited for Spider to get out, kick his ass, whatever. Just do it. Get it over with.

"OK, Dredgie," Spider said. "Don't get your panties in a twist."

"You mean you'll take 'em off?"

"Yeah, yeah. Just get back in the car. We got to meet Lum."

Dredge did.

Spider gave a ripped-to-the-tits smile as he patted himself down, searching his pockets. "I hate to say this,

Dredgie, but I seem to have misplaced the key to the handcuffs."

"Shit, piss and fuck!" Dredge got out again, slamming the door, hard, matching his heartbeat. He lumbered into the garage, found the world's biggest bolt-cutters, just lying on the floor next to Pearl. He couldn't remember where he got them or how they got there. But they were heavy as hell, and he had to grunt like a he-man to pick them up. He went back out, yanked open Eva's passenger door.

Spider was giving him the red stare from the front passenger seat.

"What the fuckin' *hey*, Dredgie?"

"Put your arms out, Eva. Keep 'em still so I don't cut your dang fingers off."

Eva turned, perched on the edge of the bench seat in her cutoffs and motorcycle boots, her heels hooked on the running board, holding her thin wrists out. Everybody was getting too skinny. Everybody was getting too damn wasted. Dredge closed one eye to concentrate, snipped the chain between the cuffs and then one of the cuffs themselves, giving the bolt-cutters a good crank to get through the metal. It scratched Eva's wrist, but she shook her arms over her head like a dancer on a bar top when he was done.

"Th-anks, Dredgie." She slipped him a cross-eyed grin. His chest liquefied. Either that or he was going to croak.

"Hold still, Eva. I'll get the other one."

"Nah, leave it." She held up her wrist and examined the thick chrome cuff resting against a delicate silver bangle. "It's punk."

"If you two are all done," Spider said, "do you think we could, like, get on the motherfucking road? You don't keep Lum waiting."

Dredge threw the bolt-cutters in the back. They set off, making it partway out of the driveway.

"Whoa, stop," Spider said.

"Now what?"

"As in 'stop the car'. As in *now*. And don't give me any more of your lip. You already pushed it enough for one day."

Dredge stopped, halfway in the street.

Spider got out, stumbled up the driveway in his stone walk, the skull on his jacket with the reefer in its teeth mocking Dredge. The door to Gramma's house opened and Spider went in.

"You OK, Eva?" Dredge said.

"Define 'OK'."

"I'm keeping an eye out for you."

"Is that what it's called?"

"I'm gonna get you out of this."

"Dredge," she said to the window. "You don't have what it takes. You're a coward. That's just the way you are."

His chest sunk as quickly as it had soared only a moment before. He fought something pulling at his eyes.

Spider reappeared, grinning like the skull on the back of his jacket, hugging five tall green cans. He got back in the car, and Dredge's heart jumped again when he saw the handle of the Charter Arms Pit Bull sticking out the back of his waistband.

Spider handed a can of Rainier Ale to Dredge, turned around to give one to Eva.

No words as they headed off.

Spider slipped on a pair of cheap black wraparounds. "When we meet Lum, everyone needs to be cool." Popping the pull tab, he slurped some beer, then turned, ran his dirty fingers through Eva's hair. "This is an important deal for us."

Dredge sucked fast breaths, trying to calm his growing agitation as his head swam, and motored north. He slowed the bucket down into a BP station just before Highway 9. Everything seemed to shimmer. He got out to pump gas and check a leaky tire that had been giving him grief. He pumped five bucks of regular into the tank, filling it halfway, and caught Eva's face pressed against the glass, staring at him with a haunted look. She looked like he felt. He went inside to pay.

And saw a familiar face.

The foxy mom from next door with her little weird kid, in line to pay for gas. Dredge went over to the dairy case and fooled around with some baloney while she paid. No point in her seeing him.

"You need the restroom, Juss?" he heard Mom say.

"No, Mom."

"I need to make a pit stop. Come with me."

"That bathroom is gross. There isn't even room!"

"You wait in the car, then. Make sure to lock the doors."

The kid left, went back out.

By the time Dredge got back out on the forecourt, both doors on the right side of the Country Squire were open and Spider was hauling Eva back to the wagon, giving her a ration of shit. She must have tried to take off on him.

"Did I say we shouldn't bring Eva?" Dredge dumped himself back into the driver's seat. Eva was thrown into the front between him and Spider, breathing tight and shallow, looking straight ahead.

"Shut the fuck up," Spider growled, glaring through his porno shades. "Drive."

Across the forecourt, in the beater Pinto, the little girl was staring at them.

"That fucking kid," Spider hissed. "I've got a good mind to burn their motherfucking house down."

"Might be a tad extreme, Spider," Dredge said, starting up the Country Squire. Bald tires squealed out of the station.

"Bitch and a half," Spider muttered.

Through dirty glass, trees started to thicken, and the sun began to slip. They passed through the state park in silence, the redwood branches breaking, late afternoon light on and off the hood.

Just after Boulder Creek the rear tire went *slug-slug-slug* around a turn. The car wobbled.

Dredge pulled over.

"Now what?" Spider said.

"That tire," Dredge said. "It's got a slow leak. I meant to fill it up back there. Now it's flat."

"Motherfucker," Spider said softly, peeling off his shades. He spit on the floor of the car. "This is your fault, Eva!"

Dredge got out, the door creaking, went to the back, popped the gate, uncovered the tire well. He pulled out a jack and a tire iron.

"God damn it!" Spider got out, dragging Eva with him, up to the rear of the station wagon. Dredge heard a click. He looked up.

Seven inches of Pit Bull were shaking in Spider's hand. "You're gonna change that fucking tire," he said to Eva, grabbing the tire iron out of Dredge's hand and throwing it on the ground. It clattered, ringing like a bell.

"Spider," Dredge said, "Lighten up, man. *Please.*"

The Pit Bull swung on him, monstrous and fierce. His

heart went aflutter, not in a pleasant way. "I've had about all I'm gonna take from you, pudge."

"Cool," Dredge squeaked, his hands going up in little flags of surrender. "*Cool.*" He began to assemble the jack with trembling fingers. Eva glowered, her eyes dark, picked up the tire iron, wiped her hair back, went out in the road, crouched down and started on a lug nut, her single handcuff banging the wheel rim. Spider slipped the Pit Bull into the back of his waistband and seized the jack from Dredge as Dredge hauled out the spare tire.

The hum of a car approached. A new blue and white four-wheel drive with Wisconsin plates. It came up and stopped in the road just ahead of where Eva was squatted, loosening a lug nut.

A sweet mid-Western lady with permed gray hair peered out. "You folks need some help?"

"No," Spider barked. "We don't."

A man's voice spoke. "You fellas sure? You shouldn't have her changing that tire, big guys like you. At least pull over. Look at her, out in the road like that?"

Spider sauntered up to the open passenger window. He blew his nose into his hand and shook it off. "I got an idea, Goober: Why don't you mind your own fucking business and go the fuck back to Idaho? How about a little of that?"

Birds twittered in the trees.

"You got some kind of a problem, pal?" the man said.

"Yes, I do, as a matter of fact. Want to find out? It can be easily arranged."

Dredge saw Eva stand up with the tire iron and slowly begin to walk off down the road. Spider and Dredge were left standing there, the people in the four-wheel watching.

"Eva," Spider said, turning. "Where you think you're going?"

"Fuck you, Spider!" Eva broke into a staggered run.

The four-wheel drive sat there. Dredge saw Spider reach for the black handle in the back of his leathers like he was going to shoo the tourists off for good.

Dredge clutched Spider's arm. "Spider," he whispered. "Stay calm, man."

Spider pushed Dredge away, turned, took off after Eva.

Dredge stuck his frizzy head in the window of the four-wheel drive. The gray-haired lady reared back, just short of terrified. The man had steam coming out of his ears. His big waxy face looked like it was about to melt.

"My friends are newlyweds," Dredge said. "It's best they work this out, you know?" He could hear Spider down the road after Eva, boots clipping on the asphalt.

"Who are the Dead Boys?" the man asked. "And what has she got on her hand? Looked like a handcuff to me."

"Are you with a cult?" the woman squeaked, her voice high and brittle.

"We respect all faiths." Dredge backed his head out of the car. He stood back and pressed his palms together in what he thought was a convincing sign of prayer. "God be with you."

"California granola," the man said. "Nuts and flakes." The four-wheel moved off.

Dredge tore off down the road. He heard something in the trees. He pushed through the branches, gasping for air.

Eva was on her knees. Spider had the Pit Bull on her. Shivers ran down Dredge's spine.

"Gimme one goddam reason why I shouldn't just blow your brains out, Eva."

"Fuck you, Spider. Fuck you."

"Spider," Dredge panted. "Stay cool, bro."

"She's going to get us busted."

Dredge approached slowly, hands up. Gently, gently, he pushed Spider's gun arm to one side. "We got to change that wheel and get moving. Lum's waiting, remember?"

Spider rested the barrel of the gun on the side of his neck, blinking. Dredge saw his forehead was scabbed where he had been picking at it. He was more far gone than Dredge realized. They all were.

"Yeah," Spider said. "That's right. We got to meet Lum."

CHAPTER 9

MOM'S PINTO crossed over High Street, toward the university.

"It's awfully quiet in this car," she said, taking off her sunglasses to examine Justine.

Justine watched the textured concrete of the buildings whip by.

"You haven't said a word since we stopped for gas," Mom said.

Justine thought of the red-haired Bird Lady in the gas station, getting pulled around by the Spider.

"You were a chatterbox before Daddy left."

She didn't have anything to say.

"Juss," Mom said as she drove. "We're moving soon. To another place. A better place."

Justine liked that. But what about the Bird Lady? Who would watch her, make sure she was safe? "When?"

"As soon as I get the money. I wrote Grandpa."

The Spider and the big one and the Bird Lady were going to the mountains in the car. They were going to Lum's party, the Spider said, but it didn't seem like much of a party because the Bird Lady wanted to run and leave them in the gas station, but the Spider went and got her and squeezed her. The Bird Lady looked at Justine after the Spider pushed her back in the car.

"Juss, are you listening to me?"

"Yes." And the big one wasn't doing anything. And it looked like the Bird Lady was saying: *Don't look at me, don't look at me like this.*

"No, you're not." Mom patted Justine's head. "I said that just because your Daddy's not here right now, it doesn't mean he doesn't love you."

"Oh, OK."

"He loves you almost as much as you love french fries. You know that, don't you?"

"OK," Justine said.

Mom looked over at her, puzzled.

"Mom..."

"Yes?" Mom said quickly.

"The Bird Lady next door? The one we're not supposed to talk about anymore?"

Mom sighed. "What about her?"

"I saw her getting smacked. Sort of. Just before. At the gas station."

"Oh, honey..." Mom put her sunglasses back on. "No, you didn't. You're just confused ... we're going to move soon."

"Uh-huh!" Justine was watching Mom now, looking for clues. Mom was smart. Why didn't Mom know about the Bird Lady?

Mom kept one hand on the wheel and gave Justine's hair another tousle. "Come on, now. New subject. I think we have time for some french fries."

"I did so see her. The Spider was pushing her. In the gas

station. He said they were going to a party in the mountains. I saw it. I didn't make it up."

There was a long silence as they pulled up in front of Irene the babysitter's peeling-paint bungalow by the campus.

"Justine?"

"Yes?"

"Remember when we called the police? And they went over to the house next door?"

"Yes."

"Well, it's the police's job to look into any trouble from now on. Not you. Not me. Do you understand? There is nothing else we can do now for that young woman."

"But Mom, he was..."

"Justine," Mom said evenly. "Sometimes we just have to say we did our best and there's nothing else we can do, even if we really, really want to."

"Like with Daddy."

Mom let out a breath. "Yes, like with Daddy. Now give me a kiss."

Mom was wiping her eyes in that way she did when she pretended that she wasn't crying. Justine kissed Mom and got out at Irene the babysitter's and Irene came out in her big-ass muumuu and waved bye to Mom and stood there with Justine and they watched Mom's Pinto leave. Justine remembered the way the Bird Lady looked at her. It felt like a bad secret. Then she unclenched the palm of her small hand. And looked at the silver bird earring the Bird Lady had dropped during the fight with the Spider in the gas station. She'd have to get it back to her. The Bird Lady wouldn't be able to fly away without both of them.

By the time Dredge swung the bucket onto the dirt road, the sun was slipping into the gleaming Pacific. Grannie's Country Squire bounced along until it came to a clearing amidst tall redwoods. Dredge remembered Gramma bringing him up here for difficult picnics when he was a boy. He liked the way the sky used to come down out of the trees. Gramma said he was a special boy then.

He could hear Eva jostling on the fold-down seat behind, under an old yellow moving blanket, out of sight. Spider had tied her hands and ankles.

A gold Mercedes 200 sedan sat under the reach of a redwood by a picnic table on the other side of the clearing. Dredge squinted. Two figures were sitting in the car. Smoke drifted out of the open windows. It didn't look particularly good. But what did, anymore? One more time he told himself he was going to find a way to get Eva and himself out of this. And soon. He just didn't know how.

"Park over there." Spider pointed to a spot halfway to the tree and the Mercedes. "Not too close, now."

Dredge jerked the Squire up to the middle of the open space, shifted to park, let the engine rumble.

"Jesus fucking Christ," Spider hissed. "Lum's not here." Zipping his jacket up, Spider pulled it down over the stock of the gun. "He sent two nobodies instead. He'll learn to show some respect."

That's what Dredge was worried about. Maybe Spider would get out and he could take off with Eva.

"Going somewhere?" Spider reached over, twisted the ignition key. The motor chugged off and Spider pulled the key, slipped it in his jacket. He gave Dredge a sharp look. "I need you to watch my back. You stand there and try to look hard. If you can. Don't open your mouth."

"Don't I need a gun of some sort?" Dredge said.

"Make do. You better not fucking punk out on me, Dredge. You have a tendency to do that."

They could hear Eva trying to say something through the rag in her mouth.

Spider looked back at Eva writhing under the blanket. "Shut the fuck up, Eva," he whispered. "Or I'll shut you up. You're getting to be more trouble than you're worth."

Eva went silent.

Dredge took a deep breath, his chest pounding and twisting.

"Go time, Dredgie." Spider got out of the car. Then he leaned back in, his dilated pupils dark with the falling daylight. "You know, it's a shame: a big boy like you, Dredge, 'fraid he might have to bump titties with a gook."

Spider left the door open, swaggered off across the clearing toward the Mercedes, like the *Keep on Truckin'* dude out of the Crumb comic.

"Come on, Dredgie," he yelled as he walked. "The hills are alive!"

Reaching over the seat, Dredge pulled the blanket back. Eva's glazed eyes were a cross between fury and fear, her red hair smashed to her head.

"Hang in there, Eva," Dredge said. "I'll figure something out."

Her eyes glared back. He pulled his hand away, hopped out of the station wagon, hoisting up his leather pants, went after Spider. Spider was almost to the gold Mercedes when Dredge caught up, breathless.

"Decided to join the party," Spider said.

The front doors of the Mercedes opened, and two young Asian men got out on either side. The one coming up to Spider was compact, dressed in a shiny gray double-breasted suit and pointed black shoes. His hair was sculptured back in a wave, his narrow, honey-colored face moving with the gum he was chewing.

"CC," Spider said. "Where's Lum?"

"Couldn't make it." CC slipped his hands into his baggy pants pockets. "And you are late."

Spider eyed the tall kid. "Why couldn't Lum make it?"

"Who is *this?*" CC gave Dredge a smirk.

"Dredge. And I don't think you answered my question."

"'Dredge'?" CC laughed. "Where do you guys come up with these names?"

The other Chinese boy was tall and double-breasted too. It was like a uniform. A small jade earring, a crescent-moon, shone from his lobe. He stood back. Dredge could make out the bulge under his left arm. Hard for a skinny teenager to hide a gun. Dredge felt naked.

"I'm speaking for Lum," CC said, getting close enough to breathe on Spider. "And if we decide to work with you, there are some ground rules."

"Ground rules, my ass. We already have a deal."

"Well, it changed, my man. It changed. Ever since Pana and three of his crew got waxed. Lum doesn't like the way things went down with Barrio Cruz. Cruz were his main distributors in SC."

Spider grinned. "Good thing he's got the Dead Boys to backfill then, huh?"

"Kind of worked out that way. Didn't it?"

"Yeah, I think that's what I'm sayin'. Which is fortunate for you. Because we got this town secured now. So it's copasetic."

"OK, here's the deal: one K a pound. In advance."

"One K?" Spider reared back. "No fuckin' way, Jose."

"Lum says *way.*"

"We talked on the phone," Spider said. "Lum and me. Lum said eight bills for an elbow. And my credit is good."

"Well, things have changed, my man. Lum doesn't dig being played."

"Lum," Spider said, spitting on the ground.

"I'll tell him you did that," CC said.

The tall boy laughed without smiling.

Spider said: "What you laughing at, zipperhead?"

The boy's face turned into a scowl. "You, trailer trash."

"What's that?" CC said, turning back around, one ear high.

The rumble of motorcycles drifted up the dirt road to the clearing.

"That must be my buddies," Spider said. "Guess we can talk more when they get here, huh? About your motherfucking one K per motherfucking pound. In advance."

"You know what?" CC said to Spider as he put his hands down by his side and flexed them. "This deal is *off*. All deals are *off*." He turned to the tall boy. "Come on, we got to jet." He turned and headed back to the car.

"You set us up?" The tall Chinese kid said to Spider, hand going inside his jacket.

"Hey, stay calm," Spider said. His hands went up in a motion of appeasement. "Listen up."

The tall boy stopped momentarily.

Spider's hand shot behind his back.

His Pit Bull came out in a blur.

The kid pulled a weapon out of his jacket.

Dredge dived for the ground.

Spider's big gun went off with a single thunderous blast. "Take *that*."

The tall Asian kid bolted back, teetering before he dropped his gun on the grass. He looked down at his chest, dumbfounded, before he stumbled backward and went down flat on his back with a hard thump. His head bounced.

The sound of bikes echoed up from the road. Two Harleys appeared.

CC had jumped into the Mercedes and started it up with a grind. He took off, one door flapping, the car skidding in an arc, off toward the exit. Spider ripped off two rounds, resounding in the clearing, punching a hole in the gold trunk lid as the car swerved for the dirt road where two more bikes had appeared. They fishtailed out of the way, either side of the Mercedes, and one toppled onto the grass, its rider flipping on the ground as the car peeled off down the road into the remnants of afternoon light.

Dredge lay there, wheezing. He watched Spider march up to the kid lying on his back. The kid pushed himself up on an elbow with what seemed an immense effort.

Spider stood over him, the Pit Bull hanging in his hand.

"Now you're messin' with a son of a bitch," Spider muttered.

"No," the kid said. "No."

"Lum is going to respect me." Spider took aim at the kid's chest. "One way or another."

"No," the kid said again, raising one hand, as if that might block a bullet.

Spider fired, the shot snapping the boy's hand back onto his neck like a fish, driving him back down to the ground.

"Respect," Spider said.

Dredge scrambled to his feet. In the waning light the kid's torso was dark and shiny with blood. He was still heaving his lungs out. Spider stood over him, watching, smiling, the Pit Bull dangling.

Two bikes came roaring up on the grass.

Beano got off his Harley, walked over. Fritter got off his bike too, knees bowed, damaged from too many spills. His windswept blond hair fluttered off his bald crown.

"Where were *you*, Spider? We waited down the road, like you said. When you didn't show, we split. Good thing we decided to come back."

"We got a flat." Spider said, staring at the kid. "How you doin', zip?"

The kid panted.

"I guess it's not his day," Beano said.

Spider put a boot on the kid's chest and leaned into it while he looked at Fritter. "Lum wanted to charge us a grand an elbow."

The other two motorcycles veered up. Sawney got off, muddy from the tumble coming into the clearing. His hair was short and white, his face grizzly with a trimmed white beard.

"What's the problem with your mate, then?" Beano said. "He looks a bit cheesed off, he does."

"He is," Spider said, pushing the heel of his boot into the kid's chest. "He is cheesed off." The boy's face clenched in agony. Blood frothed on his lips.

Dredge's stomach clenched involuntarily. "You can't do this, Spider."

"Someone tell Dredge to get a pair of balls," Spider said. The rest of the Dead Boys laughed. Spider rested his gun arm over his knee, looking down. "Die like a man."

Fritter wiped his nose, bent on his knees to watch.

"Spider," Dredge gasped. "You can't, man. You can't."

"*We*, Dredge. *We*. And we already did."

Dredge's insides were turning to water. "Someone'll find him, trace it back."

"Dredgie, there isn't gonna be anything for anyone to

pin a name to. But Lum'll know. And that's all that matters."

Dredge's stomach erupted as he vomited onto the grass. It reeked of malt liquor.

Spider spit on the ground before he looked at Dredge and shook his head. "Now that you got that out of your system, Dredge, go get them bolt-cutters."

Fourteen thirty-two Divisadero, Apartment 201, where Leon had said Pamela used to live, had been vacated for some time. The manager standing at the door facing Colleen was scratching his extended belly through a white T-shirt with a coffee stain on it. Upstairs a TV blared a game show. Joker's Wild. *Where knowledge is king and lady luck is queen*, the deep-voiced announcer crooned.

"So you don't know where Eva went?" Colleen asked the manager. Eva was the name Pam had used.

"If I did, I'd go get the back rent she owes me. Her and that hippie roommate of hers. You say you're her mother? Then maybe you'd like to settle up for her."

The hallway was littered with old newspapers and had a saturated smell of cat pee. But it was a step up from hanging out with bikers, she supposed.

That's who she'd go find next. Dead Boys. Santa Cruz.

But she wouldn't do it unarmed.

Over in the Fillmore, a few minutes into foggy evening, Colleen stood outside a place where you could get things you couldn't steal. *Barracuda* thumped out of the bar on the corner.

"Nothing fancy," she said to the shaky kid standing in front of her, smoking a cigarette at ninety miles an hour under blue streetlight; Colleen could see the film on his face.

"A nine," the kid said, "is what you want." He scoured Fillmore up and down, while he took quick hits off the cigarette. "Four bills, it's yours."

"Too rich for my blood," Colleen said. "I told you my budget."

"Hundred and fifty bucks." The kid practically spit the words out at Colleen. "Lady wants a trey-eight for a hundred and fifty motherfucking dollars."

"I'm on a fixed income," she said.

"I can see that," the boy said, "But it ain't worth no hundred and a half to get my ass out this time of night." He wiped some sweat from his forehead.

"Seems to me your ass is already out," Colleen said. "But let's do this." More moisture built on the kid's forehead, him needing a hit of something. "Two. But that's all. And a box of rounds."

"OK," the kid said, shaking his head. "See that bar over there?"

It was an old blue-collar bar. "Doolittle's."

"That's where you be, one hour from now."

Colleen watched him go up Fillmore, the kid shaking in the light rain the fog had turned into. It was different these days, and she felt older because of it.

CHAPTER 10

"YOU'VE HAD THE DRUGS!" the college DJ screamed out of the speakers on Spider's floor. "You've had the booze! Now get down on your knees and smell those pan-ties!"

The guitars opened up, heavy metal thunder ripping through Spider's living-room disaster, the drums punching so loud Dredge could see the grills of the speaker cabinets bounce. Grating music plowed through his ears like a chain-saw. Angry tribal noise from the UK. Screaming music from Mars. He watched Beano and Fritter doing the slam in the middle of the living room, bashing into each other like spastic marionettes. Sawney was cooking up a spoonful of meth and Spider was sitting slit-eyed in a torn chair on the other side of the chaos.

The bikes were outside, the boys were inside and Eva ... Eva was out back in the shed, locked up where Spider had put her when she tried to run. She wouldn't be going anywhere. He wasn't going to risk her snitching again.

Just another crazy Saturday with the Dead Boys.

They'd been up since yesterday, since the Chinese kid, and now they were burning a big hole into Saturday, with crystal meth to keep them up and smoke and booze to keep them jolly.

Dredge took a long slug of King Cobra, trying to fathom what they'd done.

He'd always thought he was a loose one but look at these boys. Beano getting up and doing a strange dance he said the Hell's Angels UK did, boots fixed to the floor, twisting his shoulders back and forth to some guy shrieking at the top of his lungs, on top of the chunk-chunk-chunk guitars. The Dead Boys shouting along. Maybe if they screamed loud enough, they'd forget what happened on Highway 9.

But Dredge didn't think so. The Dead Boys weren't forgetting; they were making sacred. Forging a link to their ancient past. Sawney getting all the words right as he bellowed along, a Brit missing the soccer fields, putting the boot in on the terraces.

Dredge finished the can of Cobra. Last night Spider made them all shower together, down by the shack in the woods. Where Eva was.

Spider's house, up by Sky Londa, was way out in the trees, on the edge of the Santa Cruz Mountains. Facing east, desolate, acres gone to hell. And Spider's broken-down house, brown and sunken, was buried under a canopy of twisted branches.

Where no one would find them.

Last night, when they were done with the Chinese kid, they stood silent in the woods by Highway 9. Silence seeped into them as they hovered around the body, sensing what they'd done. No words. Beyond words.

Spider said no one would recognize the Chinese kid because to do that, he would have to have fingerprints, teeth, hair. And he wouldn't have any.

Spider said it would look like the work of crazy people. That got some looks from the other leather jackets. Then Spider qualified it: Arabs, Viet Cong, Cambodia. You didn't need a copyright for this kind of shit. It had all been done before. Old news.

They were just dealing with the enemy.

Ben and Fritter nodded at that. Yeah, you got to know who your enemy is.

"Just another way to burn a sucker," Fritter said.

Spider liked that.

Fritter said William Burroughs wrote it.

Spider didn't know who William Burroughs was. Fritter said he was a famous doper, old as shit now. Spider said he must have wrote it down for someone to read then, to make it concrete.

By the shack, Spider made them burn the kid's clothes and scrub their leathers, leathers splattered in the frenzy. They stuffed the taupe double-breasted suit, the shoes, everything, into the oil drum out back, by the shack. Where Eva was. Spider, thin and strong with speed, kicked holes in the rusting can to feed the fire. The Dead Boys stood around, watching the sun descend and the flames take over. Bonded together. They gathered under the outdoor shower-head by the shack, stripping off together, burning evidence as well as souls. Under cold water, Dredge watched them while they slowly, silently lathered. Then the horseplay started. Delirium as they showered off the Chinese kid. Fritter grabbed for Sawney.

Be a man, kill a man.

The guitars and drums screeched to a halt. And Dredge knew what the Dead Boys were thinking. He watched Fritter and Sawney leer and roll. The DJ had screamed out their sodden thoughts. Yesterday they had committed murder. Today they were ticking away. They wanted the panties. And Eva was wrapped up, tighter than a tick.

And Dredge knew what Spider would do to bind them forever.

Make sure Eva didn't snitch or squeal.

Make sure they stuck this one out together.

Brothers into the gates, he said.

Dredge couldn't let that happen.

CHAPTER 11

WHEN DETECTIVE DANIEL MORAN'S Motorola Pageboy went off before the Serenity Prayer, he figured it was Grisset again, with another question because he had Moran right where he wanted him. Grisset, recently from San Jose Narcotics, who used his connections to land himself a homicide slot at Santa Cruz, where he could work on his fog tan and muscle Moran out of the way. They didn't call Grisset a replacement exactly, but you didn't need a crystal ball to see what was coming. Grisset never tired of paging Moran on the newest electronic contraption the department had adopted. An electronic leash on a cigarette-sized box you had to carry around on your belt like you were some kind of robot.

But for once, Moran didn't mind the interruption; he'd had enough AA for one day, holding hands with the other drunks who couldn't drink anymore. He left the meeting early and went outside and dropped a dime in the payphone and dialed headquarters.

But it wasn't Grisset who'd paged him. It was Krieger, the Santa Cruz County Medical Examiner, calling from a site up in the mountains, where the San Mateo Sheriffs had found a DB—dead body—in pieces. No one else called Moran much anymore, not since he'd been sent up to Alta Bates for the third time to dry out. Krieger was still OK with Moran. He and Krieger went back a ways.

Krieger said there might be an issue of jurisdiction. Highways 9 and 35 ran close to the San Mateo County border. Moran said if it was just before the intersection, it was Santa Cruz. Krieger said yeah, he thought so, too, but Sheriff De Lucca was saying different. Moran should hurry, Krieger said, this was a hot one.

To Krieger, every DB was a hot one. It didn't matter if it was an old woman whose time had come, lying peacefully still in her cold bed, or a drifter rotting by the freeway. Moran was going to get there before Grisset got involved. He was going to die with his boots on.

A glorious sun was leaning in from the Pacific on a Sunday afternoon as Moran drove up to the site. Light blue sky hinted at wisps of vapor. By late afternoon that vapor would be fog, sucked into Santa Cruz, high fingers of cloud reaching inland.

Well, Moran really had no one to blame but himself, drinking like a fish for how many years? How could anything he loved so much treat him so poorly?

By the time Moran pulled into the gravel road off Highway 9, the San Mateo Sheriff's deputies had the yellow crime scene tape up around the far end of a clearing under a lone redwood. There were San Mateo green-and-whites angled around the field, a green-and-white van and De Lucca's black LTD sitting in the middle of the clearing, staking ownership. Krieger's red County Medical sedan was nestled off to one side. The video specialist—another new contrivance—was videotaping something under the redwood. Investigators crawled over the crime scene like maggots.

Moran figured in close to thirty years on the job he'd seen most every kind of John Doe there was. But when he got past the yellow tape, to where the video guy and Krieger were, and got a good look at this particular Doe, he had to remove the clip-on tie Daphne had bought him and loosen the collar of his short-sleeve shirt and take some deep breaths. He had to pull his glasses off his big nose and blink a few times while his stomach settled.

Maybe it was the lack of booze made it look the way it did.

Krieger said, "San Mateo had the video camera outfit up here before they even called Santa Cruz County Med. These bastards want to pull this one out of the bag before we do."

But Moran wasn't really listening as he stared at the poor, naked, hacked-up Doe. No head. No hands. Darker skin. Not Mexican, like the ones found at the summit. Probably another drug-related homicide.

He knew the Doe probably had it coming.

But that didn't matter either. Thirty-five days without a drink might have had something to do with it. All Moran knew was that this Doe—possibly the last—was his.

"Like the Mexicans," Krieger said. "Dumped off the summit."

"Except they weren't mutilated. They were shot execution-style."

"Don't forget the one force-fed dope," Krieger said. "But look. Now someone's into heads. This poor slob got his lopped off. Badly I might add."

"Yes, I can see that, Krieger. But this one isn't Hispanic."

"Someone's showing off."

"Flexing their muscles. A drug war, perhaps." That's what the four Mexicans found off the summit were up to. Maybe someone wanted them out of the way.

"You think that's what this is?"

"You bet," Moran said. "Speed. No more kicking back, smoking a joint, listening to hippie music. Kids get amped up now, stay up for days at a time. Start seeing things, turn psychotic. And the people who sell it are worse. Not that they were much to begin with." Moran realized how he must sound. He'd always understood criminals. But not so much anymore.

"No shit, Danny. Someone cut this guy's head off."

"But if he's in Santa Cruz County—he's ours."

"You best tell De Lucca that," Krieger said. "Here he comes now."

Moran turned his head. Across the field, De Lucca, the San Mateo Sheriff, came a-waddling.

"What are you doing on my site?" Moran said innocently enough when he finally arrived.

De Lucca didn't like it.

"Where's Grisset?" he asked, trying not to look at the Doe. "I distinctly told County Med to call Grisset."

De Lucca had spent close to $800,000 of San Mateo's money in a joint effort with San Jose to combat escalating crime rates. It had been a flop, with two San Mateo deputies brought up on corruption charges. De Lucca was up for re-election. Solving a nice grisly murder would be a badly needed feather in his cap. And Grisset was a golf buddy.

"Well," Moran said. "I'm here now. And I'll take it. Thanks for your help, Sheriff."

"Now hold on just a minute," De Lucca said. He wore a freshly laundered uniform and had a drinker's nose going blue in middle age. Moran smiled because somehow he had escaped that particular damnation. "This is a joint investigation if nothing else." De Lucca continued: "I insist that my men be utilized. Parts of Highway 9 run into San Mateo County—as you know."

"Not this part. *As you know.*"

"Until the location is resolved, I insist that my men continue to assist."

"I've got Krieger and I can always call Grisset."

De Lucca squinted. "Didn't you just get out of rehab again?"

"Yeah, I did, as a matter of fact. But I still know how to read a map. And any map will tell you this is Santa Cruz."

A long-limbed San Mateo deputy tapped the Doe's torso with the toe of his boot like it was a wet log.

"Do you want to tell him to quit doing that?" Moran said, loud enough to make the deputy stop, give Moran a sheepish look.

De Lucca made an annoyed face. "Dimick's going to hear about this."

Dimick, Moran's chief.

"Fine," Moran said. "See if you can get him to believe this is your jurisdiction. Until you do, you're in my way."

Moran waited until they were gone. He'd be hearing from Chief Dimick soon enough. He'd have to work fast. Krieger used Moran's police radio in his unmarked to called County Med for a wagon.

"Well, Krieger," Moran said, removing his glasses and cleaning them with a handkerchief. "Is this a hot one you can figure out quickly?"

Krieger, bobbing on his haunches like a big chubby kid,

scanned the area around the headless body under the redwood. He looked solemn in a fat-faced grimace as he rattled off the details. It was a butcher job, done with a blunt-edged instrument, a shovel maybe. No, the edges were too jagged. Machete? But with short, ragtag cuts. Multiple instruments he concluded. He had thought the victim was a Mexican at first, but after what Moran had said, wasn't so sure.

"What's that?" Moran pointed at a smear of nearly dried blood on the Doe's shoulder.

Krieger peered around as if someone might be watching, then rubbed his thumb over the splotch of blood, wiping most of it away, revealing a tattoo of a curved shape about two inches long and half an inch wide.

"Looks like a crescent moon," he said.

"That's exactly what it is," Moran said. "It's a Tong badge."

"A Tong badge."

"Tongs. Gangs."

"Orientals?"

"You're supposed to call them Asians now," Moran said.

"Well, call this one *gone*," Krieger said, pulling up the knees of his khaki pants and squatting by where the head had once been. Krieger touched the corner of what had been the neck with the nail of his little finger, pushing at a glob of congealed blood. "Pretty recent. But without the liver temperature, I can't say exactly." Krieger dipped his head to examine the open neck. "Rigor mortis has set in."

Not only was the head gone. So were the Doe's hands. Krieger was like a child on the beach as he looked this way, that way.

"Chinese gangs," Moran said, thinking out loud.

"Don't you mean Asian?" Krieger said, grinning.

"They started in Hong Kong. Moving into California now. Members get a tattoo when they've made the club."

"Nice little club. But whoever did this, Danny, was one twisted puppy."

"*Puppies.*"

"Yeah." Krieger looked around, nodding. "Too much work for one man."

"Someone went to a great deal of trouble to make sure we don't find out who he really is," Moran said. "But it's enough to send a message to the other side in a gang war."

"The Mob?"

"Too rough for the Mob." Moran wiped his glasses with his handkerchief. "They like to put a 22 behind your ear. Nice and clean. But not for guys who do a lot of crank."

"You thinking those guys who did the Mexicans?"

"Bingo," Moran said. "Getting carried away. Out of control. Speed will do that."

"So who we talking about, Danny?" Krieger said. "We got a Mexican gang, and an Oriental Asian gang."

Moran looked around, at the tire tracks. Everywhere. Many of them single tire tracks.

"Motorcycle tracks—just like up on the summit. Even though the sheriff's deputies have managed to drive all over them."

"You're right, Danny," Krieger said, looking around. "Plain as day. I'm gonna be sorry to see you go."

CHAPTER 12

A COLD WIND whipped up 101 as Colleen headed to Santa Cruz. The car heater probably hadn't worked since 1968. But Colleen had several things going for her that she didn't have before: the loan of Leon's '65 Cutlass with half a tank of gas, and twenty-one ounces of Off-Duty Police Special, sans numbers, hanging in a gym sock under the dash. And a lead: the Double Deuce: a bar in East Palo Alto, owned by Maurice, owner of the Hornet in SF, where Pam used to work, under the moniker of Eva.

Maurice and the Dead Boys were connected. Somehow.

Colleen pulled off the freeway, wondering how Pamela was spending her Sunday. East Palo Alto looked like Detroit with palm trees.

She edged the Oldsmobile in front of the Double Deuce, open at 6 a.m., parking behind a fat black Harley with a German Iron Cross painted on the tank. Mariachi music blew out the open door. *Alla en el rancho grande!* reminding her of West Denver, the Mexican side of town. Used to go there in better times with her ex.

Long before she killed him.

She sat in the Cutlass eyeing the place. Old pickup trucks. Beater cars. Blue collar at best, illegals too. *Campesinos.* Farm workers.

Men, most of them Latinos, were checking out Colleen as she walked into the dive bar, Colleen giving it some swagger in her jeans and leather jacket despite her apprehension. Defense mechanism. The place had that tenuous feel. Drugs. People who worked a lot of long hard shifts frequently needed something to keep them going. One of those pinball machines sat in the corner, with no flippers, where the bar paid off if you hit the right numbers. Christmas tree lights strung up around the ceiling, year-round she'd bet.

And there was a white guy, the kind who would drink in a Chicano bar. Stringy blond hair, bald as a coot on top. A face battered by alcohol and a few fists. Wearing biker garb, a black leather sleeveless jacket over blue denim. One of the Dead Boys, the gang her daughter was rumored to be hanging with?

She'd have to play it cool. But stay tough. A balancing act on the high wire of her nerves.

Colleen walked up to the bar. The place quiet now that a new female was here.

A Latino bartender with slicked-back hair and a tight white T-shirt was shaking a metal cocktail shaker. Colleen pulled up a wooden stool. A few men playing Liar's Dice turned to give her the once-over. A soundless TV over the bar, something old in black and white.

The bartender flicked his chin at Colleen, acknowledging her, then walked down to the end of the bar, kicked opened the little door, walked through, put the frosty shaker down in front of the bald coot biker. The biker didn't acknowledge him.

"On the tab, Fritter?" the bartender said.

"Yeah."

The bartender came back behind the bar, up to Colleen. Another little flick of his chin.

"Draft," Colleen said.

"We're out of draft."

"Whatever you have in the way of beer that doesn't cost an arm and a leg, then."

The bartender dug out a can of Olympia, put it down in front of Colleen, unopened.

"On the house."

"Hey, thanks." Sometimes it actually paid to be a woman. Colleen picked up the can.

"Haven't seen you in here before," the bartender said.

"That's because I haven't been here before."

Out of the corner of her eye, she saw the biker he'd called Fritter turn his head, eye her.

"You don't happen to know a guy named Spider, do you?" she said to the bartender, loud enough for Fritter to hear.

The bartender grimace, as if not sure what to say.

"Who did you say?" Fritter said.

She turned to Fritter. "Spider. Know him?"

That was good for five seconds' worth of silence. Which translated to eight bars of *El Rancho Grande* bouncing along.

"Who wants to know?" the biker said, pouring his drink into a martini glass.

She walked over, stood in front of his table. "Me. Can I sit down? You won't have to buy me a drink. I already have one."

That got a crooked smile. "Suit yourself, babe."

She pulled a chair out and sat down. "I bet you want to know what a nice girl like me is doing in a place like this."

He sipped his drink. Grinning. "Sure."

"I'm looking for Pamela."

"Who?"

"Maybe it's Eva—I think she's a friend of Spider?"

Eyes narrowing, he signaled *no* with a single shake of the head. But she saw enough to see that he knew something.

She felt a dark encouragement. Push ahead.

"I'm a friend of Pamela—Eva, whatever she's going by now. All I want to do is get hold of her. That's it."

"Wish I could help." He drank, put his drink back down. "But I can't, babe."

"So, are you a Dead Boy? I didn't get a good look at the back of your jacket." Colleen popped the beer. "My ex used to ride with a crew. In Denver." The froth fizzed over the side of the can, and she held it away from her, letting beer drip onto the floor. Then she took a slug. "Spider's a Dead Boy, too, right?"

The biker poured another two inches of rust-colored liquid into his martini glass.

"You know what? I think it's time for you to beat it."

She sat there for a moment, eyes locked with a guy who called himself Fritter. She was getting antsy, but this wasn't the time to back down. To guys like this, in a place like this, that would be an admission of defeat.

Full strength ahead. Into he breach.

"You guys sell dope, right?" Colleen said. "Speed? Isn't that what you call it? The stuff you Dead Boys sell? Speed? Crank? Nitro? Bullet? Amp? Blue Belly? White Cross? Barney Dope? Blizzard? Boo-Yah? Kryptonite? Methandfelony? Satan Dust? Am I gettin' through to you at all, *hombre?*"

"You just walk in here, talking shit."

"Yes, I do." She drank gassy beer. "Have you seen her? Eva? Pamela?"

"Get the fuck out. Before I twist your panties into a knot."

The bartender coughed and said, "You best go. For your own good."

She turned. "How about that?" The Latinos were no longer watching TV. They were watching her. "Do you have Spider's phone number by any chance?" she asked. "Or his address?"

She could hear Fritter standing up, pushing his chair back. She turned back around, trying to stay cool, like she wasn't going to get rattled.

Fritter was standing. He was big. There was a smell of oil. And other less pleasant odors. He hitched up his pants.

"Spider's unlisted," he said.

"But you deal dope for him right out of this bar, right? Scap? Sugar? Yammer Bammer? I guess Maurice won't let you work in his good bar. The one in Santa Cruz?" Colleen took her last pull on her beer, put the can down on the table, stood, reached into the pocket of her brown leather jacket, held her 38 there, ready.

"I don't have much of a sense of humor anymore," she said. "So just tell me where I can find Spider and I'll be one my merry way."

Fritter's teeth were brown when he spoke. "You're gonna get your ass kicked, bitch. After I fuck it. Which is just what you need."

Colleen sighed, pulled the gun. Pointed it at Fritter.

Fritter flinched but to his credit not too much. There

was taut silence around the bar. She was keeping one eye open, make sure the barman didn't have a weapon.

"OK," Colleen said. "Where's the dope?"

"What fucking dope?" Fritter's voice wavered just a hint.

"The Wigg? Ugly Dust?" She waved the gun. "Is any of this making any sense, douchebag?"

"Easy now."

"Easy as pie. As long as I get the shit you sell to these people. I'm serious. I'm not leaving until I get Spider's address or your stash."

They eyed each other for a long moment.

"Carmen," Fritter said to the barman. "Give it to her."

A freezer baggie full of wax packets, which she assumed were powder, appeared on the bar. Colleen stepped over sideways, the gun on Fritter, scooped up the bag. It weighed a pound or so. She shoved it down the front of her jacket, zipped the jacket up.

Fritter shook his head.

"If you see Spider before I do, tell him if he wants his dope back, I need to see Pamela. Eva. In one piece. Think you can remember that?"

Fritter said, "You *will* be sorry."

"I'm past that point."

Colleen walked backwards, the gun steady, all eyes on her. She backed out the door, slipping the pistol in her pocket, just as a patrol car cruised by. Walking to the Cutlass, hyperventilating with the adrenaline of the stand-off, Colleen got in, turning the ignition key. The car sputtered to life as Fritter and a couple of patrons sauntered out of the bar.

Down Bay Street, in the rearview, she could see Fritter

walking out to watch her drive off. Nothing like starting a little fire.

CHAPTER 13

IT WAS STRANGE, Detective Daniel Moran thought, the things that caught your eye when you wanted a drink. On his way into Center Street Station this gray Sunday morning, the place smelling of fresh paint, he noticed a stuffed animal, a black spider, furry legs dangling over the arm of a small girl. She was standing with a woman, barely old enough to be her mother, who was talking to Grimes, the desk sergeant.

Maybe it was the spider that caught his eye. You were supposed to see insects and such when you were drying out.

"We still want to make a statement," the woman said to Grimes. She was an attractive brunette, wearing faded jeans and a man's white Oxford shirt tied in a knot around her slim midriff. The little girl with her was cute, quiet, with a pretty nose like her mother. But a serious-looking child.

Grimes's black face was glazed over with desk-duty ennui. The Sunday paper was spread open in front of him.

Moran went upstairs to where one of Grisset's hilarious pink *While You Were Fucking Off* message slips was taped to his desk phone.

The *urgent* box was ticked.

Grisset wasn't in the office so Moran had him paged. Technology was moving too fast as far as he was concerned. He would have been quite happy to ignore Grisset. But with the electronic-leash thing, he had to follow protocol.

When his phone rang, he answered. He couldn't even get a sentence out.

Grisset already knew about the Chinese John Doe—Chinaman Doe, Grisset called him. Sheriff De Lucca had told him all about it.

"Look, Moran. San Mateo had Chinaman Doe under control before you loused it up."

Steam rose slowly from Moran's ears.

"So you've talked to Sheriff De Lucca," he said. "And he says it's his case?"

"Something wrong with that?"

"Only if you look at a map."

"San Mateo got there first. San Mateo also has most of the evidence."

Moran could hear the laughter and clinking of glasses in the nineteenth hole wherever Grisset was calling from. "San Mateo had half a dozen men walking all over the evidence up in the woods. They didn't even call the DA." He paused, heard Grisset take a long pull on something, probably cool and wet. "But I'm taking care of this."

"I already told De Lucca the case is his," Grisset said.

"Why the hell would you do that? It's not your call."

"He wants to help out."

"All he wants is the press and TV. He's running for reelection. Everybody's up in arms about drugs and gangs. Especially Chinese gangs. Ever since Viet Nam, they think all Asians are out to get us."

"Moran, will you lighten up, already? I already told you…"

"I'm still the lead here. So hold your damn horses."

There was silence on the other end of the line. Moran heard people laughing in the background of the bar Grisset was calling from.

"Tell De Lucca I want the remainder of the evidence sent over. De Lucca might have pulled a few strings so you could transfer to Santa Cruz, but that doesn't mean he does your job for you. And get a new message pad. The old one was funny about five years ago."

"You know what your problem is, Danny?" Grisset was obviously puffing on a cigarette now, his voice smoky with anger. "You need to unwind. Why don't you head over to Arni's and sink a few? You used to suck those babies down, right? You can even put 'em on my tab."

"Seriously?" Moran said. "I can do that—stick drinks on your tab?"

"Knock yourself out, buddy."

Moran jerked the phone away from his ear when Grisset slammed it down.

Moran hung up the phone, headed downstairs.

The furry spider was still drooping from the little hand. The good-looking young woman was still sitting on the wooden bench with her daughter. Sergeant Grimes flipped a page on his newspaper.

Moran walked over to the woman.

The girl clutching the spider was shaky, but you had to look. She was trying to hide it, like an older child.

"You look like you could use some help," he said to the woman.

The woman shot Moran a look. She had sharp green eyes.

"My tax dollars at work," she said. "I've been here close to an hour. I want to make a statement."

Moran turned to Grimes. Grimes rolled his eyes.

"Have someone take her statement, Sergeant," Moran said.

"We're short-handed. It's Sunday."

"I'm aware of that." Moran turned back to the woman. "What's the problem?"

"Little girl here saw some bikers in a gas station," Grimes said, flipping a page.

Moran spoke to the girl's mother. "What gas station?"

"The BP station on Highway 9."

"On the way up to the mountains?"

The women nodded, then the little girl, not too sure of herself.

"I'm sure it's nothing," the mother said, her voice softening. "But Justine was so insistent ... And we've had problems with the same bikers. They're staying next door to us. I already made one statement about one of them this week and he was brought in. But next day, wouldn't you know? He's back at the house. Some system you got."

"Really?" Moran said. "Thank you for coming in. I'll be back in a few minutes. Don't go anywhere. I'll take your statement. Grimes, find them somewhere to sit, and get me a copy of her earlier statement, and get them something to drink, will you?"

———

The Center Street Station off-duty crowd went mute when Moran walked up to the bar.

"Danny," Arni said, blinking in surprise from under a mop of curly hair. "I thought you weren't..."

"Drinks!" Moran said, shaking his fist in the air. "Drinks for everyone!"

A roar of applause erupted around the bar.

"Danny," Arni said quietly. "Daphne called last week and said you were most definitely *not* drinking..."

"Hell, make it two rounds. You too, Arni. I mean it."

Arni squinted at him. "You sure about this, Danny?"

"I'm celebrating," Moran said firmly, slapping his hand on the bar. "Yes, I'm celebrating. So it's drinks for everyone."

"OK," Arni said, pulling up a bottle of Jim Beam and a shot glass. "The usual?"

"Oh, not for me, Arni. I'm on the wagon. I mean everyone else."

Arni whispered, "I can't run a tab, Danny. Daphne said..."

"And I wouldn't expect you to," Moran said. "Not with my history. Hell, you'd be nuts. Grisset said to put it on his tab."

"He did?"

"He most certainly did. Ask him. I just talked to him on the phone."

"Your word's good enough for me, Danny. What are you celebrating?"

"Thirty-six days without a drink."

———

The ancient roller coaster emerged from a cloud of morning fog. The clacking of an empty string of cars rolled over its hump. Colleen drove the Cutlass into Santa Cruz, dipping down into the basin of land that cupped the beach, edging to the water where the Boardwalk lay. There was a pier, a long one, the wharf they called it, running out to sea, had to be half a mile long. At the end of the wharf was a bar—The Brass Rail. Owned by Maurice.

Colleen parked at the base of Municipal Pier, left the Off-Duty Special in its sock under the dash. But she grabbed a handful of Fritter's stash of five-dollar bags and shoved them into a plastic baggie.

A few Sunday strollers moved along the pier. She couldn't believe people wore shoes with three-inch platform soles as she watched them negotiate the weather-beaten planks. The Boardwalk, with its faded amusement park ambiance, caught hints of sun. Out in the ocean bodies in wetsuits were pedaling out on surfboards. Gulls squawked.

At the end of the pier, with its etched glass and over-sized windows, The Brass Rail was a far cry from the hole Colleen had left in East Palo Alto not two hours ago. The entrees started at $7.95. Prices had gone crazy in ten years.

Unzipping her leather jacket, she pushed open the door and went in. There were red velvet booths. In one, three well-to-do thirtysomething women were lip-sticking Bloody Marys and Virginia Slims as if they owned the place. Big hair, bell bottoms, paisley print dresses and high boots. No men. Out on the town at eleven in the morning. Behind the bar a young stud with a silly perm arranged long-neck bottles in a glass and chrome case. His body was a sculpted, bodybuilder V.

He had a black-and-white nameplate that read Clifford.

"What'll it be?" He wiped a glass, checking Colleen out. It was nice to know she still had it. She had been feeling less than pristine in her Levi's, T-shirt, and old bomber jacket, especially next to the party girls in the booth.

"I'm here to see Maurice."

Clifford set the glass down. He spoke quietly. "And you are?"

"Colleen Hayes. I've got something belongs to Spider." She raised her eyebrows. "I got it from some character named Fritter in a place called the Double Deuce."

Clifford leaned forward on his elbows. "OK. Leave."

"Ouch. A minute ago, you were looking at me like I was a pastrami sandwich."

"Now I'm looking at you like maybe you better beat it."

"Just like that? I need to see Maurice. Seems he runs things—more or less. And no one wants to tell me where I can find Spider so—."

From the booth the women were quiet, watching the building confrontation.

Clifford reached for the phone. "I'm calling the cops."

She pulled a baggie containing some of the powder packs she'd taken from Fritter out of her pocket, partway, enough so Clifford could see it.

"You sure Maurice isn't around?" she asked.

Clifford put the phone in its cradle. "Put that away. I'll take you back."

Colleen slipped the bag back into her jacket pocket. "No, bring him out here—out in the open."

"Do you have any idea what you're doing?"

Colleen's hand came out of her jacket with the baggie again.

"OK," Clifford said. "OK!"

Colleen put the baggie back, sat down on a barstool. The women in the booth went back to their drinks. She turned to them.

"How're the drinks here?" she said, brushing hair out of her face.

"Not bad," a woman with a platinum-feathered mane said.

Colleen heard footsteps coming through the bar.

She turned to see Maurice's bronze face, creased in anger. If looks could kill.

He slid one hand in the pocket of flared black slacks. He wore a roomy sport coat over a red silk shirt. Crushing out an inch of cigarette in an ashtray on the bar, he said, "Are you for real?" He came around the bar and stood so that the two of them had their backs to the booth women. Colleen's body tightened as Maurice stared into the mirror behind the bar, straight into her reflected eyes. She noted the telltale spot of dried blood under his chin where she had pressed the bottle into it a couple of days ago. "You got a hell of nerve," he whispered, patting Colleen's shoulder affably.

"I found something. In one of your bars."

"I got no idea what you're talking about."

"Oh, OK. Well, it's dope. Speed. I took it off someone named Fritter. Weird name, huh? He was selling it in the Double Deuce. Did you know that? You probably should. You own the place."

"Nice story. None of which can be proved. Or means anything. But your point is...?"

"My daughter Pam—Eva—used to work for you. We both know that. Just tell me where she is. And I'll give part of your dope back now and the rest when I meet her. And then all of this is forgotten."

"Or you'll do what? Go to the cops? I get on pretty well with the police. How about *you*?"

Colleen stared into the mirror. "I don't think those bikers are paying for their drinks, by the way. Where's Spider?"

"Spider?"

"Yeah, Spider. The biker my daughter is hanging around with."

"Maybe your daughter doesn't want you looking for her. You ever think about that?"

"Sure. But you let me worry about that and you focus on those bikers not paying for their drinks."

"*Those bikers* just might hurt you—you given that any thought?"

"All I want is my daughter." Colleen frowned into the mirror. "Just give me an address where I might find her. Then I won't have any reason to ever bother you again. Except to give you the rest of your stuff back."

Maurice seemed to mull that over. "Believe it or not, I know what you're going through. I got three girls of my own. The first two are good kids, my eldest is getting married September. But the youngest..." Maurice gave a shrug. "She's gonna give me heart failure. It's her boyfriend with the earring and the long hair. I almost wish she'd start hanging around with bikers." Maurice smiled. "So, I'll do you a favor. One parent to another."

"You know, I really appreciate it."

"Sure you do. 239 Delaveaga Park Road. Up by the municipal golf course. I'm not saying Eva's there now, but she was at one time. But you best hurry. Because you got twenty-four hours to get her. That's one day. After that I'm done with you—*and* your daughter." He patted Colleen's shoulder again. "Do we understand each other?"

"We do." Colleen pulled the baggie from her pocket, set it on the bar. Clifford immediately removed it from view. "Have a *great* day."

She had a deal. Not the best but better than she had before, which was nothing. She'd have to watch her back. But Pam was her daughter, and she was her mother. And

Pam needed to be removed from whatever situation she was in.

Colleen zipped up her jacket and left the bar.

Maurice stood at the window of the Brass Rail, hands in his pockets. The three women in the booth finished their drinks, collected handbags, waved for the tab.

"On the house today, ladies," Maurice said. "Enjoy your day."

"Why thank *you*," big blonde said, slurping the last of her Mary.

They left, the cry of seagulls floating in as the door opened and closed. Outside, one of them lit up a cigarette while the other freshened lipstick. Maurice gave her a smile and a small wave through the window.

Clifford came out of the shadows.

"Want me to take care of that Hayes woman?" he said to Maurice.

"Think you could?" Maurice said, turning halfway to smirk at Clifford.

Clifford seemed offended. "Sure."

"Women are changing, Cliffie. Right in front of our eyes. It's the Age of Aquarius or some such bullshit. No, tell Spider I said that woman has permission to get her daughter."

"Tell Spider?" Clifford said, "Isn't that like ordering someone else's dog around?"

"Just do what I say. She's got one day to get her daughter back."

Down on dry land, another line of cars clattered over the roller coaster's hump, arms raised and waving. Poised to make the drop. Colleen got to the Cutlass, heaved the door open with a squeal.

She sat there, watching the roller coaster hurtle to the bottom of the dip amidst screams, thinking how she had failed her daughter. She had killed her ex in a fit of rage, and now she seemed to be back on a familiar path. Whatever transpired this time she had to think of Pamela first.

Next stop. 239 Delaveaga.

CHAPTER 14

"I CAN'T FUCKING BELIEVE," Spider said as he chopped up a small pile of white powder with a razor blade, "you let some *woman* pull a gun on you."

It was dark in the back of The Double Deuce, mariachi horns drifting out of the jukebox up front where the Mexicans were hanging around the bar. Carmen, the bartender, stared into empty space. Dredge nursed an Olympia, watching Spider slice lines with the edge of the blade, playing with the white powder, dragging it along the center of the table, avoiding the wet rings the beer bottles had made.

"What was I supposed to do?" Fritter said, his shades on, just like Spider, only Fritter had his on to hide his embarrassment. "Bitch pulls a gun, man ... what would *you* do?" Fritter punched his open hand for emphasis, like he was tough. "And then she rips us off."

"Rips *you* off," Spider said. He was making three big lines, Dredge could see, the crystal powdered out so it wouldn't sting so much. "I know you can't stop a woman, is what I know. I know you let her walk out of here with our rock is what I know. I know Maurice thinks we're a bunch of pussies now is what I know."

"That Colleen chick said she'd give him the rest of the crank back," Dredge said, hoping one of those fat lines was for him. "If we let her take Eva."

"It was *our* crank to begin with, dumbshit."

"OK. But why not think about it?"

Spider looked up, his black plastic wraparounds motionless for the longest time, facing Dredge while the enchilada music played.

"Whose fucking side are you on?" Spider went back to chopping.

Dredge couldn't stop thinking about Eva, up at Spider's place, doped to the gills for the second day. And so were Beano, Sawney, Helmet.

Eva's mother had come to get Eva. Dredge liked that idea. Eva could be free in twenty-four hours. He just needed to find a way to keep her safe until then and send her home with Mom.

"So," Dredge said. "We get the speed back—whoever it belongs to. Then we let Eva go, so we can get on with things. Right?"

Spider pointed the razor at Dredge. "You think we're gonna let some bitch fuck Fritter's ass, then have Maurice tell us what we can and can't do?"

"Hey," Fritter said. "It wasn't like that."

"'Wasn't like that,'" Spider mimicked, slicing and sneering. "Well, the fuck was it like, then, Fritter? You mind telling me 'cause I would really like to know."

Fritter sat there with his arms crossed tight.

Spider peeled off his wraparounds, eyes cracked red. "I can tell you how it's gonna be." With that Spider bent down, pulled an old straw off the floor. He placed it on the table, cut it in half with the razor. Taking one half of a straw, Spider bent over the table, snorted up a fat line. Then he sat up, eyes flickering. You could see his neck vibrate as the shit raced through him.

Dredge was thinking he just should've smacked Spider's head with the back of his fist while Spider was down there, smashed it wide open. Jam the straw up his nose.

He was good at thinking of things he should have done.

Spider said, "That Chinaman's gonna look like nothin' when we get finished with Eva's old lady."

Dredge gasped.

Fritter nodded sullenly, eyeing the two remaining lines.

"Hear that, Dredgie?" Spider had the straw stuck up his nose, hanging. He pulled the straw, wiped his nostril with his thumb and forefinger. The jukebox switched to a fresh tune, noisier than the others. The bar started singing along.

Dredge picked up the remaining half-straw and twiddled it. He needed a hit of courage. All he had to do was keep Eva safe one more day. Then he'd find a way to get her out. Him too. He cleared his throat. "But Maurice said to let Eva go ..."

Spider put his straw down, stood up. Sauntering over to the jukebox. The Mexicans at the bar turned, stopped singing. Spider swung his spindly leather leg back and heaved his boot into the metallic-looking fabric at the bottom of the jukebox.

The record squealed off and died.

"Call that shit music?" Spider walked back to the table, sat down, grabbed the straw, snorted up the second thick line. When he came up his face was clenched. "You assholes want to be Dead Boys? Well, now you are, like it or not. We all cut that dude."

Fritter nodded behind his black shades. "Damn straight."

"I didn't," Dredge said quietly, that tiny bit of courage a struggle to get out.

Out of nowhere, Spider slapped Dredge's face with a blinding smack.

Dredge's head was a golf ball being hit by a club.

Spider took a long slug of beer, watched Dredge while he rubbed his flame-on cheek.

"Brothers," Spider said. "No one backs out now."

Spider made a fist in the air. So did Fritter.

"Dredgie?" Spider said. "We're waiting for you, sweetheart."

Dredge massaged the sting out of his cheek. He was thinking about Spider. And Fritter. And all of them. And how he would like to do, He just needed an opportunity.

He just needed courage.

He raised his hand in a fist.

"Brothers," he said. He'd have to play along until he got a shot at rescuing Eva. If such a thing was even possible.

CHAPTER 15

"AND WHAT DID the Bird Lady do when the man hit her, Justine?" Moran asked. "In the gas station?"

Justine was sitting on the sofa in her mother's house on Delaveaga, Moran across from her in an armchair that had a blanket over it to hide the fact that it was torn and ratty. Student housing.

Justine looked down at the floor.

"What did you say his name was?" Moran asked.

She looked back up. Her mahogany eyes were still and unfocused. Her silky brown hair was in a tail today. Moran forced his best smile. He needed the girl to talk to him. She didn't at the station. He was hoping she'd be more comfortable at home. So he had stopped by. "Was he like the stuffed spider you had at the police station? Spider, did you say his name was?"

"Yes," the girl's mother said. "But I think it's time to put a stop to this. Justine is going through a rough patch. Ever since her father walked out, she's been obsessed with the scum who live next door. They drink and fight and take drugs—then repeat. Justine watches them. She's taken with the girl, a pathetic young woman. Justine says she saw her and one of them—Spider—fighting yesterday, when we stopped for gas but, to be perfectly honest—I didn't see a thing. Now I'm wondering if Justine's imagination might have gotten the better of her. I think she may be simply disoriented, suffering a loss. Since her father took off. She's a sensitive little girl and her psyche ..."

"I understand," Moran said. "Completely. But I have to chase down all leads." He turned back to Justine. "I'd like to hear what Justine says." Justine's brown eyes were glazing over. Getting scared.

"No," Laura Quinlan said, her voice rising. "I don't want you egging her on to believe events that never happened."

"I wouldn't be here if you hadn't made a statement."

"And I told you *I made a mistake*. Justine was over-wrought the other night after she said she saw Spider threatening the Bird Lady, or whatever she calls her, so I called the police. They took Spider in, but the next day, he was back out. I don't need him coming over here. The neighbors around here have become notoriously silent calling the police on them, and for good reason. One woman had her window broken, another man his tries slashed. I think I'll take the hint."

"Are you sure you made an earlier statement, Mrs. Quinlan?"

She threw her hands up. "Isn't anyone paying attention to what's going on down there?"

No, there just hadn't been anything on record. Moran had checked. They'd brought Spider in but let him out the next day. No charges filed.

Why?

Moran stood up, exhaling frustration. "Thank you, Mrs.

Quinlan," he said, taking his shades out of his shirt pocket, slipping them on. "That will be all for now."

Laura stood up, hands on hips in her cutoffs. "No, Detective: I think that will be all—period. I want my daughter left out of whatever this is."

Damn. This had been a decent lead. He'd give Mom a day to cool off.

"Justine," Moran said, but unable to catch her eye. "Thank you. You've been a big help." Then he asked Laura: "May I talk to you outside for a moment?"

She gave a sigh but nodded.

Outside, on the porch with the front door shut, Moran said, "May I give you some advice?"

"Do I have any choice?"

"You said you were moving. That's an excellent idea. Do it sooner rather than later. In the meantime, I'll see that someone stops by on a regular basis, keeps an eye on this place."

Like himself.

"Thank you, Detective."

Moran watched her go inside, cursing himself. In thirty-five years, he still hadn't learnt how to talk to a child. Or people for that matter. All he knew how to do was drink with them. And without them. Especially without them.

He eyed the dump of a house next door, where the bikers hung out. Delaveaga was one of those neglected streets in a nice part of town, by the municipal golf course. The eucalyptus trees were shaggy. As he headed for his unmarked LTD, Moran noticed a beater car, a white Cutlass, mid-sixties model, built when gas wasn't sixty-five cents a gallon. It was parked across the street under an unkempt tree. A lone figure sat behind the wheel, a woman with her shoulder-length hair combed back, staring at the biker house.

From the driver's seat of the Cutlass Colleen saw the plainclothes cop heading her way. The woman who lived in the house next to the house where Eva supposedly stayed, must have called the cops on her. There was no way Colleen could take off now without looking suspicious. The compact cop crossed the street, mustache, sunglasses and short sleeves, no jacket, the shoulder holster, and cannon sticking out from under his armpit a giveaway. Headed her way. Colleen saw him look the Cutlass over as he approached. Hoping he wouldn't search the car and find the 38 in the sock under the dash.

The cop came up to the window. She rolled it down.

"And who might you be?" he said.

"Colleen Hayes. I was just leaving."

"You can leave when I say you can. What are you doing parked here?"

She took a breath. "I'm looking for my daughter. I'm sorry if I caused a disturbance."

"Who says you caused a disturbance?"

"I thought someone might have called me in."

"And why do you think that?"

"Didn't someone call?"

"Just tell me what you're doing here."

"I think my daughter is staying in that house—239. But no one's home. I'm waiting."

"You better let me see some ID."

Colleen got out her Colorado license. Handed it over.

The cop read it, flipped it over, then back. He tapped it.

"Out of the car, please," he said. "Hands where I can see them."

Jesus wept.

Colleen got out of the car.

"Turn around, put your hands on top of the car."

Colleen did as she was told. It all felt familiar. Ten years and yesterday.

The cop surveyed the car while he patted Colleen down. "Is this your vehicle?"

"It's borrowed," Colleen said, feeling the cop's hand run down her inner thigh. He was decent about it at least, didn't go for the gold.

"OK," he said, finishing up. "You can turn back around."

Colleen did.

"Registration?"

In the glove compartment she found a plastic wallet with a clear side to it and a piece of paper that said State of California. She pulled the paper from the wallet, handed it to the cop.

"Where are you staying?" the cop said, reviewing the registration.

"Nowhere just yet."

"California registration, a Colorado driver's license and you're not staying anywhere?" he said. "Imagine what I'm thinking."

"I borrowed the car from a friend up in San Francisco."

"Who's your friend?"

"Leon Smith."

The cop checked the registration, verified that she knew who the car belonged to.

"Can I please explain something?" Colleen said.

"Just stay put for the time being—where I can see you." The cop went off with Colleen's license and the registration, heading over to the LTD. Got in. Colleen saw him pick up the radio.

Christ. She fought the urge to jump in the Cutlass, crank it up, drive to Mexico. But the 38 was well stashed. The baggies of snort were in a locker down at the Boardwalk.

What she needed was to stay calm. She hadn't really done anything she could be arrested for. Maurice or the Dead Boys would not have called the cops on her.

Maybe someone else had called, when Colleen was prowling around the back of the biker house. But she hadn't seen anyone.

The cop was still running his check ...

Stay cool.

Colleen fought three and a half minutes worth of silence under the eucalyptus, standing next to her car. Finally, the door to the LTD opened and the cop got out, came back over.

"You have a record," he said.

"Yes, I do."

"Just got out of prison, as a matter of fact."

"That is also true."

"Looks like you missed your first parole meeting, if I'm not mistaken."

"I waited all day in Frisco and the parole officer never showed up to verify my address."

"Only tourists call it 'Frisco.'"

"I didn't know that," she said.

"What am I going to find if I search this car?"

She forced a smile. "Half a pint of brandy in the trunk.

About half full. So, what's that—a quarter of a pint?" She grinned. "I've been under a lot of pressure."

"You're on parole. Get rid of it."

"I will do that immediately."

"See that you do."

Colleen took her license and Leon's car reg back.

The cop leaned down and stuck his face in. "Do you know the people at number 239 Delaveaga, Ms. Hayes?"

"I'm not sure."

"That's not really the answer I was after."

"I'm hoping to find my daughter. I'm worried sick about her."

"And why is that?"

"She's with a bad crowd."

The cop was watching her closely. "And you came out to California to find her?"

She nodded.

"Have you seen her since coming out here?"

"No, I haven't." Colleen was starting to feel emotional in the constraints of interrogation. "This is as close as I've got. Not very far, is it?"

The cop bent down some more.

"Do not stay parked here. It looks suspicious."

What was that? A friendly warning? Or did he know something? "I won't."

The cop handed Colleen a business card. "Call me if you find your daughter. Call me if you don't and you think you might have any new information. Maybe I can help."

"Thanks." She took the card. "Thanks a lot."

"OK." He patted the roof of the car. "Now you can go."

Colleen started up the Cutlass, pulled a tight one-eighty, drove past the LTD. From the rearview, she saw the cop get in his car, then drive up Delaveaga. Colleen drove most of the way into Santa Cruz, stopped for a drive-thru burger, pulled over, ate the burger with the engine running, spun another one-eighty, back up to 239 Delaveaga to the biker house. It was insanity, but she didn't have a choice.

CHAPTER 16

COLLEEN PARKED the Cutlass further up Delaveaga this time, out of the way. She was still just able to see down the street to the biker house.

She remembered the day she killed Pam's father. All she had been capable of when she found out about her ex and Pam was getting twisted into that corkscrew of anger. After all Pam had been through, what Pam needed was for Colleen to be there for her, like a mother.

But Colleen couldn't do that then.

She saved up from her prison pay, sixty cents a day, and bought Pam the silver magpie earrings for her thirteenth birthday. Pam had just gotten her ears pierced.

And Pam had loved them. It had made being a mother worth it.

If she ever got another chance to see Pam again, she wouldn't mess up again. She'd be the most grateful mother alive, if—when—she found her.

Maurice had given Colleen twenty-four hours to find her. Several had already ticked by. And it didn't look like anyone was home where Eva—aka Pam—supposedly had lived.

Colleen got out of the Cutlass, surreptitiously got a tire iron out of the trunk, tucked it under her arm, and strolled down Delaveaga, looking at the scattered homes, most of them above average. As she got closer to number 239, she saw how rundown it was, and wondered how Pam had wound up there.

Did bikers live in an old beater house tucked away by a golf course? Maybe in California they did. That might account for the stack of tires and tossed furniture. A pool of oil slicked the driveway. Which was otherwise empty. Where were they?

The gray afternoon stalled in the air as she walked up to the front door.

No one was home. But she kind of knew that already.

Colleen rang the doorbell anyway, insurance in case someone was watching. Looking up and down Delaveaga. She sauntered past the crapped-out car seat torn to hell, past the stack of tires, along the side of the house. To the back.

A garage. Padlocked shut with a chain.

Facing the house. A kitchen door in the back.

Locked. Colleen peered into a window that hadn't been cleaned for decades, wiping some grime off with her fist.

A pile of beer cans on that kitchen table. Brown grocery sacks on the floor stuffed with garbage. Cans mostly. All over the place. Yes, this looked like a place Pam might wind up. Some weird posters on the wall, a line of cars on fire on one of them. Adolf Hitler on another. Yeah, this looked like the place all right.

Colleen stood up, gazed around nonchalantly, readied the tire iron.

Edge the tip between the door and jamb here. Perform a little wood surgery.

Suddenly she felt eyes upon her. Her hackles went up. She slid the tire iron down flat by her leg, peered around the corner, up the driveway. The side window of the house next door, another rundown special. A girl, five or six, her hair in a ponytail, watching her. A heartbreaker in about ten years. Her eyes fastened on Colleen's. Well. Colleen couldn't very well snap the back door open now, not with Miss Curiosity watching. Colleen waved with her free hand. Big smile.

The cutie waved back, not smiling. A lonely little wave.

Colleen stood in the driveway, thinking she could go sit in the Cutlass. While her twenty-odd hours ran down. Or she could go on over to the house next door, see if someone had actually seen Pam. She leaned the tire iron down next to the back door, walked around to the house next door.

On the porch, she knocked.

She could hear the little girl going, "Mom? Wake up!"

Colleen waited, knocked again.

She heard the chain come off the door and then the door opened and there she was, all three and a half feet of her, in wild yellow shorts and a T-shirt with a big yellow bird on it. One knee was scabbed, crusted over. The girl teetered back and forth on the heels of her sneakers. She eyed Colleen, sticking her index finger in her ear. If she didn't take Colleen back, coming home from the job at Gate's Rubber in Denver, find Pam waiting on the stoop.

"Will you look at that?" Colleen said, smiling at her T-shirt.

"Are you a policemans, too?"

"Ah, no..."

"Is it about Daddy?"

"No," Colleen said. "Is your mother ... are your parents home?"

"My mom is," she said, hanging on the doorknob. "But she's sleeping. She was up late studying. She's a college student. My dad ran off with a tramp."

"Wherever did you hear something like that?"

"I heard Mom say it to Irene. Irene's the babysitter. *My* babysitter," she said proudly.

"You know," Colleen said, crouching, meeting the child's gaze at eye level. "It's not such a great idea to open the door for strangers."

"Then why did you knock?"

"You just have to be careful, that's all."

"Justine, who is it?" A voice rang from the back of the house. "Justine!"

And then Justine's mother was there too, beside Justine, in a white shortie robe. Straight elegant nose and green eyes burning from under a sweep of thick dark hair.

"Who are you?" the woman said, putting her hand on Justine's shoulder. She had painted nails, something that still caught Colleen's eye after seeing plain hands for a decade.

"Colleen Hayes," Colleen said, standing up from her crouch. "I was just telling your daughter here to be careful opening the door to strangers."

"And who are you?" she said icily.

"She was at the Bad Boys' next door, Mom. I saw her go around back. She was in the car across the street before, too, watching."

"Justine. Shssh."

"It's a long story," Colleen said. "I can explain."

"Perhaps you better leave."

The door shut in her face. *Shit.*

Colleen walked down the path, stopped at the sidewalk, thought about her twenty-four hours sifting through the hourglass, turned back around, went back up to the flaking blue door, knocked again.

The front door cracked open on a chain.

This time it was Mom.

"You again," she said.

Justine appeared around her leg, watching Colleen.

"I'm sorry if I came off weird," Colleen said. "But I don't have a lot of time. My daughter's name is Pamela. I understand she goes by Eva, too. *Eva Braun.* Go figure. I think her hair is red now. I think she's living next door at 239. I'm really worried about her—Pam—Eva, whatever her name is. I came all the way from Colorado to find her. I'm wondering if you've seen her?"

No response.

Colleen pushed ahead. "I know she's in some kind of trouble. If you don't want to get involved, I understand. With the people next door, I mean—bikers, right? If you've seen Pam—Eva—please just say so, and I'm out of your hair. But I can't afford to waste time hanging around if she hasn't been here. That's all I wanted to ask."

The little girl stared up. Mom was blinking in doubt.

"The Bird Lady," Colleen heard the girl Justine say.

"What did you call her?"

"You better come in," the woman said, unhooking the chain, standing back, holding onto Justine's shoulder.

"And," Laura said, sitting on the sofa, her bare feet tucked under her, "that's all I know. I'm sorry I can't be more positive about your daughter."

Despite the news that Pam had been living next door in

the biker house, Colleen actually felt a strange sort of relief. As bad as things were, it *was* something. She could almost say she was getting somewhere.

"And you haven't seen her in two days?" Colleen said.

"Yes." Laura rested her eyes on her daughter. "I've told Justine how important it is for everybody to tell the truth."

It was as if she were trying to convince herself.

Justine nodded, finger back in her ear.

"Remember?" Laura said to Justine. "At the filling station?"

Justine pulled her finger out of her ear.

Laura said: "You said you saw the two men and the Bird Lady? Is that true, Justine? Not pretend? It's very important to this woman. The Bird Lady is her daughter. She may be in trouble. I already told you I didn't see anything in the gas station, so you must remember and remember correctly."

"Two bad boys," Justine said softly.

"Bad boys," Colleen said. *Dead Boys.* As Leon had said. A shudder ran through her.

"Yes," Justine said. "And the Bird Lady."

"The Bird Lady," Colleen said again. A distant bell rang in the back of her mind. "Why is she the Bird Lady?"

"Her earrings."

The magpie earrings. Another jolt rattled her.

"She wore earrings, Justine? Little silver birds?"

"Yes. To fly away."

Jesus Christ, Colleen thought. But at least it meant Pam was alive. Or had been. Colleen took a deep breath in through her nose.

"What kind of a car were they driving?" Colleen asked.

"The station car," Justine said, pointing a small finger at the window. "The one from next door."

"A station wagon?"

"Yes."

"Are you sure, Justine?" her mother said. "Really, really sure?"

"Yes," Justine said. "Really, really."

"It's a Ford Country Squire," Laura said to Colleen. "With those fake wood side panels."

"Please tell me what you saw in the filling station, Justine," Colleen said.

"The Spider and the big one. In the car. And the Bird Lady."

"What were they doing?"

"They were smacking." Justine made a tiny fist and punched her open hand.

Colleen shook off the image of some human scum slapping her daughter around. "Fighting," she croaked.

Justine's eyes grew dark. "Mom was inside going pee and the Spider got mad when the Bird Lady tried to run away, and he smacked her and got her in the car and then all three got in the car. And the Spider said they had to go to a party..."

"Wait," Colleen said. "What party?"

"A party in the mountains," Justine said.

A party in the mountains. Colleen's backbone stiffened.

"Mom," Justine said. "She wanted me to tell. The Bird Lady. But you wouldn't let me. She told me to tell on the Spider."

"When, Justine?" Colleen asked. "When did the Bird Lady tell you this? When?"

"At the gas place. She looked at me and told she was afraid."

Laura said, "Now, Justine..."

"Please," Colleen said. "Let her finish..."

"Then she told me," Justine said, pressing her small hands on her chest. "When I was asleep. She told me."

Colleen went over to the tattered sofa and crouched in front of Justine.

"She told you in a dream."

"Yes."

"Thank you, Justine," Colleen said. "I believe she did tell you that."

"That's enough," Laura said quietly to Colleen. "Please leave now."

"Very well," Colleen said, standing up.

"No!" Justine shouted. "Wait!"

"What on earth is it, Juss?" her mother said. "What's gotten into you?"

Justine hopped off the sofa, thumped off into a bedroom. Thirty seconds later she returned, something clutched in her hand.

She came up to Colleen.

"You need this," she said to Colleen.

She opened her hand.

A single silver earring. A magpie, one of a pair Colleen had given Pam when she turned thirteen. Two years prison pay.

Memories came flooding back, good and bad. Pam had kept the earrings. She had kept them! She still wore them! For a moment Colleen felt a sudden closeness that had been absent for years. A flood of tears welled up inside her and she pushed them back.

"Where did you get that, Juss?" Laura said.

"At the gas place, Mom. The Bird Lady dropped it. She wanted me to have it."

Colleen looked at Laura.

"Are you giving it to her, Justine?"

"Yes. The Bird Lady. She needs both of them."

"May I?" Colleen said to Laura.

Laura frowned. "Take it. Then leave. Please. I don't want Justine involved in this anymore."

"I understand." Colleen took the earring, squeezed Justine's hand. "Thank you, Justine." She turned to Laura. "And thank you."

At the door, Colleen dropped her voice. "May I say something?"

"I think you're going to regardless."

"I had a daughter like Justine not too long ago, and I wished I'd taken better care to keep an eye out for her. Please don't make the same mistake I did." Colleen Hayes, winner of the Bad Mother of the Decade award, dishing out advice. The irony didn't escape her.

Laura ignored that. "I hope you know what you're doing," she said, shutting the door.

CHAPTER 17

DREDGE SHIFTED DOWN TO SECOND, twisting the throttle so he could keep up with Spider and Fritter who were ripping up the curves to the summit. From there Highway 17 would drop them back into Santa Cruz. It was after midnight, frigid ocean breezes over Loma Prieta Ridge dragging fog into Scott's valley.

Spider and Fritter's headlights swept the curved road ahead.

A ride like this should have been righteous: zero traffic, a slew of mountain curves, Harley pipes reverberating through the canyon—the reason Dredge shelled out most of Gramma's inheritance.

But the thought of Eva, up there right now in Sky Londa, with Sawney and Helmet and whoever else to keep her company, gnawed away at Dredge's insides. And no way for Eva's old lady to find her. Maurice had told Spider to let Eva's mother pick her up. Spider said sure, Maurice. Sure he would. And then to Dredge and Fritter, Spider said: Would he? —would he, *fuck*.

And now they were on their way back to Gramma's

house: he and Spider and Fritter, to wait for Eva's old lady—without Eva.

Eva had tried to run again, and Spider locked her up in the shed, out back, where the Dead Boys had showered off the Chinaman. Eva was sedated, stoned out.

Dredge knew what he wanted to do to those motherfuckers. He did. His mind flashed with an image of a shotgun exploding. Wet hairy wallpaper.

Then Dredge remembered where he was.

On a bike. Highway 17. Going around a tight curve. Nighttime. He braked, took a deep breath. Keep an eye on that. He'd been high a few days too long.

If anyone was going to save Eva, it would have to be him.

He'd have to man up.

Lexington Reservoir disappeared behind in wet vapor. The rearview mirror on the handlebar dripped, flickers bouncing off the droplets. Highway 17 turned into a snag of hairpin turns. Dredge milked the curves. Rumbling downstrokes thundered off the ridge. Then the bikes were on top of the summit, fog rolling through the spokes ahead. Indigo sky, white moon, a midnight sun turned inside out.

The Rat's brake light came on. Spider pulled over into the gravel by the side of the road, Fritter behind him. Dredge braked, tossing up a sloppy rooster tail of gravel as he skidded to a stop behind the two of them.

But why come back here? Where Pana and his crew were offed. Wasn't that tempting fate?

Sitting on his chopper, Spider turned around to face Dredge, gave him a prison-yard stare, eyes sunk in a skull with dirty blond hair. Spider dismounted, strutted over to the ridge. Fritter and Dredge followed. It was hot in the helmet. But Dredge wore one, even if Spider and the others made fun. A mock German WW II thing. His ball of black frizzy hair sprung out when he pulled it off.

"Why'd we stop?" Dredge asked, Spider's back to him as Spider peered down the slope into the boiling fog.

Pana and his compadres were gone. It'd been on the news all week.

"You think anyone found that Chinese guy?" Dredge said, chewing his lip. Wondering again why they stopped. Not a good feeling in his gut.

Spider turned round slowly. The moonlight caught his black pupils. "They didn't find all of him."

Dredge took a defensive breath. "I'm not so sure the cops can't put two and two together, even without the hands and head. They got all sorts of shit these days, Spider. Guy up at Santa Rita told me..."

"We're covered." Spider looked down the slope, to his left, then to his right. He spit off the ridge. "Next up is Lum's crew." Spider turned back to the canyon. "Lum takes us on, he's chop suey." Spider cleared his sinuses. Something he did a lot now with all the crank.

"You sure you got it taken care of?" The cool wind blew Dredge's hair back. He'd heard Spider and Fritter talking about some dirty detective, supposed to be helping them out.

"You know what, Dredge? You talk too fucking much." Spider ambled over to the Rat, swung a wiry leg over and jostled his skinny butt into the saddle.

"We need to line up a new source to score," Spider said. "Since Eva's old lady snagged our stash, we are running low on product to sell. Aren't we, Fritter?"

Fritter didn't respond to the implied insult.

"What about that friend of yours?" Fritter said to Dredge. "That pussyboy deals speed at UC?"

"He's a woman now," Dredge said.

"Well, does *she* got any shit to sell?"

"Last time she ripped me off. I think she was more honest when she was a man."

"Men are more honest in general," Fritter said.

Dredge was just gonna say it.

"Spider—when *are* we gonna let Eva go?" he said in a shaky voice.

Spider tilted the bike upright, resting it vertically between his stick legs.

"Do whatever you want, Dredgie. She's there for the taking. Go on. Rip yourself off a piece. You know you're dying to."

Fritter laughed.

"That's *not* what I meant," Dredge said. "I notice we didn't bring her, for her old lady to come and get. Like Maurice said."

Spider grabbed the handlebars and put his boot on the kickstart. He jumped up and landed on it. The bike failed.

"Spider," Dredge said. "We *got* to let her go, man!"

Spider was about to kick it one more time. Then he stopped, turned, and gave another thousand-yard gape. "Eva goes when I say she goes."

Dredge's heart was pumping like a rabbit. "Just do me a favor, Spider, just fucking humor me, once in your life: just let her go, man. Just let Eva's old lady come get her. Puh-lease."

Spider stared from the bike, motionless. "And what makes you think Eva wants to go anywhere, Dredgie boy?"

Dredge felt his voice lose volume, wanting to hide from the world. He hated the way his body went counter to what he wanted it to do. "She does, man. I know. So just let her go. OK?"

Fritter whined: "*So just let her go, Spider,*" then laughed through his nose.

Spider kicked out the bike stand, tilted it back, peeled himself off the Rat, strolled over to Dredge, standing by the ridge. Dredge shook as he fought the instinct to turn and run. Spider stood glaring for a moment, then his hand flashed and grabbed a fistful of Dredge's hair, snapping his head to one side. It hurt, it hurt. Dredge dropped his helmet, moving his arms to block, but Spider sunk his other fist into Dredge's big gut like a drill.

Dredge folded, thought he might vomit. He felt it coming up his throat.

Fritter came crunching up behind. Dredge threw an elbow out. It hit wet air.

Spider whispered, clinging onto Dredge's ear. "Is Dredgie in love?" He jerked Dredge's head down. "You in love with that skank? Are you, Dredgie? Eva'd lick your dead grannie for a crumb of smack."

Head bent back, all Dredge could see was black sky. All he could hear were his frightened heartbeats in his ears.

"That really hurts, Spider," he gasped.

Fritter's arm clamped around his neck from behind. Dredge's lungs collapsed from the absence of air. His ear was burning where Spider gripped onto it. Then Spider let go. Fritter had both arms around him. He began to shuffle Dredge over to the edge of the drop-off. Spider followed.

Fritter growled into Dredge's throbbing ear, "You're way out of your league, pal." He clamped his arms tighter around Dredge, locking down Dredge's big torso. "Way out."

Dredge eyes fluttered from lack of blood.

"Let's beat his ass," Fritter said.

"Calm down," Spider said.

Spider said to Dredge, "You and me don't need to get into it, Dredgie—not if you help us out. Me and Fritter are gonna go to your place first, stash the bikes, hide out. You follow, make it look like you're on your own. Leave your bike out front. Leave the lights off. Then we're gonna wait for Eva's mommy. When she shows, you answer the door, let her in, like no one is around. *Then* we'll see about letting your sweet little Eva go."

"You mean it?" Dredge panted, locked tight in the clinch. He wasn't cut out for this courage shit. The pain was blinding. The dark sky was turning white around the edges.

"You want to see Eva go free, you'll play along. Sound good to you?"

Dredge nodded as best he could.

Spider gave Dredge's ear one final, searing twist. Fritter released him and kicked him in the back of the leg. Dredge lurched, over the precipice, falling, spinning, skidding. Grabbing at a bush to keep from going where the Mexicans had gone. He pulled himself back up, grunting, his field of vision pulsating with the blood returning to his head. He crawled back over the top, on his hands and knees.

He heard crunching in the gravel. Fritter and Spider's boots leaving.

"The Chinaman should have smartened you up, Dredgie." Spider moseyed over to Dredge's bike. "But you had your eyes shut the whole time."

"Pretty bike," Spider whispered. "Pretty bike."

Fritter lit a cigarette. He lumbered over to his motorcycle in his busted knee-walk.

"Don't forget I know how you got that pretty bike, Dredgie." Spider picked up Dredge's helmet, climbed on the Rat, pulling the helmet onto his head. Weird, Spider never wore a helmet before. He kick-started the bike. It rumbled low in idle, belching exhaust.

Dredge felt invisible hands tightening around him. Eva too.

"So don't get any ideas, Dredgie. Just do what you're told, and you and Eva might get by."

CHAPTER 18

WHEN JUSTINE SAW the policeman's car settle in under the tree across the street, Mom smiled and said, *there,* he *was* checking in on them and hey, it was late. Time for bed. Mom slipped Justine's blue nightgown over her upstretched arms, kissed her on the forehead and told her to get into Mom's bed while she double-checked that the house was locked up. There was nothing to worry about, Mom said.

Nothing to worry about, Justine thought, wondering why the policeman with the big nose and mustache would come back if there was *nothing to worry about.* Wondering why they waited until this late to go to bed if there *was nothing to worry about.*

Wondering why the Bird Lady hadn't been back since the Spider hit her at the gas place. And why was the other lady, the Bird Lady's mom, so worried about her if there was *nothing to worry about?*

Mom slid in under the covers next to Justine in her white nightgown. Mom said the two of them were being roommates now. Mom gave Justine a long warm hug and clicked the light out. There was nothing to worry about. Within minutes Mom was snoring.

Nothing to worry about.

Anxiety sprinkled down her neck as she heard the policeman's car outside starting up, then rumbling off down the street. He was leaving.

Nothing to worry about.

She tried to sleep but couldn't. She listened to night sounds, carrying farther than normal, cars whooshing by, far away.

Then familiar engines popped in the distance. The growling of the big motorbikes. Justine's back tingled, prickling up to her skull. The bikes droned up the street, pulled into the driveway of the Bad Boys' house next door. The engines died. Justine heard the Bad Boys mumbling, two of them she thought, speaking low. They normally didn't bother to keep their voices down. Why now? It was the Spider and another one, another creep. The big one wasn't there, Fridge, the one who looked like a big little boy, the one Mom said had a problem. She heard the garage door creak open, slowly. Then they were rolling the motorbikes into the garage. Then the garage was getting shut. The back door to their kitchen opened and closed, their quiet voices trailing off as they went inside.

Mom had told her not to look out that window. Told her.

Justine slipped out of Mom's bed and padded quietly into her bedroom.

When Justine got to the forbidden window in her bedroom and lifted the blind an inch, there wasn't anything to see. The Bad Boys' house was black dark. But she had just heard two Bad Boys go in through the kitchen.

What were they doing in the dark?

. . .

Dredge sat astride his silent bike, waiting, watching the fog float down Delaveaga. He thought of not going back to Gramma's house at all, maybe just head downtown to the cop shop, turn himself in, put an end to all this. He felt a bruise forming on his leg where Spider had kicked him. Yeah, he might just go downtown, turn himself in. Turn them all in.

But that wouldn't be the best thing for Eva. Who knew if the cops would get to her in time? And who knew when—and if—they would do anything.

He could see the wall of his new cell.

And a cellmate, some big guy with a grin and a hard-on.

Dredge straightened himself up, kicked Pearl the Harley over. Dumped the clutch, dropped her into first.

Minutes later he pulled into Gramma's driveway, acting normal, if there was such a thing. He left the bike out front, like Spider had told him to, trying to look nonchalant as his boots clopped up the driveway.

Checked the street. Empty.

Next door looking quiet, a two-hundred-watt bulb burning bare on the porch now. The sexy mom chick worried about the Dead Boys. Who could blame her? Dredge was worried about the Dead Boys too.

Then he saw the window blind in the little kid's room, showing just a crack of black. The gap fell shut. God damn it. Why didn't that kid just mind her own business?

Dredge went inside Gramma's sour-smelling house, not turning lights on, like Spider told him to, on through to the kitchen. The poster of a line of burning cars was lit up by the streetlight dripping through the kitchen window. Then he saw the two of them, Spider and Fritter, standing in the corner of the kitchen, clutching cans of Rainier Ale. Spider looked freshly gacked judging by the sparkle in his eyes.

"Anyone follow you?" Spider took a shaky pull on his beer.

"No," Dredge said. "Maybe Eva's old lady won't show."

One could hope.

"She'll show." Spider took another long gulp of beer, said, "Fucking kid next door. At the window again. She saw us coming in."

"I didn't see anyone," Dredge lied.

Dredge felt Gramma's crippled ghost hobbling over his grave as he dug into the fridge, got out a cold Cobra. Opened it. Drank some. Tasted like shit. He drank it anyway. Shit was what he deserved.

"Better scare her off, Dredgie," Spider said. "That kid."

"Fuck it," Dredge said, as a tear moistened his weary eye. He drained his beer, dumped the can on the floor on top of the others with a tinny clank.

Back to the living-room window. Pulling back the lacy piece-of-crap curtain Gramma had put up, fuck her anyway, fuck her and her oppressive bullshit. Made him stand there naked, to teach him not to do some thing or other he wasn't supposed to do. The curtain was dirty with oil stains, stunk of cigarette smoke. The top of a little girl's head at the window across the way again. Fuck it, there she was again. Why couldn't she just leave it be?

What a dismal fucking situation.

Spider hissed from the kitchen: "Are you fucking *crying*, Dredgie? Get a fucking grip. Eva's mom might show any minute."

What choice did he have? He thought about Eva. He went through to the back, out the kitchen door, under a bleached moon, around and up to the weird kid's window.

.   .   .

The big one was walking up to the window, Justine could hear his big boots in the driveway. Scraping. Here he came, like a sad buffalo. His wild hair was blowing, and he had his great big leather jacket on. Justine moved back, plastering herself to the wall next to her window, flat and out of sight.

She heard him crunch up, stuck his big face up to the window, trying to see in. He was breathing heavily.

Justine tiptoed to the corner of her bedroom. The streetlight coming in was broken by the silhouette of his fuzzy ball of hair, bouncing across the floor as his round head moved around.

Oh, why didn't she ever listen to what Mom said?

"I know you're in there," he said, low and croaky, from the other side of the glass. "I know you've been watching us again. Why? Why do you do it? It's not good."

Maybe he would leave. If Justine kept quiet. Her heart sure wasn't quiet, though.

"I don't want to hurt you," he said. "But you know who does, right?"

Yes, she did.

"He wants to hurt your mommy too. You don't want that. So why do you keep watching?"

Justine wondered about saying something, but whatever was in her throat caught.

"If you tell anyone anything—the police, your mommy ... well, you know what kind of trouble you'll be in?" the big one whispered through the glass. But his voice was high, like he was scared too. "I can't stop them. I have to do what they say. You understand—don't you?"

In her mind, Justine could hear frightened birds,

screaming from a hundred miles away. She froze against the wall, wanting to become part of it.

Then she heard a third voice, calm, not frightened, in the driveway, behind where the big one was standing.

"Get away from that window," the Bird Lady's mommy said to the big one. She was holding up a big stick, like the kind that went on a shovel.

CHAPTER 19

COLLEEN HAD both hands on the pickaxe handle she'd bought, like a batter coming up to the plate. The big freak's head turned her way as he stood in front of Justine's darkened window.

Justine was staring out the window at her.

Colleen's chest pounded like rocks falling onto cement.

The big guy was gawking at her. Weird wasn't the word.

She blinked to focus and licked her dry lips. She had the 38 tucked in her waistband. Cold metal pressed against the base of her spine.

The house had been dark, and it didn't seem like Pam—Eva—whatever she was called these days—was around.

"I guess you didn't hear me," she said to the big guy, her hands twitching on the handle.

His mouth fell open, his hands going up in appeasement, and he backed away from the window.

"Justine," Colleen said to Justine at the window, not taking her eyes off the big dude in the leathers. "Get away from the window. Now."

Justine moved back, but in the shadows, Colleen still saw the top of her head.

"Get away from that window!" Why didn't kids ever listen? Why hadn't Pamela ever listened? Why hadn't Colleen ever listened? Why hadn't she ever opened her eyes? Seen what Pam had been going through all that time?

"Which one are you?" Colleen said to the big guy, feeling the grain of the pickaxe handle move in her palm, as if it had life.

"Dredge," the big biker said. "This is my place." He pointed behind him to the broken-down house.

Dredge was big but off-kilter. He wasn't tough. Colleen cocked her head. Silence.

"Where is my daughter?" she said. "That would be Eva to you—Pam to me. Pamela Hayes. You know who I'm talking about, right?"

Dredge blinked like Baby Huey about to cry. He nodded.

"And you know who I am," Colleen said, the handle up. "Maurice told you I was coming, right?"

"Yeah."

"Well, is she here? Or isn't she?"

Dredge's eyes seemed to flicker out a message. He dropped his voice. Almost no voice.

"You need to be careful," he said, barely audible. He pointed at the house.

Colleen let that register. This guy was trying to warn her about something.

"Bring Eva out here," she said.

"They aren't gonna let that happen," Dredge mouthed without speaking. "Leave."

How many in the house? she said with just the movement of her lips.

Two.

Armed?

He gave a single nod.

"She's not here," he said.

"No?"

Shook his head.

She'd come all this way. She was going to find out what was going on.

"We'll talk inside," she said, loud enough for her voice to carry. She dropped her voice. "Point them out. Lead the way. But don't get any ideas."

Dredge turned, stiff.

Colleen saw Justine peering through the window.

"I thought I told you to get away from that window already!" Colleen hissed in a low voice.

Justine's head disappeared.

Colleen let the pickaxe handle down and followed Dredge past a custom Harley around to the back of the house to the kitchen door she had almost forced open.

The house was dark.

"Anyone else here?" Colleen said, playing along with Dredge.

"Just Eva," Dredge said, playing along as well, let Spider think she didn't know he and Fritter were there. Opening the kitchen door. He went in, stood in the middle of the unlit mess.

Colleen entered the kitchen, pickaxe handle down, pulsating with the moment. Everything was heightened but at the same time it was a blur. The kitchen stunk of garbage.

"Want a beer?" Dredge said.

"No, I don't want a fucking beer. I want to know where my daughter is. Now turn a light on."

The kitchen light went on and Colleen eyes shifted

from pitch black to blinding light. Dredge was squinting, like a frightened puppy.

Beer cans everywhere. Sacks full. And all over the floor. All over the place. Weird lacy curtains on the windows. What was this? A set of works on the kitchen table. Right out in the open.

"Where is she?"

Dredge was going watery on her.

"Where is she?" Loud enough for others to hear. One eyelid began to flicker.

"Sleeping," Dredge said. "In the living room." Dredge pointed to a part of the house. Then she saw his lips move around more words. *She's not here. They're in the living room. Waiting.*

"OK," Colleen said, her heart thumping. She simply had to trust this guy, as whacked-out as he was. He was all she had. But he had a certain amount of credibility. "You go first."

Dredge turned awkwardly and headed down a dark hallway.

Colleen followed with the handle raised. Into the dark living room. Jesus, what a stink.

The curtains were drawn.

"I'll turn a light on," Dredge said, fumbling around.

She didn't need to be seen.

"No!" She swung at the light fixture overhead, hanging from the ceiling. It shattered and fell to the floor in a rain of glass.

"Get her!" someone yelled.

Boots came scuffling from the other side of the living room. Here came moving shadows. Colleen swung the axe handle. *Whip.* She blundered forward, swinging for all she was worth.

Something crashed.

Dredge shuffled out of the room, thumping down the hall. Running away.

Colleen swung again.

Crack. The handle connected. Someone yelled. She pushed forward, where the shouting had come from. She swung harder. The handle stopped short, crunching on flesh and bone. Someone screamed about his nose and tumbled, crashing into Colleen, knocking her backwards. Colleen fell back onto a coffee table, back over it. That hurt. A cacophony of beer cans. The pickaxe handle slipped from her fingers.

Colleen scrambled up on her knees, grabbing the 38 from her waistband. She was safer down here on the floor. She remembered a cellmate telling her: *All fights go to the ground.*

"Get 'er!" another voice growled. Bodies came in close, the black air full of menace in motion. There was an almighty crash, something metallic hitting the coffee table in front of her, sending the remaining cans into the darkness.

A chain.

"Hi Mom!" the voice hissed. The air zipped with the rattle of metal. It missed her, thank God, smashed into the coffee table again. "You're dead meat."

Nerves leaping, Colleen scooted backward. If she got too close to the window, they'd see her in the streetlight leaking through. She shifted to the wall, straining to see. Her eyes were full of crazy flickers. Her heart thrashed. She could hear their boots again.

The gun shook in her hand. On her knees, she brought it up. "I've got a gun!" she yelled, pointing the gun into darkness. "I've got a gun!"

"Jesus Christ!" Dredge yelled from the kitchen. The kitchen light went out.

Colleen squeezed that trigger; the gun went off. Roar of thunder, a flash in the dark.

"Jesus, Spider! She does have a gun!"

The chain snapped her clasped hands, more than hurting. The 38 flew across the room, smacked the wall.

"I got 'er!"

Another shot went off.

A big boom, *big*. Plaster fragments flew, clots of mortar showered down.

A shotgun.

Colleen kicked out, caught the coffee table, flipped it over, a thousand crashes, smashing into a moving form. A man yelled.

Smack.

The chain cracked her shin, wicked pain. Colleen fell, scrambling backwards on hands and knees, dodging the chain coming at her like a scythe through the air. Clattering back through cans. Two bodies coming at her. She backed over something on the floor.

The pickaxe handle. Under her aching shin. Colleen grabbed it.

She jumped up, ripped the handle through air as she hopped on one leg, swinging at ninety miles an hour.

"Watch the fuck out!" someone yelled.

The shotgun went off again, a mighty explosion. A fresh storm of loose plaster sprinkled.

Colleen turned to the origin of the blast, swung, line-driving into black. The handle connected. Nice and hard. Someone's head? Colleen's hands buzzed as the handle vibrated. It tumbled to the floor again.

A helmet. Guy was wearing a helmet. Colleen sunk to the floor, scrambling for the handle.

There it was! Her fingers clutched onto it.

A boot sunk into her ribs. Screeching pain.

Up again, she swung the handle like a madwoman, keeping it low.

Direct contact! A satisfying crunch. Howling in the darkness. Colleen kept swinging, pummeling the source, beating it for all it was worth in a bone-breaking frenzy. Something sticky splattered her face. A body crashed, heaving and swearing over the upturned table.

"Stop! Please!"

That left one to go.

Colleen's eyes finally adjusted. One lone shadow was back against the wall, not moving.

The air whooshed where the shadow stood. The chain.

"Come to poppa," Shadow said.

"I'm coming." Colleen held the pickaxe handle up, crouching forward. "I'm coming, sweetheart."

The chain flayed the air. "Come on, then. Come on, bitch."

Colleen took one more step. "You the one wearing a helmet? Too bad. I was hoping to beat your brains into putty. Guess I'll have to make do with the rest of you. Or you can give me my daughter back."

A nasty nasal laugh. "Your daughter's too busy giving head."

Trying to get her mad. Colleen could hear the other body she'd beaten, on the floor, groaning. She took one more step forward, the handle up over her head.

"Eva's a sweet little piece," the voice said. "Ain't nothin' her ass can't do."

The air whooshed twice, the chain trying to find her. Colleen jumped back, dodged it.

"Tits and ass for days."

Colleen stepped closer. Could see the skinny shadow, a sharp black profile looking beyond, not seeing her though from this angle. Probably out of his brains.

The skinny face staring right past her in a helmet. Guy couldn't see in the dark. Dorked out on powder.

Colleen heaved the pickaxe handle down, catching the chain, ripped it out of the skeletal hand. There was a sharp gasp. The chain sunk to the floor.

She plowed ahead, battering the shadow's torso. It doubled up under her blows, grunting.

"Did you say something?" Colleen yelled. "Something about my daughter?" She kept heaving the handle into the thin body.

The body rolled up into a ball.

Colleen shouted, landing the pickaxe handle with grim satisfaction. "I could have sworn I heard you say something."

———

The house with the tires, the Bad Boys' house, was still dark, even though Justine could hear crashing and yelling in there. She squeezed her eyes shut and opened them again and looked out harder, out the window, until the gray of the house was a sharp blue outline in the moonlight.

Then she heard something else, like the back door being slammed shut.

There went the big one, lumbering to the garage, heaving open the door.

That meant the Bird Lady's mom was in the house, alone with the Spider and the other Bad Boy.

Justine had to do something.

She tore out of her bedroom, in her frayed blue nightgown. Thought about waking Mom but there was no time and Mom would only scold her and say she didn't see what she saw.

Justine fought with the deadbolt on the front door. Tugged it open.

Outside, the air was cold and wet.

Running across the gravel, the stones hurting her feet, to the Bad Boys' house. Up one of the cement tracks where the cars went in the driveway, dodging rocks.

Something clanked in the garage. Justine darted over to the house, pressed herself against the wall.

The garage door opened up. The big one appeared. He looked up. He had some bags that go over the back of the motorbike in his hands. He dropped them, surprised.

"Hey!" he yelled. "Get out of here. I told you. Go on, scat, beat it!"

He came toward her. She turned, toward his kitchen door. Into the kitchen. The big one right behind her.

"What do you think you're doing?" he screeched. "Don't go in there!"

Justine dived, landing on the kitchen floor with a thump, skidding into crumpled cans. The place smelled bad.

Noises from the hallway. Fighting. Yelling. Crazy.

The big one was at the kitchen door behind her. He was swearing bad names. Panting, breathing hard.

"Come on, kid! You need to get out of here! I mean it!"

Then more noises from the hallway. Someone coming.

The Colleen lady. She had a big stick.

"What the heck are you doing here, Justine! Beat it!"

She stepped around Justine and up to the big one by the kitchen door.

"Wait," he said, dropping his bike bags. "You don't understand. I was trying to h..."

She swung the stick like a bat and hit the big one. *Ooof.* He staggered in a circle. The Bird Lady's mom smacked him again, *swoosh-smack,* and the big one screamed and held his stomach.

Swoosh-smack. The big one fell, crying like a hurt dog, in a ball on the floor. Colleen hovered over the big one with the stick raised.

"Where is she?" she yelled. "Where is my daughter?"

"Sky Londa," Fridge yelled in between gasps. "A mile or so past the 7-Eleven."

"Go on, Justine!" the Colleen lady shouted. "Get out of here! Scoot! Now!"

Justine scrambled over the big one. Almost free.

"Run, Justine! Run!"

And run she did. Like a bunny. And didn't care if the gravel hurt her feet. Or if Mom was going to get mad. Justine looked up as she tore down the driveway.

Mom was running for her, in her nightie, across the gravel.

Sirens howled in the distance.

CHAPTER 20

"OK, HAYES," Detective Moran said, pushing his glasses back up his nose. He paced the gray interrogation room, a windowless box humming with cold fluorescent light. "I'll ask one last time."

It was five in the morning.

"I told you," Colleen said. "I've got nothing to say."

Moran stared across the table at Colleen Hayes. In the glare of the overhead tubes the prisoner looked bad. Her face was masked by a sheen of exhaustion, a fresh bruise under the right eye. Moran resumed walking back and forth. "You did nine years for homicide in Colorado. Released less than a week ago. Now you're caught on a breaking-and-entering in California. Along with a grievous assault." Moran stopped. "And let's not forget possession of an illegal firearm."

"Lawyer," Colleen said from her chair.

Moran rubbed his face. "How about coffee? Because it looks like we're staying up."

Colleen worked a crumpled Winston out of her pack. Felt her pockets, but Moran knew they'd taken any matches away when they brought her in. Moran pulled a book of Arni's matches from his chinos, tossed them across the table. Colleen lit up the bent cigarette with a shaky hand she managed to disguise fairly well. Let out a billow of gray smoke.

"Who was it who told you about those bikers on Delaveaga in the first place?" Moran asked.

She blew a smoke ring, studied it.

"You're in trouble, Hayes," he said. "Henry Beaumont—Dredge—is going to press charges. You can look forward to another stretch."

"Ha." She took a drag, blew a smoke ring across the cell. "You really think that loser will press charges?"

No, he didn't. "Where did you get the gun?"

"Who says I did?"

"Because it'll have your prints all over it."

"Because I had to take it away from one of those dirt-bags when he pulled it on me."

"The gun's hot. In more ways than one. It was recently fired."

"I wouldn't know." Colleen released another plume of smoke. "But it doesn't surprise me."

Moran crossed the small room, waving away the cigarette smoke. "I'm in the middle of a murder investigation. *Murders,* to be exact. 239 Delaveaga is under surveillance." He went back over to the table. "A convicted felon—you—barges in and beats one person to a pulp. A gun fight ensues with members of a motorcycle gang. Now how does that look?"

Colleen's eyes narrowed. "You know why." She took a crackling hit on the Winston. "My daughter. I explained when you stopped me yesterday." She exhaled smoke.

"You still haven't told me how you got the address for Dredge's place."

"I can't remember."

Moran put both hands on the table and glared at Colleen through his shades. "A man was found murdered up in the mountains, Friday afternoon. We're still looking for his head and hands. The bikers on Delaveaga are connected." Moran watched Colleen hold the last of the smoldering cigarette, staring at him. "We're also interested in them on four other murders. Is it a war, a biker gang taking out two other gangs who also deal speed in Santa Cruz? Looks like it. Then *you* break into a house and go ballistic. If the police hadn't arrived, someone else might be dead too. No telling what Colleen Hayes would have done. She's violent. Has a criminal record for homicide, stabbing her ex with a screwdriver. No address, no money. She's from out of state. A drifter. Seen hanging around the house at 239 the day before, questioned." Moran began pacing again. "Maybe Hayes is the killer. That's all the prosecutor needs to hold you."

"Even though you know it's utter bullshit."

"Do I? You almost murdered Henry Beaumont —Dredge."

"If I wanted to, he'd be dead. Ask my ex." She took a drag.

Ballsy, Moran thought. She wasn't going to give in easily. "What about the other two people fleeing the house on motorcycles?"

"I'm not sure who you're talking about."

"Why are you trying to do some vigilante thing on your own? Against bikers? Drug dealers? And what about the mother and daughter next door? The Quinlans? The arresting officers said they saw the girl and her mother with you when they arrived."

Colleen studied the floor. "Please. All I want to do is find my daughter. I told you all that when you questioned me."

"The jury can decide that. When it goes to trial. In about six to nine months. In the meantime, you'll sit in a cell. No bond. Your daughter goes wherever she goes. While you rot, Hayes."

Colleen stood up, flicked the burning cigarette butt. It skidded across the table, sparks erupting, splashing embers on the leg of Moran's pants. "What would *you* do—if it was your daughter? Turn in a bunch of bikers? Who might kill her? All I want is to get her back."

Moran brushed the cinders from his pants and stepped on the smoking cigarette butt. "Or we can do it another way," he said. "You tell me what you know, and I do my best to get you out first thing this morning."

"Do your best?" Colleen had her hands on her hips. "The word of a cop? That's how I ended up spending over nine years in prison for killing a man who couldn't keep his hands off his eight-year-old daughter. I signed a statement and they promised they'd work with me. Worked *on* me, more like it. You know full well I had nothing to do with any murder. You also know that whoever is living in that haunted house does. Suppose I tell you what I know, then what? Maybe my daughter winds up dead in the mountains too. While you're thinking about getting me out in the morning."

"Tell me and you have my word. Don't tell me, you're in a cell. You have my word on that too."

Moran watched the prisoner stand there for a lengthy

moment. She hooked her thumbs through the belt loops of her Levi's.

"Look," he said. "I could have pulled you in when you were parked in that car outside the Quinlan's house. I knew something was up. But I let you go."

Colleen Hayes pursed her lips.

"You used me as bait," she said slowly. "Didn't you? To lead you to those guys. That's why you let me go so easily. Like you want to keep right on doing if you let me go now. You'll use my daughter the same way."

"Tell me where you got that lead on the Dead Boys," Moran said. "And you're out of here. My word."

Colleen took a breath through her nose, let it out slowly.

"Maurice," she said finally. "Maurice Navarro. He owns several bars. One in Santa Cruz: The Brass Rail. The Dead Boys run dope for him. He gave me 24 hours to get my daughter back. Now please help me do that. I'm almost out of time."

CHAPTER 21

"THE 187 UP ON HIGHWAY 9?" Moran asked the young balding lab tech in the gray basement room that smelled of fresh paint. "Shipped over from San Mateo last night? Three tire impressions, seven footprints, one handprint."

The techie hunched over a thick sheaf of paper logs, his narrow face drawn and pale in the incandescent light. "Nothing."

"Look again. It was expedited." Moran's suspicions were kicking in.

The clerk's fingers flipped through a desk full of papers, then the in-basket. Finally he checked the Telex machine. Looked up, shaking his head.

"What about Forensics? Maybe they know something."

The techie picked up a phone, dialed. He asked a few questions. Hung up, didn't return eye contact. "Looks like that report already went out."

Moran stiffened. His voice rose. "Already went out *where?*"

The clerk continued to examine papers, avoiding

Moran's iron gaze. "Seems Lieutenant Grisset called in, had the forensics report sent to him. I wasn't on duty yet."

Moran's face darkened as anger set in. "I expressly asked for that report to be given to Krieger or myself only. Look at me when I'm talking to you."

The lab tech looked up with weary blue eyes. "If you want to know where that report is, I suggest you talk to Lieutenant Grisset. He *is* your partner, isn't he?"

Moran swore under his breath and trudged up the black diamond-bar metal stairwell. He stood on a stair for a moment, trying to think.

Grisset had plenty of friends to help him out. Moran knew what they thought of him, drunk half his life.

He stopped in on Central Records on the first floor and pulled Henry Beaumont's—Dredge's—sheet. A 311—indecent exposure—over a year ago, knocked down to loitering with intent. Another thing outside a high school. Then another, dropped to a 288 Lewd and Lascivious, when the 15-year-old hooker didn't show up for the arraignment. That earned Dredge thirty days in Santa Rita County. A dismissed possession for sale, last December, right after he got out. Now what would a sad sack like Dredge be doing with the Dead Boys?

New friends for Dredge? His Harley was new. And Moran would bet a bottle of Jim Beam that Dredge's Country Squire—still registered in his grandmother's name—was a lot like the one that left those tire tracks up at the murder sight.

Maybe the Dead Boys were humping dope for someone a little bigger. Hayes had mentioned Maurice Navarro, the bar owner. And Navarro had connections to Sio Lum, Dragon Master of the Hip Sing Tong.

Krieger slid his wide butt into the red padded curve of Moran's booth in Arni's bar. "You had to page me at six a.m., Danny?" Across the table Krieger's pudgy face was irritable, but still curious.

Moran drank from a tall glass.

"Moran, what the hell is this?" Kriger pointed to Moran's glass. "You drinking again?"

"Fizzy water." Moran took a long slug of Calistoga. "You know what really gets me, Krieger? More than anything else?"

"I'm not gonna listen to whining." Krieger got up and came back with a stein of beer and a fresh Calistoga in a glass with ice and lime. He sat down, pushed the Calistoga toward Moran. Moran remembered having morning beers. He wondered when he would stop missing them.

"The Asian Doe's gone," Krieger said, drinking. "What there was left of him to begin with."

Moran looked up, startled. "Tell me you're joking."

"Grisset had him moved over to San Mateo," Krieger said "Busy little cocksucker all of a sudden. After he dragged his feet?"

Moran took a swig. It looked like a gin and tonic but tasted like nothing. "This case stinks to high heaven."

"The Doe," Krieger said, draining a third of his beer, leaving a white mustache of froth on his thick upper lip. "I took a quick look at him yesterday before Grisset swiped him. A young blood. Chinese. Nineteen or twenty. About six foot. That would be *with* the head, of course, which wasn't fastened on. Blood type O."

"You opened him up?"

"Shot twice in the chest with something big." Krieger

licked the froth off his upper lip. "I managed to pull a slug. Forty millimeter or I'm a hack."

"Big gun," Moran said. "Was that the cause of death?"

"Someone shot him and cut his head off?" Krieger drank. "That will generally do it."

"Nicer for the Doe if one happened before the other."

"The cuts suggest a struggle. Done with multiple instruments. Looks like they resorted to a shovel in the end."

"Jesus." Moran stared into his drink. His non-alcoholic drink. He looked at the off-duty cops at the bar, drinking boilermakers. He pictured Krieger digging around in a dead body. Would he talk to it?

"Whoever aced our Doe, Krieger, was a pro in some ways, though. No hands. No head. Straight out of *The Godfather*."

"A professional job?" Krieger said.

"In some ways. But not others. Someone ripped someone off, moved in on someone's territory. Retribution."

"Yep."

"Well, it's De Lucca's case now." Moran wanted to draw Krieger out, see how he would react.

"De Lucca," Krieger said, shaking his head. "Grisset. You gonna let those butt-slammers do this to you, Danny?"

Moran took his glasses off and cleaned them with a bar napkin. "No. I am not." He studied Krieger for a minute. "Our Doe had a tattoo, a Tong brand. Get a picture of it?"

"I didn't figure on De Lucca swiping the body."

"It was a crescent moon." All Moran could think of was killers who wanted to be like the big boys. Boys not disciplined enough for the mob or triads. Boys who'd get into a frenzy with a shovel, got a charge hacking a head off. But working for bigger boys. Bigger boys like Maurice Navarro. Thanks to Hayes, Moran had the connection made.

"What I'm going to say is strictly for your ears, Krieger."

Krieger drank beer. "No one else listens to you anyway."

"Anne Marie Beaumont."

Krieger's eyes flickered in thought. "299 Delaveaga?"

"Not bad. 239."

"Yeah." Krieger pursed his lips. "Henry Beaumont," he said. "The license plate on his bike reads DREDGE."

"You do have a memory."

"I haven't been hammering away at it for thirty years with Jim Beam," Krieger said. "Henry Beaumont. Anne Marie Beaumont. His grandmother. Bit it last December. Old broad, eighty-one. I did the papers on her. She wound up with a County burial. Kid didn't have any money. Or didn't want to spend any on her."

"Dredge."

"Yeah, the kid was the only surviving relative. Granny raised him. I had to approve the burial for Deacon. The coroner? I went out to the house to get her myself. The kid didn't even come down to the morgue to sign the papers. I remember now. It was typical; he had no money to bury the old lady but had bucks for a new Harley FXR. Just bought it."

"Sign of the times," Moran said. "What did she die of?"

"Asphyxiation," Krieger said, obviously staring back into his thoughts. "Choked on something in her sleep. Happens often enough. But it was a rush job, Danny. Out of a cold bed and into the ground. County job." Krieger shrugged. "You know?"

"I'm afraid I do."

"But now..."

Moran pulled his shades off, eyed Krieger.

"We never even opened her up, Danny. I guess we

should have. But it's a common enough way to go—at eighty-one."

"Sure." Watching Krieger.

"It's fucked, Danny. An old lady raises a big asshole like that, then goes out on half-digested meat. The lady was a mess when we found her. At least a day old. At least."

"So why the fuss, Krieger? Everybody knows no one looks after the old ones. Like you said."

"But it makes the kid look funny now, like…"

"Like you wish you'd done an autopsy on her?"

CHAPTER 22

MORAN WIPED the all-night grime off his face and took another look at Henry Beaumont's rap sheet. The sun was just up, casting pale pink outlines over Moran's desk and Henry's—Dredge's—anxious stare into the camera. His hair wasn't as wild yet. He wasn't wearing biker garb. He didn't look so strung out. He might have still had a chance back then. Just a couple of years ago.

Moran's eyes were jumping at shadows.

Ever since he quit drinking, pretty much.

Outside, in the parking lot, he heard more cars arriving. Day shift was starting up. Moran was keeping an eye—and ear—out, checking each one that pulled in, watching the officers get out, reporting for duty.

An orange Datsun 1200 darted up, with its hair-dryer engine. It cut into a stall, coming to an abrupt stop. A tall, slender man hopped out, locked up the compact with a key, broke into a light jog toward the building.

Moran rose from his chair, hurried downstairs to intercept the officer before he made it to the changing room.

Moran caught him coming in the back door.

"Officer Stoll," Moran said. "If I might ask you a quick question."

"I'm on duty in a few," the tall man said, checking his watch. He had dark hair, thinning, combed over. He smelled of mouthwash.

"It won't take long."

Stoll frowned. No one wanted to waste time on Moran anymore. "If you could please make it quick."

Moran only had himself to blame. But he couldn't let it jeopardize the case. Push ahead. He dropped his voice. "I heard there was an arrest the other day—up on 239 Delaveaga ..."

"Domestic abuse case. We brought in a biker, called himself Spider."

"That's what I heard, but when I looked for your report —well, there's no trace of it."

"Are you sure?" Stoll gave him a questioning look, as if Moran's lucidity might be in question.

"I double-checked," Moran said. "Triple-checked."

"I filed it myself."

"Maybe it got misplaced," Moran said. "Hadn't even been entered in the mainframe." He cleared his throat. "I'm wondering if you can tell me the details. High level."

"I made a copy. I always do."

"Excellent," Moran said. "I need that copy—for a case I'm working on."

Stoll gave an audible sigh.

"A homicide," Moran stressed.

"Of course," Stoll said. "I can't believe they let that animal out. After the shootings up on the summit? But that's the way it goes with domestic abuse." He reached into the pockets of his slacks, came out with a set of keys. He selected one key, removed it. "You know where I sit? Bottom right drawer. Green hanging folders. Should be in the first one. Lock up when you're done and leave the key under the blotter. I've got to get changed."

"Thank you very much, Stoll."

Back upstairs, minutes later, Moran reviewed Stoll's report.

And now had a pretty good idea why it had been "mislaid."

"What's the matter? Couldn't sleep again?"

Moran spun in his swivel chair to see Detective Steve Grisset filling the doorway, looking breakfasted and rested, dressed for success in a stylish two-piece suit with a wide, trendy tie. His blond hair was blow-dried and feathered back.

Moran checked his watch: 7:25. "You beat your record by almost two hours, Grisset." He placed the copy of Stoll's report in a file folder.

Grisset smirked, dumping his briefcase on the chair of his desk in the office he shared with Moran. He put his hands in his pockets and stared.

"Dimick wants to see you," he said.

It wasn't hard to figure out now: Grisset in early on a Monday, the Chief of Police wanting to see him.

"Why did you move the Doe over to San Mateo in the middle of the night, Grisset?"

"Dimick wants to see you *now*."

"I didn't realize you had time to kiss De Lucca's ass so early." Moran stood up, put the file he was building in his center desk drawer, locked it. "You must be exhausted."

"Have a nice day, asshole."

Chief Dimick's office was upstairs, with a view of the rooftops and the roller coaster, fuzzy with morning fog. Dimick sat in his swivel chair, facing the window, his back to the door. Stale cigarette smoke hung in the air. An ashtray on his desk already had two dead soldiers, the first of many.

"You wanted to see me, John?" Moran said.

The leather chair turned. John Dimick was a heavy, bald man with Himmler glasses. His face was scoured and pink. His neck sagged over a starched white collar. He waved a stocky arm at the guest chair.

Moran took a seat.

"I hear you've had a busy weekend," Dimick said through a layer of smoker's phlegm.

"Pulling threads on the 187 on Highway 9, John. I'm making some progress ..."

"Why haven't you been keeping Grisset up to date?" Dimick folded his hands over his round stomach.

"Because Grisset has not been helping. In fact, just the opposite. He's itching to give the case away."

"Not what I hear." Dimick's hands remained folded.

Dimick was pissed.

"John," Moran said. "If I might explain..."

"Wait." Dimick held a palm up. "Last night I get a call from De Lucca. Told me—no, let me rephrase that—ripped me a new one, regarding a 187 up by 9 and 35." Blue sky began to lighten behind Dimick's shiny head. "Over the fact that you've been interfering with a murder investigation he's conducting."

"*He's* conducting?" Moran said. "In *our* jurisdiction?"

Dimick's hand went back up. "Not what De Lucca says. And he's a little higher up the chain than you and me." Dimick's hand went back down. "He also tells me that you and that nosy-ass Medical Examiner Krieger took it upon yourselves to remove a Doe from the scene of the crime, thereby impacting a sensitive investigation."

"Sensitive? Because De Lucca's going to get voted out unless he can pull a rabbit out of the hat? Our Doe being the rabbit."

"Moran," Dimick said, his pink face getting pinker. "Shut up."

Moran watched the sky turn a dirty shade of teal.

"De Lucca's already got a suspect. He would have preferred it if you had not hindered."

Moran nodded slowly, biting back on his anger.

"De Lucca specifically requested Grisset on this one," Dimick said. "Apparently told you as much on Saturday. But no, you had to get ambitious. All of a sudden. Now let me explain things, Moran: You've fucked up once too often. Remember your last bout in Alta Bates? Strike three? Do you? Because I sure as hell do."

"John..."

"Now, you may not like him much, but you damn well better not prevent Grisset from doing his job. This was an opportunity for Grisset to make us all look good. But no. Moran charged ahead, did as he damn well pleased. Again."

Moran opened his mouth.

"Did I say you could speak?" Dimick raised his eyebrows for a moment. "On top of all this horseshit, Deacon the Coroner is pissed beyond belief because that jerkoff Krieger went ahead and did a partial autopsy on the Doe. Now I got another guy wants to pound my ass and it's not even eight a.m. Monday yet."

Moran waited.

"Sounds like the work of an amateur, right?" Dimick put his hands flat on the desk in front of him. "But this is what I get from a thirty-five-year veteran. Who can't stop drinking. But wait, there's still more. Santos, who happens to be Santa Cruz Sheriff—remember him?—calls me in the middle of the night, after De Lucca burns his ass, and wants to know why the Sheriff's Department in my own fucking county isn't even aware of what's going on until they hear it from De Lucca."

"I thought this was De Lucca's case to begin with," Moran said dryly.

Dimick shot up out of his leather chair, finger aimed at Moran. "And I thought I told you to shut the fuck up!" He dropped his arm. "What we have here is another example of Detective Moran going it alone, making wild assumptions, pissing the world off—at my expense. Before he wanders over to Arni's to scramble his brains."

"I've arrested a lot of killers over the years, John. Closed a *lot* of cases."

Dimick, standing, cleared his throat. "You've gotten your ass into a sling more than a few times too. And I've always covered for you. That little drinking binge that's been going on for the last three decades? One small example of how much I went to bat for you."

"I haven't had a drink in over thirty days, John."

"And I'm supposed to be impressed?"

"John? Will you please calm down for a minute?"

Dimick sat down. His anger had been spent for now. "You got one minute."

"Forget about De Lucca's politics. We're talking about a dead body. Beyond politics. If De Lucca has a suspect he thinks committed this murder, then I'd like to interrogate him. The whole thing's crooked, John. In two days, I've gotten pretty damn close to what is really going on, and it's right here in Santa Cruz. A biker gang, connected to a local bar owner, dealing speed. Add a drug war. Those four Barrio Cruz members found dead? As for Grisset, he's done nothing but try to hand this case over to De Lucca. Why?

Here's some more food for thought: One of the bikers we're keeping tabs on, a guy named Spider, was arrested last week. Domestic abuse. The woman who made the statement claims Spider was bragging about killing four members of Barrio Cruz. Pretty interesting stuff, right?"

Dimick shook his head. "The drugged-out girlfriend who was slapped around claimed the guy who beat her up said this? She wouldn't have any reason to make it up, would she?"

"I know. I know. But the next day, Spider was released. Grisset OK'd it. And the woman's statement is nowhere to be found." Moran realized *he* was standing up now.

"Big deal, Moran. Some small-time biker? In for slapping his cycle slut around? Jesus Christ. We're not babysitters. What do we want him for?"

Moran was blind-sided for a moment. "John, Grisset is covering up for Spider. Why else did that report disappear? Spider and the Dead Boys murdered that Tong gang member, and they killed Pana and three of Barrio Cruz."

Dimick shook his head. "Why would Grisset do that? Cover up for him?"

"Good question. Let's get him in here and ask him."

"Do you have any idea what you sound like right now, Danny? Accusing your partner of working with bikers and drug dealers? Covering up a murder?"

"*Murders*. John, I've got this. Tight. By the end of the week I'll have a suspect for you. And it will be Spider. I bet you a fifth."

There was a pause before Dimick gave a sympathetic smile. "Drop it, Danny."

"John, something smells bad. Something about Grisset. If I don't have anything for you by Friday—well, I'll back off. No questions asked."

"*No questions asked?* You still don't get it, do you?"

"Get what?"

"Sit down." Dimick's voice softened.

Moran sat down, feeling his legs wobble.

"Danny," Dimick said. "It's time for you to move aside."

Moran's stomach dropped. "You can't throw me off the case, John."

"Danny—you're off the case. For good."

Time stopped.

"John," he said. "I'm ... fired?"

"I'm not firing anyone. You should have seen it coming. You've already caused enough embarrassment to the department with your drinking. Now this paranoid bullshit about De Lucca and Grisset?" He shook his head. "It's gone too far. You've got three weeks to go, Danny. Until full retirement."

"I don't want retirement, John."

It was as if Dimick had not heard him. "So take three weeks. An unofficial gift from me to you. You'll get all your bennies. Come back in three weeks. We'll have a nice sendoff."

"I don't want the three weeks."

"Well, you've got no choice in the matter."

Moran took a deep breath. What could he salvage?

"John, give me the three weeks to solve this case. One week. Then I'll go quietly."

The hand went up one last time. "I don't think you're hearing me, Danny. I said *take the time off*. I didn't ask. It's not an option, see?"

"John," Moran said. "I haven't had a drink in a month."

"So you said," Dimick said. "And you've said that before. And I said *I'm not asking you*."

Moran felt waves of defeat wash over him as he looked

at the weak dawn rising behind Dimick's bald head. Sometimes he hated daylight. But what could he do?

What could he do?

"John. There's a prisoner downstairs: Colleen Hayes. Came in last night on a B and E. She's got a sheet. But she gave me a strong lead, and worked with me, and I said we'd work up a release for her. Waive charges, get her out today."

"You shouldn't have done that, Danny."

"Christ, John. Cut me some slack here. I gave her my word."

"Danny, you're way off-track on this case—believe me. Grisset's done some nice work and we now have the murderer behind bars. I shouldn't be telling you this, but Grisset's gonna send her over to San Mateo this morning. So take the fucking three weeks off already. That means clear out your desk, go home to Daphne and if you don't, I'll have you escorted out of the building. And *that* will impact your retirement. I don't want to do that."

"*Her?*" Moran was dumbfounded. "You mean *Hayes?* Grisset's going to book Colleen Hayes? For murder?"

"Colleen Hayes went to prison once for killing a man, Danny. Looks like she did it again."

CHAPTER 23

MORAN STUMBLED back to his desk in a haze of defeat.

He flinched when he saw Grisset, sitting in *his* chair, legs up on Moran's desk, hands behind his head, his square jaw out, sneering victory.

"How'd it go with Dimick, buddy?"

Rage gripped Moran's neck like a vise. With a sweep of his arm he flung Grisset's legs off the desk. He heaved Grisset back across the room on his roller-chair, banging him into a metal file cabinet with a clatter.

"Didn't go well, I take it?" Grisset asked, rolling back toward him. "I'm sorry."

Moran got his keys out, but when he went to unlock his desk, he realized it was unlocked. He yanked open his top desk drawer. The file he was building. Gone. He looked up, gave Grisset a furious glare.

"I'm not going to ask where you got a key. But give that file back, or I'll blow the whistle."

"You don't have a whistle to blow, Danny." Grisset put his hands back behind his head.

Moran reached under his arm and unsnapped the Ruger from its holster. He whipped the gun out in one fluid motion, letting the sight at the end of the barrel settle on Grisset's nose. He flicked the safety up with his thumb. It felt good, that motion.

Grisset's smile vanished like a thin cloud in a windy sky. His hands were still behind his head, but frozen.

"Moran—what the hell do you think you're doing?"

Moran squeezed one eye shut. "The file."

"Have you gone nuts?"

"The file."

Grisset's hands dropped. They were shaking. "Sure, Moran. Sure." He turned slowly in his chair, keeping his eyes on Moran the whole time, while he rolled over to his desk where he pulled open his desk drawer, got Moran's manila folder out. He stood up, came back, handed the file over, his arm quivering.

Moran took the file folder with his free hand.

"Thank you, Grisset."

But he kept the Ruger in the center of Grisset's face. "I'm going to kill you, Grisset. You know why? Look at me when I'm talking to you. I'm just a crazy old cop, half in the bag, right? You cost me my job. But you're a damn filthy crook. We both know it. Now put your hands up."

"No, Danny! Honest. I..." Grisset's lips trembled as he put his hands up over his head. He changed color. "Danny ... get a grip." He gulped. "*Please!*"

Moran dropped the gun to his side and grinned. Then he started laughing, a low chortle at first, working his way up to the first good hearty laugh in years. "You slay me, Grisset," he said. "Jesus wept, you thought I was actually going to shoot you?"

Grisset seethed. "I ought to turn you in."

"You do that. Then I'll make sure the *Sentinel* knows exactly what kind of cop transferred over from San Jose— and how he does so well on a lieutenant's salary." Moran raised his eyebrows.

"Go to hell." Grisset let out an angry breath. "No one will listen to you. You're history."

Moran snapped the Ruger back under his arm. He left Grisset shaking and headed downstairs to see Grimes, the desk sergeant.

To Moran's surprise, Laura and Justine Quinlan were talking to Grimes again. Moran walked up to the desk.

"Ah, Detective Moran," Laura said. "Perhaps you can help us."

"With what?"

Grimes rubbed his Black face as he gave Moran a knowing, private look. "Lady wants to bail out a prisoner, Danny. A woman brought in last night. For B and E."

Moran eyed Justine, in her overalls and bright yellow shirt, brown eyes serious as a heart attack. Then Laura, in jeans and down jacket. "I don't understand."

"Colleen Hayes saved my daughter from those maniacs," Laura said. "And she was arrested? I can't believe it. If anyone should be thrown in jail it should be that scum who live next door. They were going crazy last night. You know, there were times I thought Justine was imagining things. Now I see how sick those bikers really are. Forget bail. I want to see the Chief of Police, now. Where can I find him?"

Moran looked at the young woman and her doe-eyed daughter. He hoped someone would look after them. But he wasn't feeling overly optimistic.

"Actually, the charges against Colleen Hayes have been dropped," he said. "I was just on my way downstairs to see to her release."

"Good," Laura said, crossing her arms.

"I didn't hear anything about releasing a prisoner, Danny," Grimes said. "You sure about that? I thought Grisset..."

"Sergeant," Moran said. "Am I in the habit of lying to you?"

"Why no," Grimes said. "It's just that Grisset..."

Moran dropped his voice. "I'm taking Hayes over to Superior Court for processing," Moran said quietly, winking at Grimes to let him know he was placating the Quinlans. "I'll be bringing her back forthwith."

"Ah," Grimes said, winking back, playing along. "Where's the paperwork?"

"Grisset it getting it filled out. He'll bring it down. We're kind of in a hurry, Grimes."

"Got it. No sweat."

"Processing for what?" Laura said. "What is she accused of?"

Justine looked up. Her face was pink, but her eyes were dark with suspicion.

Moran said: "Oh, it's just routine." He glinted at Grimes again, letting him know that he was trying to go easy on the Quinlans.

Grimes looked theatrically serious. "I'll call down and have the prisoner brought up, Detective."

Moran had to move before they realized he was out. "Don't bother, Grimes. We're in a hurry. Have one of the men meet me at the prisoner's cell to let her out. I'll take it from there. The Quinlans can wait outside in the parking lot. Come on, step on it."

. . .

Outside, in the lot behind SCPD headquarters, Moran and Colleen stood by a green Pinto. Colleen Hayes stood with her hands cuffed.

"My advice to you," Moran said to Laura, sitting at the wheel of her car, "is to find another place to live—as soon as possible. Now would be ideal. That house next door is not safe to be around."

"I plan to," she said.

"Hayes," Moran said. "We've got to get out of here."

"Just a minute," Colleen said to Laura. "I've got something for you." Colleen tried to work her hotel key out of her jeans pocket. With her hands bound together it took a moment, but she managed it. "If you need somewhere to stay away from those wackos." Hands together, Colleen pressed the key into Laura's. "It's paid up until the end of the week. I'll call if I need to stop by. It's not much but it's somewhere to go."

"Thanks," Laura said, her sea-green eyes locking onto Colleen's for a moment. "Thanks a lot—I ... really appreciate it."

"You bet," Colleen said, wondering what was going on.

"Good luck to you, Colleen," Laura said. "I hope you find your daughter. Soon."

Justine looked at Colleen seriously from inside the car. "Don't get smacked again."

"I won't, Justine."

Laura started up the Pinto and it rattled to life. She backed the car out into a puff of exhaust, ground it into first gear, bounced out into the street. Colleen watched them go.

"Get in the back of my car," Moran said to Colleen Hayes.

Once they were in Moran's Ford, Moran said, "I'm driving you to San Jose. Then you're on your own. Don't go to the airport. You need money for a Greyhound? Somewhere out of state?"

"You're letting me go?"

"I don't really have time to discuss it."

"In that case, my car's right where I left it. Up at Dredge's house."

"Forget that. You can't hang around Santa Cruz. They'll be looking for you."

"I'm not leaving."

Moran narrowed his eyes. "You're wanted for murder now. You realize that?"

On top of everything else, being charged for murder seemed like a grim joke. But it was something she would have to worry about later. Pam came first.

"Murder? Really? Well, that sounds about right. Because I feel like murdering someone. But I'll have to take my chances."

"You need sleep. Get some on the bus out of town. I know there were three of them in that house last night, but the police only found Dredge."

"I didn't see. It was dark."

Moran started up the car. "And I'm off the case. I've been fired. So you've got no one to look out for you. So let's go."

That got Colleen's attention. "That's crazy. But you'll still bust this thing, right? They'll have to see it your way. You'll be in the clear soon enough."

"It's a long shot."

"Not with the two of us working together," Colleen said.

"No," Moran said, shaking his head. "You're headed out of town."

"I'm in too deep. I've met this Spider. I'm not going anywhere. So save your breath."

"Forget it."

"Then how come you let me out?"

"Because I said I would. Even though you didn't believe me. Maybe *because* you didn't believe me."

"Well, how do you like that?" she said. "A cop who keeps his word. But what did you think I'd do? Leave town? With my daughter here? Look, you need me to shake up those bikers for you. Then you can move in, bust them."

Moran set the car into Drive and pulled out onto Center Street. "I'm going to drop you off at your car and then hope you do the only sane thing—getting out of Santa Cruz as soon as possible. Leave Spider and the Dead Boys to me."

Colleen didn't answer.

They rode in silence up to Delaveaga where the battered Cutlass was parked. Laura and Justine weren't back yet. Colleen put her cuffed hands up across the bench seat. "It's been a pleasure. But can you take these off, please?"

"Keys are in the trunk." Moran got out of the car, went to the back, opened the trunk.

Colleen peered over the front of the bench seat. There was a manila file folder. Moran's case file, she'd bet. Reaching with both cuffed hands together, she flipped it open. An address in Sky Londa was scribbled in pencil on the inside cover. She remembered Dredge saying Spider lived in Sky Londa. She repeated the address to herself three times, shut the file.

The trunk slammed. She sat back in the rear seat.

Moran came around with a set of keys, opened the rear door.

She swung around and he undid the cuffs.

"Now get out of here before I change my mind, Hayes."

CHAPTER 24

AT FIRST DREDGE thought he might be seeing things as he peered out from behind the dirty lace curtain. His head was all screwed up from the codeine they'd given him at SC General. And the battering he got last night from Eva's old lady would have him seeing double for a month. But wasn't that Eva's old lady again, the Hayes woman, getting into a beater car, right in front of his house? She was supposed to be in jail—wasn't she? But there she was, starting up the piece of shit Cutlass, black puffs coming out of the tailpipes.

Dredge pulled the curtain back a hair more. Christ on a pogo stick. There was that cop too, the one who'd been snooping around next door, with his glasses and big nose and his gun sticking out from under his arm. Just driving away in his LTD.

Jesus. Jesus. Jesus. Jesus Christ.

The fuck was going on? Dredge checked the time. Early. How'd Eva's mother get bail?

Dredge found his baggy leather pants in a heap by the bed. Heaved them on. Stumbled into the kitchen with his bandaged head pounding, just pounding. Where he'd gotten in the way of a fucking pickaxe handle. Put his hand up to it. Like a big diaper on his head.

Dredge fished in the encrusted fridge for a can of Cobra. Found one, opened it.

Man, his body hurt. He pawed his chest while he switched the can to his other hand, the one that didn't feel like all the fingers were broken. Under his T-shirt there was more diaper, where they'd padded up his ribs. That lady did a number on him. More Cobra.

On the kitchen table was a yellow prescription for Percodan. Either the doctor's handwriting was off, or Dredge was seeing bleary. There was an appointment slip for a follow-up visit.

That fucker Spider wouldn't even give him a ride home from Emergency. After all the abuse Dredge had taken. Motherfucker wouldn't even give him a motherfucking ride home. Still licking his wounds, too, him and Fritter. Up at Sky Londa.

What to do? Spider told him it was cool, Colleen Hayes wouldn't be getting out of jail, was going to take the rap for the Chinese kid.

But she was back. And so soon.

So he should focus, Dredge should, getting Eva out of Spider's mitts. He'd have to move quick. Get them both out of here.

It was up to Dredge.

He finished the Cobra. Got another one. Finished that too while he summoned what courage he had, if he had any at all, and thought about how he might get Eva out of the shed up at Spider's, patting his head, where they'd wrapped it like a big Q-Tip.

And when he finished thinking about things, he got another beer out. No more Cobras left, he had to reach back for a Mickey's Big Mouth, behind a carton of cottage cheese Eva had bought a while ago. Cottage cheese slash science project. The weak sun coming in the kitchen window was trying to burn through the heavy fog hanging in the air.

He checked the house next door while he slurped beer.

Didn't look like the girls were home yet. They'd left earlier.

As Dredge got a nice little heat-on from the beer, he thought some ice on his head might be a good thing. So he went to the freezer, above the fridge, yanked it open, only to find the ice cube trays empty and frosted with white freezer fuzz. A half-empty pack of Popsicles that Eva had bought. How he loved to watch her eat a Popsicle.

And there was a crumpled brown paper bag, in the back of the freezer, something in it.

What was that?

He pulled it out, and it was cold, and it shouldn't have been. It was hot as hell. Because he knew what it was.

But he opened the bag anyway. Just to confirm he was as big a fucking chump as they thought he was.

Spider's Pit Bull.

He checked it. Loaded.

But no doubt wiped down.

In Gramma's freezer.

Set. Him. Up.

Spider.

You.

Mother.

Fucker.

Now was the time.

Because he'd been a coward his whole life. So what if he wasn't ready, maybe Eva's mom being out of pokey didn't give him as much time as he'd of liked, but now was the time. To do it. Make up for all the shit. Make it up to Eva.

He finished the Mickey's and marched off to the garage. The fog was hanging, almost to the roof. He dug behind the boxes of Gramma's old clothes and rattan furniture stacked up crooked.

Ah yes, here it was, still wrapped in brown paper and string from Gun World. He ripped open the package, examined the box: Rossi Double Barrel Side by Side.

Very nice. He put the box down on his workbench.

Then he got his hacksaw out.

In the red plastic tray on the top of his toolbox he was pleasantly surprised by a small baggie with a decent dose of white powder lining the bottom. Some gack left over from a stash he'd forgotten about. He must have been as high as a kite. Not much, but enough to give him a temporary pair of *cojones*.

Dredge snorted a fat line right off the back of his hand and got to sawing. The saw made a whining noise, cutting the twin blue-steel barrels off the Rossi. Dredge read the box while he sawed, the crank actually making his vision a tad clearer.

Box said the Rossi SBS was similar to the single-barrel version. Only it had two. Plus it cost Dredge sixteen dollars more. But he always figured he'd use the extra barrel.

Take care of those little extras.

Like Fritter.

With the barrels sawed off, it was about a foot shorter but that still wasn't enough. So Dredge hacked the stock off, right behind the pistol grip. That shortened it down another nine inches. Made it easier to hold, too. He hefted the sawed-off in the dimness of the garage, bringing it up on the rattan chair stacked in the corner on some boxes, pretending

Spider was the chair. Making shooting sounds with his mouth. *Pow. Pow.*

Naw. Still too big.

What Dredge needed was some weed to smoke. Take the edge off this rattling speed buzz, the pounding in his head from that pickaxe handle.

Dredge put the Rossi back on the workbench, went back inside the house. None of the ashtrays contained a single roach. They'd cleaned them all out the other day when the cops had stopped by after Spider had thumped Eva around. Not one roach. So he figured he'd take a hit of codeine instead, maybe have another beer to wash it down 'cause codeine was a mite nasty and he had a sensitive palate. Schlitz Malt Liquor this time. Which he took out to the garage with him. He got the rest of the barrels sawed off, all the way down to the wooden forestock.

He held the weapon up, aimed at an imaginary bad guy. An alien invader.

Still too long.

He got the thing back in the vise, hacked the barrels down, right through the forestock, his arm aching and buzzing, bit of a butcher job, yes, but he got the thing down to less than a foot total.

Out of the vise the gun looked like a handle, two triggers and a pair of smushed nostrils over sawed-away bare wood. Dark holes where the fire came out.

Boom, boom, boom, boom...

Gonna shoot you right down.

Dredge sang to himself as he drank some beer and duct-taped the mini-barrels down and over what was left of the forestock so the barrels wouldn't come loose where he'd cut 'em down maybe a bit much.

Yeah, that worked.

Could hide it in your jacket, *mon*, and it would hardly mess with the stylish line.

Yeah, could even slip the Rossi down your pants. Baby.

One eye closed, Dredge aimed at various things around the garage. Practicing.

Then he loaded it up, knowing it was more than just the speed making his fingers like Jell-O. Trying to slip them fat twenty-gauge shells in. He was scared, that's what it was. Sure as shit.

But he was going to do it. With any luck, he'd get Eva out and not have to shoot anybody.

But if he had to, he was going to.

He slid the Squire into one of Pearl's saddlebags. Went inside Gramma's house with the last smear of crank. Snorted himself good and stupid, opened the last beer, sat in the shiny green armchair, drinking and listening to the Ramones belt out *Beat on the Brat* on the Sears Silverstone hi-fi at full volume.

Ready for the long ride up to Sky Londa.

Get Eva out of there.

CHAPTER 25

THE ROLLER COASTER emerged through wisps of gray, floating on the edge of Colleen's vision as the Cutlass' steering wheel reverberated up her arms. She held the wheel tight and motored into the basin of land in front of the Boardwalk, the old car feeling the roads.

Any elation she might have experienced about being let out of jail had evaporated. She had no weapon. As she drove into Santa Cruz, she realized she didn't have anything beyond the option to leave town before she was arrested for the murder of the John Doe that Moran spoke of.

And her twenty-four hours with Maurice were long gone.

The days in California weighed her down like bags of sand. She couldn't recall sleeping since she'd arrived. Her nerves were coleslaw. She needed an hour or two of sleep; she needed a shower. She needed a lot of things.

But Pamela needed more than that. Much more.

Colleen had to keep going.

She checked the clock on the Oldsmobile's dash. Still early. She'd head over to the Sea Breeze, where she'd rented a cheap room, take a quick shower before Laura and Justine showed up, if they even would.

She got a key from the desk clerk. Went upstairs to the dirty green door of her room facing the roller coaster. A vaguely familiar scent assailed her nostrils, a woman, not one she could place by name but familiar all the same.

She'd given Laura her room key.

Colleen ran her fingers through her hair. She must look like New York on a Monday morning. She knocked, lightly.

Footfalls padded over to the door. It slowly opened.

"I wondered who was out there," Laura said.

"Sorry," Colleen said. "I didn't think you'd be here yet. I just wanted to grab a shower, pick up my things." The window to the room was shut, as were the curtains. The lights were out.

Laura pushed the door back a foot, leaning against the edge. "Well, I'm glad it's you this time," she said, smiling sleepily.

"*This* time?" Colleen could see the bed unmade and rumpled sheets.

"The police dropped by."

"The homicide detective? Moran?"

"No." Laura shook her head. "Someone else. Grisset. Lieutenant Grisset." Laura brushed hair out of her eyes. "Lieutenant jerk. Some big cop with an attitude to match."

"Really? What did he want?"

"You, I think."

Colleen wondered how this Grisset had found her. Had she been followed?

"Don't worry," Laura continued. "He didn't know me from Adam. Didn't know I'd just been down to the station this morning. I told him I'd just taken the room." She squinted. "You're wanted? By the police."

For murder, no less. "Something like that."

There was a momentary silence.

"I don't get it. Detective Moran let you out. I was there."

"It's a long story."

"Well, aren't you going to come in? It *is* your room."

"You bet." Colleen came in.

"Grisset might have checked with the clerk downstairs," Colleen said.

"I doubt it." Laura leaned back against the door. "I didn't see anyone at the desk. Men like that think they know everything. That makes them sloppy."

Colleen realized Laura could give most cops—most men—the brushoff, if she wanted to. "Where's Justine?"

"Irene's," Laura said. "The babysitter's. I'm headed over there now. But I'm glad you're here. I needed to talk to you."

"About what?" Colleen said.

"About what you're planning to do next."

"Sky Londa." To the address Colleen had seen on the file folder in Moran's front seat. "Where those bikers have a place."

"To find Pam."

"That's right."

Laura nodded. "Maybe Detective Moran was right. Maybe you should just leave town. Maybe there's nothing you can do for Pamela. Maybe she'll come home someday."

"Maybe, maybe," Colleen said, pulling the crumpled pack of Winstons from her jacket. "But I'm going up there anyway."

"I'd like to say that I'm coming with you. After all you did for Justine. But I don't see how."

Colleen shook her head. "Justine needs you." She pulled a Winston out, put it in her mouth. "But thanks."

"Brad used to smoke those."

"Brad," Colleen said. "That would be your husband."

"Ex."

Colleen nodded. "I had an ex, too."

"*Had?*"

"Another long story."

"One I'd like to hear sometime."

"Where can I find you?" Colleen said. "When this is over?"

"Irene's—until I scrape up the money to find another place to live. I left the address on the dresser." Then Laura went over to the chair, picked up a denim bag. She unzipped it.

She came out with a shiny Colt Combat Elite, a big gun for a woman. The blue steel caught the light from the bedside lamp.

"It was Brad's," Laura said, holding it by the barrel. "I kept it under a loose floorboard, where Justine couldn't find it. For protection. The clip is full. I don't have any more bullets." She held it out. "Now it's yours."

"Don't you need it?" Colleen asked. "For protection?"

"Not anymore. We're moving on."

That gun was just what Colleen needed.

"I really don't want you to be involved in this," Colleen said.

"I already am."

Colleen took the Combat Elite, ensured the safety was on. "Then thank you."

"Have you ever shot anyone?"

"Not exactly."

"Not *exactly?*"

Where did stabbing her ex with a screwdriver fall? "Not exactly."

"Think you could?"

"Someone like Spider? For what he did to my daughter? No question."

"OK." Laura pursed her lips, nodded. "OK. I just wanted to make sure."

Laura left for the babysitter's house.

Colleen took a cat nap, refreshed herself, got up, showered, pulled on clean underwear, Levi's that had taken her shape. Found a clean T-shirt she had left in the dresser.

Then she went out, headed up to Sky Londa.

If Pam was up there, she was ready.

CHAPTER 26

DREDGE WAS sticky with sweat by the time he got to the top of the dirt road at Sky Londa. Sticky and wired. Spider's collapsing brown house seemed to be absorbing the shadows under the sprawling oak branches of the tree standing guard. From the dirt driveway, through a tunnel of trees, Dredge could hear the stereo, guitars buzzing under words of hate. He extinguished the FXR and rode Pearl silently down the drive. Five bikes were parked out front of Spider's, front wheels all slanting the same way.

He hadn't expected all the Dead Boys to be there. His pulse rate picked up. More than it already had been.

Near the house he slowed the bike down, his feet striking the ground in alternating strides as he guided the bike around the side of the house, past the hammering music coming out of an open window, Johnny Thunders tearing it up. To where the fifty-five-gallon drum was. Where they'd burnt the Chinese kid's clothes. Where the shack was.

Where Eva was.

Hopefully.

A strip of gray over the roof of the shack, under the tree canopy, showed the sky dying to the west.

Dredge pulled up, quietly eased Pearl over onto her chrome stand. The burnt wet ashes from the oil drum assaulted his nose. He pulled his helmet off gingerly, negotiating the bandage on his head, and dug into a saddlebag, retrieved the sawed-off Rossi. He stepped softly through pine needles to the shack's outdoor shower, where he and the Dead Boys had showered off after the Chinese kid. It felt like all that had happened in some other time, some other place. But it hadn't.

It was still happening.

The plywood door to the shack was padlocked with a heavy chain.

His heart sank. They key to the padlock was most likely with Spider.

He tapped on the door.

"You in there, Eva?" he whispered. "It's me—Dredge. They don't know I'm here."

He pressed his ear to the door.

He heard Eva. Her voice was muffled.

"I'm gonna get you out," he said. "I'm gonna get you out."

Bold talk for a guy whose heart was banging like an engine with a broken piston. Dredge shoved the sawed-off down inside his jacket. The pocket was deep, but the gun was bigger, and the grip stuck up past the lapel, hitting his chin. He jammed the thing down, ripping the fabric bottom of the pocket loose, forcing the gun down. That worked. It was a big bulky jacket, and he was a big bulky boy, and it hid the gun. Stepping quietly, he skulked back around to the front of Spider's house, dipping his big frame below the open window.

He heard there were places in Wyoming where you could buy fifteen acres for next to nothing. Maybe he could take Eva there.

When Dredge opened the front door, the guitars pummeled his ears, even with the bandage covering one of them.

Spider pulled himself out of an armchair and lurched to the door with a long silver pistol in his hand. Dredge jumped at the sight of it.

"What the fuck are you doing here?" All Spider had on besides the gun was a pair of grimy denims, his porno-star shades, and boots. No shirt. His chest was a blue-and-purple mottle of cuts and bruises, courtesy of Eva's old lady and the pickaxe handle. His scrawny face was beaten and puffy in places. Dredge didn't mind that.

"I wanted to check in," Dredge said. He eyed the pistol in Spider's hand.

"Look familiar?" Spider said. It was the Bernadelli the Chinese kid had had, up in the mountains.

"Waste not, want not," Dredge said. *Never mind you left the Pit Bull you shot him with in my freezer, you suck ass.*

"I thought," Spider said over the music, scratching his skinny, rippled stomach with the barrel of the gun. "I thought I told you to stay the fuck away."

Dredge saw Fritter slumped out on the sofa, his face purple from last night's fight, but obviously feeling no pain now. Sawney was passed out next to him, head back, mouth open. Beano was scratching his balls and Helmet was digging through a stack of albums. On the coffee table lay a bottle of Jack, almost half full, on its side, and an album cover of loose green leaf and a pack of rolling papers.

Next to that was a blue metal Smith & Wesson 38.

Maybe Dredge had overestimated his ability to handle the Dead Boys.

"Did you hear me, Dredgie?" Spider growled, holding the door. "The fuck is wrong with you, anyway? You look like you're out of your head."

"I'm ripped to the tits. You got a can of beer in there?"

"Where's your bike?"

"Stashed it. Up on the main road. I walked down."

"You sure no one followed you?"

"I'm sure." This was OK, Spider just a little worried.

Spider gave a tight shrug, pointing his oily nose forward. "No one? You sure?"

"No one followed me. Can I get a beer?"

Spider turned, marched into the house, left the front door open. Dredge shut it, tailed Spider.

The howling guitars finally surrendered.

A poster on the wall said How Much is the Oil Now, Asshole? A Marine on top of an Arab, holding a rifle in his face. On the coffee table Dredge saw what he was looking for, next to the bottle of Jack on its side, a small key on a thin rusty chain. That had to be the key to the padlock to Eva's shack. Spider clumped into the kitchen, Dredge behind him, a cat-urine-ammonia smell coming on strong.

The kitchen was in full production mode: rubber tubes snaking everywhere, even out of the stove, blackened up the front from a recent cooking fire. A paint bucket full of something sat on the floor. Canisters of white gas here and there. Bottles of acetone. Paint thinner. Battery acid, a road flare lying on the floor. Packs of Sudafed on the counter. The bandage around Dredge's head came half undone, hanging like a torn rabbit's ear. Uncle Adolf stared at him from the wall.

Dredge found a can of King Cobra in the fridge. He

drank half down, watching Spider rub his dirty thumbnail on his lower lip, his shades smudged.

"I got a call from Grisset," Spider said. "Some weird shit is going down. Some dude he works with is on the rampage. A cop named Moran. He let Eva's old lady out of jail this morning."

Dredge gulped beer. He knew that. He'd seen her. He crumpled the Cobra can.

Spider scratched his face, wincing as he hit a bruise, pulling the long dirty blond hair behind his ear: "The cops didn't come to your place?"

"No," Dredge said, fishing in the greasy fridge again.

"This pig Moran is likely to come after me. I got to lay low until Grisset finds him. So you need to book. Now."

Dredge grunted, opened the can of Cobra.

"OK," he said.

"You see those gooks at all? They come to Grannie's place?" Dredge almost'd forgotten about the Smoke Dragons. And the gold Mercedes 200.

"No," he said.

Spider leaned his scrawny butt on the table full of beer cans, making a black helmet roll back and forth like a kid's *tippee* mug. In the living room the stereo was blasting again. *Born to Lose*. Wasn't that the truth?

"Eva's old lady might show up," Spider said. "Her and that cop Moran."

"I thought no one wouldn't be able to figure nothing out, Spider, the way you did the Chinese kid."

"*We*, Dredgie. *We*. You keep forgetting that. Chop-chop." Spider made cutting motions with invisible bolt-cutters. "Time for you to blow now." He made a waving motion. "Bye-bye."

There was a pause while a screeching guitar solo tore through the kitchen wall.

Dredge took a long, long drink, killed the beer. "I'm gone."

Dredge left Spider in the kitchen, plodded on through the living room. Fritter was smoking a hit of ice through a light bulb, and Sawney was eagerly waiting his turn.

The bottle of JD was still laying on its side. Next to the key.

Dredge swung by the table as casually as could be, swooped up the bottle, along with the key on the chain, both at once. He'd done his share of shoplifting. He slipped the key into his pocket while he unscrewed the cap to the bottle, took a healthy, burning slug.

"I thought I told you to fucking jet, already," Spider said, standing at the kitchen door.

"Yeah, yeah." Dredge took another throat-scorching hit, capped the bottle, set it down upright on the coffee table. "Just thirsty."

Then he left, head buzzing afresh, the stereo discharging "Chinese Rocks." Johnny Thunders singing about needing a fix while his girlfriend cries in the shower stall.

Dredge lumbered up the dirt road, waited, caught his breath, out of shape and scared. Scared on too much speed and just plain scared.

And he thought about running.

But no. This time he'd do it differently.

He got off the dirt road, pushed through vegetation, branches hitting him like whips, and snuck back down to Spider's place.

CHAPTER 27

"EVA?"

No response.

Dredge pressed his ear against the plywood door of the shed. The wind was picking up out over the ocean. Even on a good day the sun rarely made it through the crown of trees out here, back behind Spider's decaying house.

Dredge would have to move fast before Spider and the others realized he'd taken the key.

The air smelled damp with coming rain.

"Eva?"

Dredge fumbled the key into the padlock, pulling the chain out of the holes as quietly as possible. Then he opened the door, quiet.

Didn't smell any too good in there. Dredge opened it wide. Let some air in. Or out.

He could see Eva in the door-shaped block of light falling into the hut. She was curled up on a cot in a fetal position, wrapped in the crumbling yellow moving blanket that had been in the back of Gramma's Country Squire. Mesh tatters spotted her tangled red hair.

She moved.

Thank God for that.

"Dredgie?" she said. "Is that you? Is that really you?"

Eva sat up, face gaunt. Beer and soda cans littered the floor around the cot, along with TV dinner trays, crumpled, congealing.

See? Gramma said. This is what it all comes down to. You pathetic, pathetic boy.

Dredge moved into the doorway, dwarfing the light.

He couldn't fathom how anyone could treat her this way.

Dredge went in, pulled the door shut, crouched by her cot.

He put a big leather arm around her, feeling her recoil at first.

"Eva, we're getting out of here."

Eva shook her head into his chest. "Yes," she said, nodding. "Yes."

She sat up, wiped her face, gave him a curious look. "What the hell happened to you? That bandage."

"Nothing."

"It sure doesn't look like nothing, Dredge. No more pretending, OK? We're *never* getting away from this."

"Shush, Eva," he said, standing up. "We're getting away from this. We are. I'll be right back."

Dredge crept back up to his bike ducking under the kitchen window.

He heard Spider talking on the phone.

"I told Dredge not to come up here, for fuck's sake."

Dredge stopped, flattened his bandage down with a hand to reduce his profile, raised his head at an angle, one eye peering through the corner of the kitchen window.

Spider was on the phone, the one hanging on the kitchen wall next to the poster of Adolf. A guitar solo spit from the living room.

"How the fuck do I know?" Spider said. "Dredge couldn't handle thirty days in Santa Rita. How you figure he's gonna handle questioning for murder? We can't leave him for Moran. I stashed the Pit Bull in his freezer. So how about you pick him up, twist his nuts off for good?"

Dredge saw Spider fumble a cigarette out of a pack on the kitchen counter. Spider lit it, phone cradled on his shoulder, playing with the book of matches. He pulled on the cigarette.

"OK, Grisset," Spider said. "We'll get rid of him now. Eva too. What the fuck."

Grisset, Dredge thought. That bent cop.

Spider hung up, dropped the half-finished cigarette on the floor, stepped it out on the linoleum.

Looked up.

Dredged dropped down fast, praying Spider hadn't seen him.

Spider thought he saw something, thought he heard something. He clumped over, looked through the bars of the kitchen window.

Dredge. Disappearing around the back of the house to the shed.

Spider thought he had split.

What did he think he was doing?

Taking Eva?

Did Dredge finally grow a pair?

Well, it only made things easier, really.

It had started to rain. That would make things messy.

Dredge hurried back to the hut, came in, pulled the blanket up around Eva, covering her neck, brushing yellow scraps of material out of her matted hair. Did he feel lucky? Spider had probably seen him at the window. He could hear the *put-put-putting* of rain on the corrugated iron roof of the hut. A little noise cover might actually help.

Eva had put her dirty white Keds on.

"Good," Dredge said, "You ready?"

"If you are, Dredgie."

"Eva," he said, "I'm gonna check if all's clear, and when it is, we're gonna sneak around the side of the house, where my bike is parked." Dredge pulled a key out of his leathers. "You know how to start up my bike?"

"Electric start, right?"

"Yeppers. Just put the key in, between the forks. Push-start button's on the right handlebar."

"Easy as pie."

"Think you can ride it out of here?" But he already knew the answer to that question, just by looking at her. Eva was frail. And Pearl weighed over seven hundred pounds.

"You head out there first," he said. "You start Pearl up, wait for me. Anything goes wrong, you just make a run for it, best you can. You got that?"

Eva nodded, taking the key, shaking in the blanket.

"Dredge, I'm scared."

Dredge stood up, pulled the sawed-off shotgun from his leather jacket. "No problem. I got this." He didn't want to say that the Dead Boys would be out there, soon enough.

"Shit, Dredge," she whispered in a screech. "Shit!" She

took a deep breath, let it out. "OK," she said. "OK. We got this. We got this."

"Copasetic?"

"Yeah," she said. "I think so."

Dredge broke the Rossi open, checked the two twenty-gauge shells in there for the umpteenth time. There were more in his jacket. "Eva," he said. "Let's do this: I'll stay here by the door and cover that kitchen window. You run around there, start up the bike. I'll be right behind you. OK?"

"OK," Eva said, standing up, wrapping the blanket around her tight. She was shaking. "OK."

She stepped around nervously in her sneakers, the key between thumb and forefinger. "Let's just go, Dredge."

The rain was starting to beat on the metal roof of the hut. Dredge edged over to the door with the sawed-off in one hand, pulling the door back with the other.

It was getting dark out there, the rain making it more so. He ventured out, peered around the side of the hut to the back of Spider's house. The kitchen light was on. Otherwise it looked clear.

"Eva—you got the key ready?"

Eva nodded, tight in the blanket, holding up the key to his chopper.

"Go," Dredge said. "I promise he won't get you. Not this time."

Eva coughed again.

"Come on," Dredge said, trying to control his shaking voice. "*Vàmanos!*"

Eva darted out of the hut, her white legs wobbly and thin, the yellow blanket leaving scraps in the air. She dashed past the outdoor shower, picking up speed, through the brush around the side of the house. The rain muffled her footsteps.

Dredge moved out, into the rain pelting through the branches. He had the sawed-off down by his side. He waited, giving Eva a moment to get clear, so he could cover her.

He moved out further. Rain hit his face.

The kitchen door creaked.

Spider and Sawney appeared, standing in front of Beano and Helmet, the light silhouetting the four of them. No Fritter. Even from the hut, Dredge could see the outline of Sawney's virulent grin. Spider was still bare-chested. Something glinted in his right hand. Dredge knew what that was. A shiver jolted up his back.

Spider saw him.

"You still here, Dredgie boy?"

"Just taking off," Dredge said, the sawed-off Rossi behind his back.

Beano spoke: "You're a bloody liar, mate."

Spider's hand moved. Dredge saw the light flicker off the pistol.

"Where's Eva?" Spider said.

"How should I know?" Dredge fingered the sawed-off behind his back. "Still in the hut, I guess."

"Bull-fucking-shit," Spider said. "You took the fucking key. You let her out."

Spider's hand came up, shaking.

A gun, real big.

Dredge whipped the Rossi out from behind his back and brought it up. No time to aim.

Boom!

The shot blew the window by the door into a thousand splinters, shattering fragments of light that spread into the kitchen. The Dead Boys hurled themselves back into the house, Spider and Sawney diving for the floor.

Missed! Fucking missed.

Dredge turned and ran into the rain, after Eva, slopping through wet pine needles, the bandage getting wet, flapping on the side of his head.

"Eva!" he screamed. "Start 'er up!" He tore around the corner of the house. "For Christ's sake, start 'er up already!"

Around the side of the house where he'd left the bike under a tree, Eva was there, next to Pearl, on the ground in the blanket, on her hands and knees, digging frantically through wet needles.

"Jesus, Dredge!" she yelled. "I dropped the fucking key! Jesus fucking Christ!"

Dredge crouched down next to her, chest lashing away. It was dark as shit. No way in hell they'd see a thing. Not a fucking thing.

"Keep looking," he said, getting up, heading back a few paces, jerking his head around to the front of the house. "I got us covered."

Eva scrambled on the ground around the bike, coughing again.

Dredge saw a figure come around the front side of the house, disappearing in the shadows of twisted branches, something long in its arms. Long blond hair trailing off its skull.

Fritter. Fritter, coming to get them. He had a rifle. Or a shotgun.

Dredge fingered the second trigger on the Rossi. One shot left before he'd have to reload.

Fritter came out of the trees, bald crown reflecting broken window light, holding up a pump action shotgun. He stopped, stood, legs apart, bringing up the weapon.

"Well, hello there, Dredge."

Dredge flipped the Rossi up. Mashed the trigger.

The blast ripped his ears as Fritter's blond hair smeared back into dark streaks. Clumps blew from one side of his head. Fritter landed on his back, rolled in the wet needles, screaming. Then he was silent. The blast hovered in the air for a second or two, teetering before it faded into strafing rain. Fritter rolled over, got on his hands and knees, panting. He crawled out, his head coming into a shaft of light from a window. His jaw hung loose. Fritter's hand clawed at the wet ground for a moment. Then he fell on his side; then he went still.

The rain came down.

Dredge stuffed the shotgun down the front of his leather pants. It was hot from the blast, burning his groin. He didn't care. He went back, scooped Eva up, threw her over his shoulder, her legs dangling over his back.

"Eva. Just hang in there."

"I will, Dredgie. Let's go!"

Dredge staggered off with Eva folded over his shoulder, heading west, into the sodden trees and leaves, down the hill that led to the black Pacific. In the darkness he heard shots, ringing out from the kitchen, Spider yelling for the others to move it. *Just move it.*

CHAPTER 28

THE BLACK SEDAN had been following her since Santa Cruz.

Rain was picking up. Colleen turned on the wipers.

She flew past the Highway 9 intersection, stomped the gas pedal around a curve. The black car disappeared behind her for a moment. She continued up 35.

But there it was again, in the rearview, right behind her.

Sky Londa went by as fast as it came, nestled in between the folds of the Santa Cruz Mountains. A mile or so to go, according to the address she'd seen in Moran's file.

But then it happened.

In the rearview she saw a hand come out of the window of the car behind, popping a plastic cylinder on the roof. Blue light swirled in the darkness.

A cop.

Colleen kept driving, thinking: could she outrun him? Should she? In Leon's crapped-out Cutlass? Maybe it was the only way to go.

Then the siren blipped, the sedan right up on her bumper.

She didn't have the power to get away.

Colleen slowed the Oldsmobile down into wet gravel by the side of the road, stopped, let it idle. She might be on a wanted list by now. She flipped the safety off on the Colt Combat Elite Laura had given her, racked a round into the chamber, nestled the gun under her right thigh. Out of sight from the driver's window. She hoped it wouldn't come to this.

A squat officer came up, puffs of steam in the starting rain. He stood at her window.

She rolled it down, looking straight ahead at the glistening road.

"You have any idea how fast you were going?"

"I've got to get to my daughter." Which was the truth. Colleen handed her driver's license over to the pudgy cop. She thought she was playing the desperate mom well, considering that's exactly how she was feeling.

"Just hold your horses," the officer said. Out of the corner of her eye, Colleen saw him stare at her license. "Colorado?"

"Please," Colleen said. "I just told you: my daughter..."

"Registration," the officer said, palm out.

Colleen gave him Leon Smith's registration. "I borrowed the car from a friend."

The cop took it, studied it with a flashlight.

The windshield wipers flapped back and forth, marking time.

Colleen had the Combat Elite ready. She didn't want it to come to this.

Then, finally.

He handed her license and registration back.

"Good luck with your daughter, ma'am. Stay safe."

Small mercies.

The sound of the Dead Boys thrashing the bushes rustled a hundred yards away.

Dredge and Eva were pressed close to the side of the hill, waves crashing on the rocks below. If you looked, in the near darkness, you could see white froth breaking. Eva was hanging onto Dredge in her cutoffs and T-shirt. Her soaking wet blanket had been discarded.

"Can't you fire at them, Dredge?"

Dredge had pulled the bandage off his head. His wound stung in the rain. "Soon as I do, they'll know where we are. Not a lot of hillside left."

Hillside, shit. It was straight-down cliff, and there were big rocks down there.

Way down there.

He could hear Eva coughing quietly, trying not to.

"Hang tight, Eva. The Dead Boys aren't Boy Scouts. They'll give up eventually."

"No they won't." She pressed her cold wet face into his neck. "You know they won't."

Dredge's heart pumped out of control.

"There's a place in Wyoming, Eva, where you can get fifteen acres for a thousand down."

"It sounds nice," she whispered into his neck.

"Doesn't it?" Dredge held onto Eva with one wet arm and checked the Rossi. He'd reloaded it with two more twenty-gauge shells from his jacket. He slipped the gun back under his wet T-shirt.

He could hear them yelling, less than fifty yards away, wild and excited, just like with the Chinese kid. Howling like dogs.

"Stay cool, Eva." He checked the sawed-off once again.

There was a cry of joy in the distance.

"Jesus," she said. "They found the blanket. Now they're going to find us."

"No, Eva," Dredge said. He peered over the top of the bushes to where the trees thinned out. The shrubs were lashing back and forth, the Dead Boys shouting. Dredge looked over to his right, to the south slope. Across fifty, maybe sixty yards of clearing there were more trees, thick ones. Could barely see 'em in the darkness. But they were there.

"Eva," he said. "See those trees over there?"

She moved her head away, looked, jammed her head back into his neck. She nodded up and down in a yes.

"That's where you run," he said. "I'll stay here, hold 'em off."

"Then what, Dredge? Then you follow me—right?"

Dredge put the shotgun down for a moment, carefully, peeled his leather jacket off. "Here, take this. It's wet as fuck."

"You sure?"

"Just take it." He handed the big jacket out to her. She slipped into it, lost inside.

"What's this?" she said, fumbling in the pocket. She came out with Spider's Pit Bull, the one he'd brought from the house.

"You know how to use that?"

"Spider showed me once. It almost knocked me over."

"Be careful."

She put the gun carefully back in the big jacket.

"You go on ahead," Dredge said. "I'll catch you up."

"Catch me up where?"

"Eva—just get out of here."

"Dredge, I want to say something ..."

"Please. If you get clear, Eva, get the hell away, find a road, people. There's a 7-Eleven just north of Spider's. Whatever you do, don't go back to my place. Ever? Understand?"

"What about you, Dredge?"

"I said I'd follow."

"Dredge..."

"Now!" he whispered. "Go!"

Eva half squatted, up, ready to run, then ducked down and turned to him quickly, pulling her wet stringy hair out of her face.

"I'm sorry I called you a coward, Dredge." Eva touched his arm. "I was totally wrong. And I'm sorry."

He felt his heart punch with emotion. "Eva—please. Go."

She reached over, gave him a wet peck on the cheek. Lit him up. The rain started to beat down, and Dredge saw Eva take off across the clearing, her skinny white legs in her white sneaks, her cutoffs droopy wet under his big black leather jacket, the one that said Dead Boys on it. Her hair was long and wet, hanging over the back of the skull with the reefer in its teeth. Running for all she was worth. Into the trees.

Then she was gone.

He knew he'd never see her again.

He could hear the Dead Boys roaring again, close enough to distinguish individual voices, Spider saying he wished he had them bolt-cutters.

Dredge checked the sawed-off one last time, both shells in there. He stood up, behind the bush, wet as wet could be and let one blast rip—*blam!*—off in the direction of the Dead Boys. It lit up his chunk of the mountain for a fraction of a second. He saw the Dead Boys ducking, then the light dying before they were all the way down.

"Chickenshits!" he screamed. "Miserable lame fuckers! Are you *blind* from doing too much speed? I'm over here, you fucking homos!" Dredge ducked down behind the bush.

A long silence. Dredge jumped up again.

"What are you—Dead Boy cocksuckers? Come down here and die, you asswipes!"

Dredge dropped back down. They were yelling again, beating the bushes. Shots rang out, zipping through the branches.

He waited for them to get closer, then leapt up again.

"Come to Poppa!"

He pointed the sawed-off at moving shadows, one eye closed, aiming as best he could. He let the shotgun rip. *Boom!* The bushes flashed and he saw the Dead Boys light up too, four of them, then they went black. But there *was* a scream. Someone fell.

"Shit! Dredge got Helmet!"

"All right!" Dredge yelled. "Al-fucking-rightie! *Shake-shake-shake!* Shake your bootie!"

Then they were bellowing again, getting closer.

He'd have time to reload, take one or two more out. Shit, he might even get out of this motherfucker alive ...

Then, with a twist of heart valve, Dredge realized. Eva had his jacket. The extra shotgun shells were in the pocket. He turned, saw the blackness of the Pacific, the rain coming at him from the clouds low over the sea. Dredge could hear their voices howling, close. *Close.*

When Eva heard the shots, from the Dead Boys up on the ridge, she ducked and cowered behind a shrub. They were shooting at Dredge. Why wasn't he firing back?

The Dead Boys were shouting. She peered over the top of the bush. She literally shook. She caught a glimpse of Dredge; he was on some rocks overlooking the ocean, just like she was.

She could see Spider, his wet hair slapping the back of his leather jacket as he ran along the ridge. Two others followed him: Sawney and Beano.

"There he goes!" Spider yelled. Dredge ran over to the other side of the crest. He didn't have a shotgun in his hand. Why not?

They had him cornered.

Arms vibrating, Eva raised the Pit Bull in both hands. The big gun was cold and wet and simply too much for her. She pulled the hammer back with her thumb. It hurt the soft flesh, hard and unyielding. She hated guns. They practically exploded in your hands. She aimed in the direction of the Dead Boys and tried to point at Spider and the others. The damn thing was shaking.

More shots echoed. They were firing at Dredge, laughing.

She had to draw them away.

Eva fired. The thunder of the shot slammed her eyes shut and the big gun kicked back and smacked her chin. It smarted. She felt something warm run down her jaw.

She peeled her eyes open.

The Dead Boys had stopped, turned, were looking her way.

With great effort, she pulled the hammer back with her

buzzing thumb. Raising the gun with both hands again, she held it straight-armed and tight so it wouldn't kick back as much this time.

And fired.

The Dead Boys ducked.

"Hey, boys!" Her voice was weak and thin, and she had to screech in order to be heard. She sounded like someone else. "You ready to go fry for killing those Mexicans? For killing that poor Chinese kid? Sure you are! Dead fuckers!"

She squeezed the trigger and fired again. You didn't need to pull the hammer back. She knew that now.

They turned, came after her. One of them fired and she found herself suddenly on her knees in the mud, gasping, holding on to the Pit Bull with one hand.

But she wasn't hit.

They were getting close; she could hear them talking.

"Eva can't shoot worth shit," she heard Spider say. "Keep going."

She turned and ran. There wasn't much to run to, just a couple of wind-bent Monterey pines out on a ledge over-looking the ocean. Her feet were cold and numb in the waterlogged Keds.

"There she goes!"

Heart slamming, she dashed out to the outcropping of rock overlooking the Pacific and slipped behind one of the pines. She squatted down, sucking wet air. She was scared, good and scared. Blood was running off her chin, dripping on her T-shirt under the jacket. It felt slippery. She wiped it off with the back her hand and readied the gun.

The Dead Boys were close, coming out.

"Put the gun down, Eva," Spider shouted in a teasing voice. "You know you ain't got no business trying to shoot that thing. Just put it down, babe."

She raked her head around the tree and squinted in the rain. Three of them.

She brought the Pit Bull up, squeezed the trigger with two fingers.

Bam!

All three of them flinched down.

She was close that time. She felt a thrill shoot through her.

"Going to prison!" she sang. "Going to *fry!*"

Spider brought a pistol up and fired at her. The bullet tore through the branches like a missile.

Shit! She ducked down.

"Hey, Eva—how many more shots you got left?"

A wave of panic overcame her. How many times *had* she fired?

Franticly, she dug in the pocket of Dredge's big jacket, looking for bullets.

And froze when her hand touched shotgun shells.

That's why Dredge had stopped firing. He'd given her his jacket. He was out of ammo.

She heard them coming for her. Slowly beating the bushes. They were maybe twenty-thirty yards away. She pulled the hammer back because it seemed steadier when she did that, rather than just squeezing the trigger, and came out from behind the pine, squatted, and fired.

Thunder.

Someone screamed. A British roar. Beano. She'd hit Beano!

"Jesus fucking Christ, Spider!" Sawney yelled. "She got 'im!"

"How about a little of *that?*" Eva said, dancing in her wet cutoffs and baggy leather jacket, waving the big gun and shaking her fist in the air. "How about a little bit of *that?*"

Sawney turned and ran into the trees.

But Spider, Spider looked at her, his eyes turning white. He raised his gun, stood there smirking. She slipped back behind the tree.

There was a shot.

It ripped through the branches, right next to her. Inches away.

"Yeah," Spider said. "And how about a little of *that?* I got plenty more of *that.* How much you got?"

She squatted, panting, the warm gun in both hands between her thighs.

"How many shots you got left, Eva? Me, I'm reloading. Can you say the same? You got my Pit Bull, bitch," Spider shouted. "I left it in Dredge's icebox. And I know I didn't leave any spare shells. What you down to? One shot? Yeah, one at most. That thing only holds five. How many times did you fire?"

Hands shaking, she turned the revolver, pointed it at her face, looked at it from the front, down into the cylinders. She didn't see any bullets. She'd fired a lot of times. So maybe she had a shot left.

And maybe she didn't.

"You got lucky when you hit Beano. You won't get that lucky again. So come on out."

"Go to hell, Spider!" she shouted, her voice cracking.

Bam.

Another shot tore through the trees.

Her heart raced like a turbine.

"Enough of this bullshit," Spider said, his voice closer. He was walking toward her. "Drop the motherfucking gun already. Or you're gonna get killed."

She sucked in a lungful of air, held it tight to keep her steady when she fired. She held the gun in both hands, jumped out from behind a tree.

There Spider was, walking towards her in his lion walk, not scared of anything.

He raised his gun lazily as he came toward her.

Grinning.

She squinted and fired.

There was a blast that kicked her gun sideways and pulled her with it. But she saw a piece of Spider's leather pants flap, right by his thigh.

"Motherfucker!" Spider spun and went down.

"Oh, dear!" she shouted. "You're hit, sweetie."

"Jesus Christ!" Spider was writhing on the ground. Then, "I can't fucking believe it, Eva. But I know you're out of ammo now. That was lucky! But you're a hard-luck case. That's why you ended up with us. The Dead Boys."

She squeezed the trigger.

Click.

Spider got up, hopping on one leg, laughing, pulling his wet hair behind his ears. "I heard that. I heard that, Eva. You're out of ammo. And out of luck, too."

He stuck his gun in the front of his pants, pulled a switchblade from his jacket. It slicked open. The thin blade looked white from a distance.

Spider smiled as he came limping toward her.

"You're gonna wish I shot you now, Eva. The Chinaman ain't gonna have nothing on you when I'm done."

She saw her short life flashing by. She had wasted it, thrown it all away.

Nothing was worse than Spider when he was angry.

Eva turned, ran. She slipped on a rock, fell, skinned her knee. It opened up and bled.

"Yep, you're gonna be begging to die," Spider growled.

She ran for where the rocks ran out, to where there was just gray rainy sky. And below that, waves crashing. But out there, in between the rain-filled clouds and the white-capped water, was sky. Just sky. Pure sky. And she was a bird. A bird that could take flight.

CHAPTER 29

THE RAIN WAS LETTING UP. It was near dark.

It took a while to find Spider's house. Colleen parked up the road, jogged down the muddy dirt lane, staying out of sight. Under an awning of trees, five Harleys were angled in front of the brown ranch-style house. Combat Elite in her waistband, she looked around. There was another motorcycle, a prettied-up gray chopper, the one she had seen in the driveway at 239 Delaveaga the other night. License plate: DREDGE. She knew him alright.

Colleen took a deep breath through her nose, nervous, anxious. Was she close to finding Pam?

She darted around to the front door. On the porch, quiet. No one home. Where were they? She checked the door. Locked. Bars on the windows. She slipped around back to where a urine-scented shack skulked behind the house, next to an outdoor shower. Piles of wet crates. A rusting fifty-five-gallon drum stank of something freshly burned. Colleen peered into the drum: wet ashes, charred rags. A recent fire.

Where were the dead boys, she wondered again. Where was Pam? Had she been here?

Up to the back door. Locked. But the kitchen window was smashed. Bars on it, too, blocking access.

The Combat Elite pressing into her lower back, Colleen scrambled up on top of the shack and hopped over onto the back of the house. Walking across the shake-wood shingles, careful to stay on the beams, because this roof was old, and the shingles were brittle. Dodging the low wet branches of an oak hanging over the house.

And there it was, just what she was looking for: a skylight.

She reached down, pulled at the metal lip of the skylight window. It wouldn't give. She stood up, put the heel of her shoe through it with a smash of glass.

She bent down, reached in carefully through the broken glass. Found the latch, soon had it open. Climbed down, hanging onto the rim of the skylight, her hands smarting, dropped into the kitchen, onto the counter, knocking bottles onto the floor, smashing a few in an ear-clattering frenzy. She clambered down to the floor and readjusted her Levi's after pulling the Elite.

Looked like a science project gone wrong. Smelled like one too. Bottles and tubes everywhere. A drug lab.

Poster of Adolf Hitler on the wall.

Gun ready, nerves tight, Colleen stepped through to the living room.

About five thousand bucks worth of stereo equipment, big black speakers hulking in each corner. Records stacked. A poster of a soldier holding an Arab prisoner. Nothing on the coffee table but a bottle of Jack Daniels, about three inches left. No dope. As dirty as Spider's place was, it was clean in an odd sort of a way. Cleaned up. That was it. Cleaned up.

Into a bedroom.

Nothing of interest in the closets. No dope, guns, or women's clothes that would fit Pam. Nothing.

Colleen went out back after unlocking the kitchen door. To where the fifty-five-gallon drum was. Up to the hut that stunk of piss. More agitated now; this shack just didn't seem right. The plywood door of the hut was open.

She went in, pitch black. Blinking to see.

She got a book of matches out, lit one up.

An old cot against the wall. A bucket in the corner, stinking of pee and worse. The match burnt the top of her thumb. She swore, shook the match out, lit up the entire book, the hut flashing with light.

And on the ground, in the yellow light blazing in her hand, a little strip of silver.

She didn't have to look any closer to know what it was.

But she did anyway. Blowing out the flaming matchbook, letting it drop to the floor. Picking up the silver earring, cradling it in her palm, stroking the beak as if it was alive, like she prayed Pamela still was.

The magpie, one of a pair. Now she had both of them back. She remembered buying them for Pamela for her thirteenth birthday.

Finally, a trace of her.

Here.

Here. Her daughter winding up in a place like this.

Salty tears singed the back of Colleen's throat. Flooding her eyes, stinging her cheeks. Couldn't wipe them away fast enough, so she let them fall, onto this piece of hell where the magpie had fallen.

A warm prickle of rage crawled up her back.

Sorrow would do no good. Colleen wiped her face.

Back into the house. Colleen dug through kitchen drawers until she found a black marker. Walked calmly into the living room, tearing the poster off the wall, writing on the wall in black letters, four inches high:

Spider—

You have until midnight tonight—Monday—to bring my daughter to the Boardwalk—alone. Any variation on this, and I go to the Feds. You, Maurice, Dead Boys, all go down. Harm her and I kill you myself.

Colleen Hayes

The Cutlass wouldn't start. After several tries, Colleen muttered to herself and sprinted back down to the house, picked out one of the bikes, an old oily beast. Key still in it. She knew bikes well enough, her ex had ridden, shown her how, long before everything had gone wrong.

CHAPTER 30

A PAIR of headlights drifted down Beach Street.

Detective Moran and Krieger watched from Moran's darkened LTD as the headlights swept by the Sea Breeze hotel. Krieger was looking nervous in the wee hours. A streetlight's misty beam crawled over the hood of the gold Mercedes as it slinked past the hotel high-lighting four men in the car. Going slow.

Moran unsnapped his shoulder holster. The four young heads watching the Sea Breeze, the Mercedes barely moving as it went by.

Moran pulled the Ruger out of its holster, flipped the safety off. Rested the gun against his thigh, ready to bring it up.

One face turned and looked at Moran and Krieger sitting in the LTD. Asian, high cheekbones, mean-looking. He spoke to the driver. All the faces turned to Moran and Krieger. Staring.

"Smoke Dragons," Moran said. "Lum's involved."

"That explains the tattoo on the Doe up at the site."

Krieger was breathing deeply. "But what are they doing here?"

"Looking for Hayes. This is where she was staying. There's a connection. Roll your window down, Krieger."

"Why?"

"In case I have to fire."

"*Fire?*" Krieger said. "What the hell, Danny?"

"I said '*in case*.' Just do it."

"You need to get a grip, Danny." Krieger hit the button on the armrest, melted back into his seat as the window wound down.

Moran squinted. He'd take the driver out first. Then the mean-looking one. Take them both out with half a clip. The other two would be dazed. He'd have the advantage.

Stay cool.

It was getting to him.

The gold Mercedes picked up speed. Moran made a mental note of the license plate. As he popped the safety back on, snapping the P-85 back into its holster, damned if he didn't see what looked like a perfectly good bullet hole in the trunk lid of the Mercedes. Recent. Anyone with a car like that kept it up.

The Dragons could tell he was probably a cop. They wouldn't care. Maurice's people wouldn't either. Lum's people, even less. They had their own cop. He knew the stories about Grisset. Flashy clothes. New Corvette. Grisset had been with San Jose Narcotics. Grisset had gotten rid of the domestic abuse statement on Spider. Moran had a pretty good idea where Grisset's money came from.

Krieger spoke: "They're saying things about you, Danny. That you're losing it. You let Hayes walk."

"You've known me a long time, Krieger. You know I had a good reason. Let's go."

They got out of Moran's LTD, went into the Sea Breeze.

The desk clerk at the Sea Breeze with the polished head didn't have too many qualms about giving out Colleen's room number. Moran did have the P-85 jutting out from under his armpit.

Moran said: "Is Hayes in her room?"

The clerk observed Moran, then Krieger in his red plaid shirt hanging out below his jacket, wide-eyed and jumpy.

"She in some kind of trouble?"

Moran wiped his face with his hand. "I said: 'Is Hayes in her room?'"

"No," the clerk said, hands on the counter as if that made him honest.

"Wait here, Krieger," Moran said.

Krieger's round face was unshaven and flushed, a sheen of sweat over it. "I don't know about this anymore, Danny," he stammered. "Those Dragon guys out there? I just don't know."

"Now's not the time to go soft on me."

Krieger didn't respond.

"Don't dare leave," Moran said. "I'll be upset if you do."

Krieger took a deep breath, gave a single nod.

Moran went upstairs.

"Are you sure that guy's OK?" he heard the clerk say to Krieger as he walked upstairs. Upstairs, Moran knocked on the door to Colleen's room. Muffled noises came from inside. He knocked again, louder.

"You know what time it is?" a woman's voice said.

"Police."

The door cracked open. Laura Quinlan held it a few inches from the jamb.

"Let me in," Moran said.

She stood back, opened the door.

Moran came into the room. It was like any cheap hotel room, even in the dark. Moran imagined a chintz bedspread and a print on the wall of some child with big eyes.

"Where is Colleen Hayes?"

"I don't know," Laura said.

"But you did at one time." Moran went over by the window. He stood by the single chair. "Would you turn a light on, please?"

The bedside light came on. Laura's profile was shapely and lean in the sheet wrapped around her. Her dark hair was tousled. Then Moran noticed Justine, huddled under the covers. He hadn't figured on her.

"What is your daughter doing here? What are you doing here?"

Laura sat down on the bed next to Justine, who shuffled up to sit against the headboard in her blue flannel night-gown, rubbing her eyes.

"It's too dangerous up on Delaveaga," she said. "You said so yourself. Colleen said we could stay here. We're waiting for her to find her daughter."

Moran processed that. "Is she planning on coming back here?"

"I don't know."

He pushed his glasses up his nose. "Is there somewhere else you can go? You need to go there now."

"What's going on exactly?"

"Colleen Hayes is in more trouble than she'll ever be able to get out of. Not only with the police, but with people far more dangerous."

"I've thought about what you said," Laura said. "And I'm prepared to have Justine testify to what she saw with the

Dead Boys. And with Justine willing to appear, that should help clear things up."

"And what would you have Justine say?" Moran waved his arm. "To *clear things up?*"

"Why—I'd have her tell the truth. I'd…"

"It's too late for the truth. I'm telling you that you and your daughter need to get out of here. Now."

"I'm not going anywhere. I'm waiting for Colleen. I told you, Justine will testify."

Moran moved to the middle of the room, put his hands in his pockets.

"With all due respect, Mrs. Quinlan," he said. "If you put your daughter on the witness stand, the attorneys the Dead Boys will hire will make mincemeat of anything she says. You don't want that."

"We're prepared to testify if it will help Colleen find her daughter," Laura said. "But not in the middle of the night."

"*We?*" he said. "There's no 'we' about it, Mrs. Quinlan. It'll be *her* alone up there, on the stand, and the defense attorney asking lots of nasty questions, tearing her to shreds."

"She'll testify."

"Until you decide she won't. Again."

"If it will help Colleen Hayes find her daughter, then we are prepared to…"

"She's not going to find her daughter," Moran said. "It's too late for that, Mrs. Quinlan." He raised his eyebrows, letting her know what had happened to Eva.

Laura's face went white.

"Oh, my God," she said, and started to cry. "Oh, my God."

"Now do you understand?"

"Yes." Laura wiped a tear from her cheek with her fingertips.

"My partner Krieger is going to take both of you somewhere safe," Moran said. "While I wait here for Colleen Hayes."

Laura nodded, wiping her face with the back of her hand. "Very well," she said.

CHAPTER 31

COLLEEN HAD STASHED the beat-up black Harley down on Cliff Street, near the Boardwalk. That had been a couple of hours ago. Around the beachfront now, there were minimal signs of life. She stayed in shadow, stamping her feet in the cold. A clump of drunken teens sauntered past the Casino Arcade entrance. One folded over and vomited into a trash basket.

"Bitchin'," one said. His eyes met Colleen's. "Who the fuck we got here?"

"Run along," she said.

The boys stared for a moment, then moved on, the puker straggling.

Colleen checked her watch. 2:25 a.m. Spider was late— if he was going to show at all. She knew it had been a long shot.

What now? What had become of Pamela?

Then the rumble of an engine caught her attention. A gold Mercedes approached. She ducked into a doorway. The sedan rolled by. Full of young Asian men. Things seemed to be coming together in an ugly sort of way.

Then she heard boots on the tiles, coming around the Casino Arcade. She stepped out with caution.

Medium height, heavy, in a brown leather jacket with a plaid shirt hanging out. Curly hair, eyes like eight-balls, round in fear.

"Who might you be?" Colleen said.

"My name is Krieger. I'm the County Medical Examiner. We've been waiting for you."

"We *who?*"

"Moran and me."

"What do you want?"

"You can't hang out here. Moran's at your hotel. I took your friend and her daughter to her babysitter's house. Moran needs to talk to you. If you stay out here, they'll find you."

"Who is *they?*"

"People you don't want to get involved with."

"I'll take the risk. I need to find my daughter —Pamela."

Krieger's mouth softened. "Please," he said, touching her arm. "It *is* about your daughter."

"She's dead," Colleen heard Moran say, as he gripped the steering wheel of the parked LTD. His voice was stiff with emotion. "I'm so sorry."

In the passenger seat, Colleen sat silent for what seemed an eternity. Her body became one huge knot of tension. She pressed the heel of her palm against her forehead, willing this not to be.

But it was.

"I'm sorry, too," Krieger said, sitting in the back of the car. "I really am."

Colleen felt hollow inside. All of her effort. Too late. For nothing.

Dead. Her daughter. And it was Colleen's fault. For killing Pam's father, going to prison, not being there while Pamela grew up. Her fault. How would she ever live with this? She was so physically tense her muscles were hurting, as if they might snap.

"Where is she now?" she asked.

"Santa Cruz County Morgue," Moran said, clearing his throat. "She was found on the rocks. Up near Sky Londa. She was medevacked after a Coast Guard helicopter spotted her. But it was too late. It appears she fell to her death."

"I was too late." Colleen's words seemed to echo inside her head.

"No," Moran said. "You did all you could, Hayes."

"We need to get to the morgue," Krieger said to Moran.

"What?"

"It's like this," Moran said, starting up the car, the V8 throbbing. "I'm not officially a cop anymore, but that doesn't mean I'm not still on this case." He nodded, as if to himself. "Yes, I'm on this. Krieger's going to let us into the morgue, while no one else is there, and you're going to ID your daughter. You'll sign a statement, then I'm going to arrest Maurice, the Dead Boys and whoever else I can lay my damn hands on."

"How are you going to arrest anyone?" Colleen said. "You just said you're not a cop anymore."

"They're not going to get away with this."

Washed out, Colleen felt devoid of anger for the moment. It was a new feeling for her. But it wasn't much better.

"If your daughter's death is to mean anything, Hayes,

then you have to help me. It's the only way we'll get any justice. It's the only way you'll come to terms with it."

He was right, Colleen thought. It would be heart-wrenching, but she had to go through with it. For whatever closure was to be had.

She'd have to see Pamela. Even if she was no longer alive.

"Yes," she said listlessly. "Yes."

The basement of the county morgue was cold, feeling all the more so for the dimmed lights. But even so, a hotness filmed Colleen's face, like a fever. She felt sick—inside. Krieger led her into the examination room, and Moran followed. Krieger shut the door.

In the shadows, Krieger headed over to the stainless-steel door of the walk-in refrigerator. He flicked on an exterior light switch and heaved back on the big iron door handle. The light from the storage room spilled out onto the white tile and the empty stainless-steel tables—and Colleen's barren thoughts. Her mind was a morgue, a storage room for empty, dead thoughts.

"It's more than my job's worth, bringing you guys here." Krieger's face, which had seemed normally round and expressive, was tense and drawn.

"We'll be as quick as we can, Krieger," Moran said.

Colleen remembered a time when Pam was four: she'd fallen off a swing and tore the skin off both knees. It was a nasty fall, one that Colleen felt vicariously, as she often did whenever Pamela was hurt. In her clouded thoughts, she recalled Pam looking up at her.

Am I going to die, Mommy?

No! Colleen told her. *Of course not!*

Not ever?

She didn't know what else to say. The truth could come later.

Not ever.

She felt Moran touch her arm, pulling her out of her memory. He led her into the refrigerated storage room. The air had a sharp bite to it, stinging of chemicals.

A gurney sat draped with a white plastic sheet. The body was small. Thin. Dirty feet with red chipped toenail polish were poking out from the bottom of the sheet.

Colleen braced herself for a lifetime of regret and anguish.

"Where did you say she was found again?" she whispered.

Moran said, "On a beach, below a ridge by Sky Londa. Near a biker house."

"Spider's."

"I believe so, yes."

Where Colleen had been, not many hours ago. But not soon enough.

"So I *was* too late," Colleen said. "Even then."

She felt Moran's hand on her arm again. "You can't blame yourself."

Couldn't she? She certainly could.

Krieger pulled the plastic sheet back, a delicate lift, revealing only the face, above the neck, trying to spare Colleen.

She stared in shock. At what she did not expect to see.

The look of dead peace, the fall from the heights sparing the girl's skull, thank God, if there was a god in the middle of all this anguish. A bruise graying on one cheek. A gash on her chin. The fluids collecting around her nostrils, the sand in the corner of her mouth.

At the dyed red hair, dyed, not natural, matted now, clogged, crusted with sand.

A twisted release filled Colleen's guts, along with tremors of guilt. Eva had suffered, suffered more than any human being should ever have to. But it was over.

"They called her Eva," Moran said quietly. "But her real name was Pamela—correct? Pamela Hayes?"

Colleen shook her head. "It's not her."

If this was relief, she would take it. A sick, guilty reprieve, but irrefutably better than the worst possible news. A discharge of emotions that left her numb.

But she would take it. Gladly.

Moran's mouth dropped open. "What?"

"We have to get out of here," Krieger said, pulling the sheet back over Eva's face. "Now."

"Hayes," Moran said. "—what the hell are you talking about?"

"This girl, Eva—whatever her name is," Colleen said. "She may be dead. But she's not my daughter."

CHAPTER 32

"SO WE DON'T KNOW who Eva is after all," Moran said, turning around to face Colleen sitting in the back seat of the LTD. Krieger sat next to him in the front, slumped over, strangely quiet.

Moran's words seemed to echo in her head, swimming in a mixture of grief and what might be called relief—relief because there was still hope that Pamela was alive.

Dare Colleen even think it?

She recalled San Francisco, a few days and a couple of centuries ago, Leon telling her that Pamela had changed her name to Eva Braun. A punk thing, he said. Perhaps more of a way to hide. Who was Eva? Did Leon even now? Who the real Pamela was?

To come all this way and only be confronted with more questions. Things she didn't know. And more heartbreak because Eva—whoever she was—was *somebody's* daughter.

The earrings. Colleen had found one in that wretched shack behind Spider's house. Half of a pair that Colleen had given Pam when she was thirteen. Justine had found the other in a gas station where Eva and Spider had fought. How did this Eva get hold of Pam's earrings?

Maybe Pamela and Eva had been friends.

Colleen's head was a rat's nest of thoughts, not sure of anything.

But Eva would—*could*, quite possibly—more than anything else, still lead Colleen to Pamela.

And Eva, whoever she was, deserved justice. Or what passed for it.

Retribution.

"Stop here, Danny," Krieger said to Moran. "This is the end of the line for me. I'm out of the loop from here on out."

This was not good news, Colleen thought, but this whole situation was out of control. It wasn't her call. She barely knew Krieger.

"Just a little longer, Krieger," Moran said as he drove. "I need your help. For just a while longer."

"You've gotten all the help you're going to get from me, Danny," Krieger said. "Stop the car now. I mean it."

Moran sighed and nodded to himself, pulling into a deserted parking lot where the red Medical Examiner's Blazer sat, collecting night dew.

"I never saw you," Krieger said to Colleen, opening the door. "I don't know you." Krieger got out, his fleshy face stern and distorted in the car's dome light. "You too, Danny." He slammed the door and trudged off, leaving Colleen and Moran in darkness.

"Krieger's a good man," Moran said in a murmur. "But he's not a cop. He doesn't have what it takes to finish this off. No one's got what it takes. Not anymore."

Puzzled, Colleen looked over at Moran. His eyes were out of focus. He was out on the edge.

They watched Krieger get in his red ME Blazer and

drive off. Moran opened the glove compartment, and Colleen heard the clank of glass and slosh of liquid as he pulled a pint bottle of liquor. It had been opened; about a quarter of it was gone. Colleen watched him twist the cap off and take a long gulp as if it was medicine.

"You better let me drive," she said, disheartened.

Moran downed another inch and shook his head.

"What the hell are we doing?" Colleen said. "Sitting here while you get blasted?"

"I'm finished."

"Yeah, that's the kind of talk that gets things done."

"I've been fired. Blocked. Stonewalled. But I thought there was a chance I could still pull this off. The way it should be done. Arrests. Criminals sentenced. But that's not going to happen. It's not."

Colleen didn't know how to respond to that. Maybe Moran was seeing it as it was.

But she wasn't going to stop now. There was Pamela. Out there, somewhere.

"If you want my help," she said. "You've got it."

"Let me ask you a question, Hayes. Have you crossed paths with the Smoke Dragons?"

"Who the hell are the Smoke Dragons?"

"Thugs who work for Lum."

"Another name I don't know. Who is Lum?"

"Underboss of the Hip Sing Tong, the triad trying to control Maurice, take over Santa Cruz. The Dead Boys are at war with him. They already killed four members of a Mexican gang that were working for Lum."

"I saw a car with four Asian guys drive by not long ago," she said. "There's your connection to Spider. And Eva died near his property."

Moran drank another half inch of liquor. "But that

doesn't explain how *you* got on Lum's radar. Why the Smoke Dragons were watching your place."

Colleen took a deep breath. "I've got something to tell you."

"Out with it."

"I took about a half a kilo of speed from the Dead Boys."

Bottle halfway to his mouth, Moran eyed her in the rearview mirror. "Why the hell did you do that, Hayes?"

"I needed leverage with Maurice. He owns a bar out on the pier in Santa Cruz: The Brass Rail. Pamela worked for him before she disappeared. I thought she came down here as Eva to hang out with Spider. I went to one of Maurice's other bars, in East Palo Alto. Met one of the Dead Boys, a guy calls himself Fritter. I pulled a gun on him and took his stash. And told him the Dead Boys could have it back when I got my daughter."

Moran drank some more. "Would have been nice if you had mentioned this when I stopped you on Delaveaga that day. I knew something was up."

"You used me as bait."

"So Maurice is in on this too. And Lum—somehow. One big happy family."

"See how many ducks you're lining up? That's why you need to see this through."

A car came down the street, music blaring in the wee hours. A funky guitar scratching.

The car passed. The music faded.

Moran said: "What's your connection to Laura Quinlan?"

"I gave her the key to my room at the Sea Breeze. So she and Justine could have a place to stay. Away from those dirt-ball bikers."

"Now it makes sense."

"What makes sense?"

"Spider beat Eva up, Justine saw it, Laura Quinlan reported it. Before you showed up." Moran took another slug. "Spider was arrested. Grisset got rid of the statement—the one Laura Quinlan made. Let Spider out of jail. I knew Grisset was connected to Spider."

"Yeah, Laura told me about making that report." Colleen knew Laura felt that she hadn't done enough.

"I thought Grisset was just working for Spider, but now I think it goes deeper than that. I think Grisset has bigger plans. Bigger than Maurice. Helping Lum move into Santa Cruz. Now Grisset is watching you too. And that means Lum. I'm driving you to the edge of town. Get as far away as you can. Out of the state to begin with."

"But then you wouldn't have any proof from me to back you up when you bust the Dead Boys. And Maurice. And Lum. And this Grisset. I know you have broad shoulders, but you can't nail half of Santa Cruz on your own."

Moran sipped from the bottle. "Your daughter had no part of this," Moran said. "You're done. You want to go back to prison? Because you will, if you're caught. I won't be able to help, not with my current situation. In fact, I'll probably be joining you. So you need to leave while you have the chance."

"*Eva* had a part in this. She was someone's daughter." Colleen wondered if Eva had anyone who cared about her. And Colleen needed to find Pam. Solving Eva was the only way she knew how to do that. And Grisset had to be stopped. Colleen felt that anger return, the needle rising on the dial of her emotions.

"I'm not going anywhere," she said to Moran. "If I'm ever going to find Pam, I can't stop now."

Moran turned in his seat. "You sure, Hayes?"

"Yes," she said, although she'd have to watch Moran. He was starting to crack.

"I already told the other cop Colleen Hayes wasn't here," the bald clerk at the Sea Breeze said. A magazine was open in front of him on the counter, a two-page shot of Farrah in her red bathing suit. Behind him, a radio played "Hotel California" at a low, late-night volume. They were playing the hell out of it, until people went out and paid a buck for the 45.

"What other cop?" Lieutenant Grisset said, although he had a pretty good idea. He put his badge in the side pocket of his taupe linen sport coat. "Small guy with glasses and a big nose?"

"And a big gun right here." The clerk indicated his armpit.

Grisset nodded, chewing the gum he should have spit out an hour ago. Moran wasn't going to let up. In fact, he was doing the opposite. Acting wild. Like pulling that damn gun on him. "Anyone with him?"

"Some chubby guy with curly hair."

Krieger. Moran's Medical Examiner buddy.

"Where'd they go?"

"They left with the woman and her kid."

"What woman? Not Colleen Hayes. You just said she's not here."

"No. I don't know her name."

"So you just let anyone crash at your *hotel*?" Grisset said with some edge. "*What* woman?"

"Pretty young thing. Had a kid. A girl. Called her *Jessie*? No, Juss. *Justine*. That was it." The clerk flipped the page on Farrah, as if covering up the fact he had it open in the first place. "I thought she was just a friend of Colleen Hayes."

Laura Quinlan. The one who made that damn statement Grisset got rid of.

Which could come back to bite him.

And then he had an idea.

"So you let the women slide. What'd she do, bat her eyelashes?"

"She was staying in Colleen Hayes' room. I had no reason to not let her go."

"Where did she say she was going?"

"I heard the kid say they were going to the babysitter's," the clerk said defensively. "They left a note. For Colleen Hayes."

"A note?" Grisset smiled. "Let me have it."

There was a pause.

"You'd best let me have it," Grisset growled. "You hear?"

The clerk reached under the counter, produced a folded-up piece of lined paper.

Grisset took it, unfolded it.

It was for Colleen. It had an address on it. Had to be the babysitter's. Grisset folded it back up, slipped it in his shirt pocket.

The clerk eyed him warily.

"You don't tell anyone I was here." Grisset put a business card on the counter. "If the other cop returns, I want to know. If anyone comes back—Colleen Hayes, the woman with the kid, anyone—you call this number, right away. My pager number."

"What's a pager?"

Grisset pulled his jacket back to reveal his Motorola Pageboy on the big belt of his checked flares. "It'll beep when you call it; you punch in your phone number. Then I'll call you back. And next time I come in here, I don't want to have to pull teeth to get information."

"Sure thing. Sorry."

Grisset pulled the stale gum out of his mouth, put it on the countertop. "Get rid of that, will you?"

CHAPTER 33

"IT IS ALMOST five o'clock in the morning," Lum said. "Where is Grisset?"

Lum cradled his teacup in his bony hands, sipping Sheng Puerh, tea that Maurice kept on hand just for his visits, costing as much per ounce as any speed or cocaine. Low light from the Tiffany lamp over the table in the Brass Rail flicked off his gold-rimmed glasses, highlighting the crow's feet around his eyes. Sio Lum, Dragon Master of Hip Sing Tong, was a trim seventy-year-old with a full head of dyed jet-black hair. He wore a boxy two-piece suit, like some guy fresh off the boat, and a gold Rolex on his wrist to counterbalance the look.

"Grisset should be here any minute," Maurice said, brushing his dark hair back over his collar in a quick, nervous motion. "Any minute."

But the truth was, Maurice didn't know.

They were sitting in the Brass Rail: Maurice, Lum, Maurice's bodyguard, and a couple of Smoke Dragons. Waiting for Grisset. Waves crashed underneath the otherwise empty restaurant at the end of the pier. Outside, fog blanketed the Brass Rail, obscuring the windows facing the black Pacific.

Things were starting to pile up on Maurice.

It should have been simple enough: Grisset told him about Colleen Hayes getting popped out of jail by Moran, Moran throwing a curve ball no one expected, caught them *all* by fucking surprise. They needed to cut her off at the knees. Enough was enough.

But Hayes wasn't at the Sea Breeze. Laura Quinlan had been, though, the woman who lived next door to that loser Dredge, with her kid. She had filed a statement against Spider. Which Grisset had gotten rid of. Then Moran had been asking around about it.

So Grisset decided he better go have a talk with Laura Quinlan. See if Hayes was there. If not, use Laura as leverage against this Hayes woman, who wasn't going to let the fuck up.

"Grisset is still looking for Colleen Hayes," Maurice said to Lum.

"The woman who stole the product from these Dead Boys?" Lum said the word *woman* with a hint of derision in his voice.

"Grisset's got her covered."

Lum sipped. "Perhaps."

"He does."

"And Grisset's partner?" Lum said. "Detective Moran?"

"He's gone. Fired. Don't worry about him."

"You say not to worry," Lum said, taking another sip of tea. "Yet every time I talk to you, there is someone new who needs managing. Someone else to be contained."

Maybe Lum's people could just step up, then, Maurice thought. But what he said was: "I know it seems that way. But it is under wraps." Maurice had to be careful. He was hanging on to what he had left by his fingernails. "If you recall, Grisset belongs to you—not me. But, for some reason, I'm the one on the hook."

Lum blinked as he held his teacup halfway to his lips. "Because it is those animals who work for *you* who started the disharmony."

"The Dead Boys?" Maurice shook his head. "They aren't *my* people. The Dead Boys aren't anybody's people."

"That's right, Maurice," CC, Lum's nephew, sitting next to Lum, said. His ducktail hairdo was freshly carved. "Try to back out of it."

Clifford, Maurice's guy, was cleaning his nails with a toothpick, but seemed to be listening to everything. "When you Dragons showed up on Highway 9, you tried to gouge the Dead Boys on the price. But you want to blame *me* for things getting out of hand?"

"*Out of hand?*" CC said. "My friend doesn't have a head anymore. Or hands." CC turned to Lum. "It's time for us to take over. Clean up this mess." He turned back to Maurice. "Because you obviously can't."

Maurice said to Lum, "Does he do your talking for you?"

CC sat back, glaring. He crossed his legs, foot bouncing.

Lum said quietly, "The arrangement by Highway 9 went poorly." He studied his cup, then looked up, fixing a steely gaze on Maurice. "Your Dead Boys went back on the arrangement."

"They were being overcharged."

"You let a *woman* rob them," Lum said with contempt. "Your tough Dead Boys. Now I have a man dead. I will have to make his parents a settlement." Lum raised his eyebrows above his gold glasses. "One which you will reimburse."

Christ, Maurice thought. All for some punk who ate fish heads with sticks. Maurice had to get out from under this. He needed some time to work things out. "First things first. If Colleen Hayes is around, we'll find her. And this renegade cop—Moran. Then we can discuss a *reasonable* settlement."

"He was my friend!" CC stood up, knocking his glass aside with a sweep of his hand. It landed on the floor and shattered.

"Then you make the fucking settlement," Maurice growled.

"You're out of business, man, just in case you haven't figured it out yet. *Finished.* You don't dictate the rules. I —*we*—do."

Clifford stood up, pulling open his jacket. The threat of his not-so-concealed gun was clear. "Just calm down, buddy," he said to CC.

CC laughed at him. "What do you think you're going to do? Shoot me? Who do you think runs things? Maurice? Look at him. Hip Sing Tong runs this area. This turf"—he pounded the table with a fist—"is *our* turf. You're lucky we let you work for *us*. But that can change."

Maurice shot up like a thick snake, his voice low and hard. "You don't tell me what to do! I had this town locked up when you were in diapers."

"Everybody will sit down," Lum said. He took a sip of tea.

Clifford waited, adjusted his jacket, sat down.

Maurice wiped his face. Then he sat down.

"This is our turf," CC said. "*Our* turf."

"Sit down," Lum said.

CC sat down, glowering.

Lum turned to CC. "You will treat this man with

respect. It is the way you will do business." He gave Maurice a dismissive wave.

A long moment went by while waves splashed on the pilings under the restaurant. CC's breathing subsided. "Yes, Uncle."

"As you can see," Lum said to Maurice, "My people are not content with what happened in the mountains. Such a killing brings unwanted attention. We are fortunate that the Santa Cruz police are understanding."

"I want this business behind me as much as you do," Maurice said.

"Then you will make the settlement I spoke of."

"Fine."

"And when this woman is caught, and this business over, you will get rid of these people you have working for you—this motorcycle filth."

Tell Spider just to go away. That was like asking a scorpion not to sting. "Understood."

"And you will grant us unlimited permission to work here."

"*Grant you unlimited permission?* You're putting me out of business."

"You have your other bars," CC said.

"I *had* Santa Cruz."

"No longer," Lum said.

Maurice went for his highball, picked up the empty glass. He slammed it down, staring hard out the window at the other end of the darkened dining room, the fog blocking in the pier. He was blocked in too. He needed time, time for Grisset to get the Quinlan woman. He needed time for Grisset or Spider to get to Hayes, neutralize her.

Then he'd worry about Lum.

Maybe he'd get Spider to take care of Lum.

Yeah, maybe that. Spider was good for some things.

Then Maurice thought he heard something. Something moving in the fog, outside the restaurant. On the pier.

A lone fisherman in a yellow slicker with the hood pulled over his head was hunkered down by the end of the pier, one side of the Brass Rail. A pole arced out over the railing in front of him, a length of fishing line stretching down to the water.

Moran and Colleen approached. Colleen had the Combat Elite jammed halfway in the pocket of her jacket, zipped up against the fog. Moran had the Mossberg down by his side.

"You need to move along," Moran said to the fisherman.

"Who the hell ..." the man began to say, looked over, saw the outline of the shotgun. "Sure, no problem." He reeled up his line quickly, picked up his bucket and tackle box, trotted off down the pier towards the mainland into swirling mist.

Moran peered around the front of the restaurant, came back.

"There's four or five people inside," he said to Colleen. "Sitting around a table. I can't see who, but my bet is most of them are who we're looking for."

"And?"

"And we're going to take them by surprise. And I'm going to take as many as I can in."

"How are we going to do that?"

"Follow me." The glint in Moran's eyes had an unnerving coolness to it. Colleen suspected he was starting to lose it.

A moment later Moran stood by a pair of heavy glass

doors with the bar's name etched on them where Colleen had been the other day. The opaque glass ran with moisture and the imprint of a hand where Moran must have rubbed the fog away to look inside. "Stay out of sight, Hayes. When the door opens, we'll move fast. We're outnumbered so there's no time to second-guess what they might do." Moran stood back, the Mossberg 500 Speedfeed in one hand. Colleen took a deep breath against her throbbing heartbeats, brought the Combat Elite out, moved off to the side. Moran beat on the door with the heel of his fist and stood back, into the mist.

Colleen sucked in an unsteady breath. She had to see this through if she wanted to find Pamela. And see Eva—or whoever that girl had been—avenged.

"Stand back," Moran said. "Be ready."

"That must be Grisset," Maurice said from the table inside. "Finally." Whatever the news, it would be something. "Clifford, get the door."

Clifford stood, pushing his chair back. Drawing his Sig Sauer, he strode into the darkened part of the bar to the glass door. He saw one figure at the door. Had to be Grisset. He pressed down on the push bar with his free hand, the gun in the other.

The door flew open on him, someone pushing it.

When the door unlatched, Colleen jumped out from the shadows, the Combat Elite in one hand, heaving the door open as Moran jumped in. He had the Mossberg ready. The guy at the door was the barman she'd met the other day. Clifford, that was it. A startled look crossed his face. He had a gun. In the back of the bar, Colleen caught a glimpse of three faces at a table under a hanging lamp. Light reflected off a pair of round spectacles.

"Lose the gun," Moran said to Clifford. "You are all under arrest."

"You and whose army?" Clifford said, obviously seeing only two of them, bringing his gun up.

Moran pumped the Speedfeed and the shotgun exploded into Clifford's midsection. He was hurled back onto the floor, where he immediately went still. The air echoed with the boom. Warm drizzle settled on Colleen's face. The shot thundered between her ears sending her nerves into hyperdrive.

Moran stepped into the dim bar area, bringing the shotgun up toward the table. "Hands up—all of you—and I mean *now*."

Colleen followed, saw Maurice, and an older Chinese man in glasses—that had to be Lum—and a young Asian guy, getting up from a round table, chairs scraping. Colleen kicked Clifford's pistol away.

Maurice's hands rose above his head. So did Lum's, eyes furious behind gold-framed glasses. CC raised one hand in surrender, but the other hand was reaching inside his jacket.

"Watch out!" Colleen shouted, bringing the Combat Elite up in both hands, firing off two shots. The gun jumped with each one and the Tiffany lamp shattered, and then the Chinese kid spun and staggered as the other two men— Maurice and Lum—dived into the shadows.

The Chinese kid stumbled but still began to reach into his jacket.

Moran fired the Mossberg. The kid twisted down to the floor as the table erupted into shreds, the air becoming a sea of fragments and buzzing noise. Maurice was crouching to one side, wide-eyed. Lum had lost his glasses and was stumbling toward the kid, his face nicked and bloody.

The Chinese kid lay on the floor, stone still. A slick of blood ran underneath him.

"Stay where you are." Moran racked the Mossberg.

The older Chinese man stopped, hovering on his haunches.

Scraps in the air settled to the floor. There was near silence for a moment, amidst the ringing in Colleen's ears. She fought to regain her senses. She hadn't expected the situation to go this far south this quickly. But it had.

Moran swung the shotgun on Maurice.

"J-just stay cool," he said to Moran.

"Frisk him, Hayes," Moran said.

Heartbeats thumping in her ears, Colleen went over to Maurice, patted him down with her free hand. "Clean."

"On the floor," Moran said to Maurice. "Face down. Hands clasped behind your head."

Maurice lay down, hands over the back of his head. Colleen stood by. She looked over at Moran's face in the half-light. His jaw was clenching, as if involuntarily. She feared he'd gone past the point.

Moran swung the Mossberg on Lum.

"We can negotiate," Lum stammered. "Name a price."

"On the floor. Next to Maurice. I'll ask once and once only."

Lum quickly got on the floor next to Maurice and put his hands behind his head. They were shaking.

Moran turned to Colleen. "You've got three minutes to ask them any questions you have about your daughter. Then I take these guys in. Three minutes."

If this was how Moran wanted to play it, she couldn't let it slip away. She'd come too far.

Colleen walked over to Maurice. Her foot was near his head.

"What ID did Eva use when she applied for the job at your bar in SF? The Hornet?"

"She gave me something that said she was twenty-one."

"Even though she was nowhere near that age."

"It was just for my books," Maurice said, voice trembling. Then, "Please, don't let this guy kill me."

"Be quiet," Colleen said. "What was the name? On the ID Eva gave you?"

"I don't even remember," he said, turning his head to look up sideways at Colleen. He gulped the words. "She wanted to go by Eva. Plenty of the kids use nicknames. I've still got her application. In my office. You can see for yourself."

"Where?" Colleen said. "Where is her paperwork?"

"Bottom drawer in the filing cabinet. Keys are under the bar—to the right. Office is behind the bar. Just don't let this guy kill us."

"Hurry up, Hayes," Moran said.

Colleen went over to the dark bar, behind it, found a set of keys sitting next to a small baseball bat. She shoved the Combat Elite in her waistband, found the office next to the bar, fiddled with the keys until she found one that fit the lock.

"You two," she heard Moran say to Maurice and Lum. "On your feet."

In a small office with a smeared window facing the lights of Santa Cruz, Colleen shut the door, put the Combat Elite on a desk next to a coffee mug that proclaimed WORLD'S GREATEST DAD, went behind the desk where she turned on a green banker's lamp. There was a picture of a younger Maurice in a tux and a Latin woman with a gorgeous smile, the whiteness of which matched her wedding dress. Colleen got down into a squat, opened the bottom drawer of the metal file cabinet and found the employee files. She flipped the folders, stopping at Eva B. No last name.

Colleen pulled the file, opened it. Her hands were shaking. Like the day she read her statement for her finale parole hearing.

There it was.

An application for waitress. Pamela Hayes, written in a childlike scrawl that wasn't Pamela's. Grandma's address in Denver, Colorado. A smudged photocopy of Pamela's Colorado driver's license. She was sixteen years old. But with a hard gaunt face, mouth turned down, preparing for a lifetime of disappointment. Damaged permanently by her father. And her mother. Sixteen going on seventy. Her birthday had been altered to make her a few years older.

Eva Braun had used Pamela's altered ID to get the job at Maurice's.

But no one ever knew Eva by that name: Pamela Hayes. Except for Maurice, and maybe he never really noticed, and certainly didn't care. Not even Leon knew what Pamela looked like, just the name she had used, the one she stole from Pamela. Colleen remembered; back when she went to the Hornet, showing Pamela's picture, and no one recognizing her. It made sense now.

Because no one had ever seen the real Pam. Just her imposter. Who became Eva.

Colleen folded up the application and photocopy of Pam's ID, stuffed the papers in the back pocket of her

Levi's. She prayed she hadn't left it too late. That she could still find Pam—wherever she might be.

She picked up her gun, turned the light off, went back out into the bar.

With a shock she saw no one was there.

The glass door was wide open, cold wet fog blowing in.

She went outside, her pistol ready.

Squatting on the wet rail were Lum and Maurice, their backs to the Pacific, gripping the wood banister desperately with white-knuckled hands. Like terrified birds afraid to let go of a slippery perch. Lum's face was a facade of pure fear. Maurice's wasn't much better.

Moran had the Mossberg pointed at them.

CHAPTER 34

LUM AND MAURICE CLUNG to the wet rail like terrified gargoyles. The fog blew around them in gusts. Lum's face was dripping with it, giving the appearance of tears. Without his glasses he blinked desperately. Maurice's hair blew in the cold wind.

Moran held the Mossberg on them.

"What the hell do you think you're doing?" Colleen said.

"Getting some answers," Moran said calmly.

She wondered how far gone he was. "What are you planning?"

"Taking these two down to Center Street."

"You sure about that?"

"If they don't give me any trouble," Moran said. "If you've got any questions left, Hayes, this would be a good time to ask. Otherwise I suggest you be on your way. There's not much I can do at this point that'll keep you from getting apprehended."

Moran had treated her fairly. He'd taken a huge risk in

letting her out of jail, done his best to get her some resolution on her daughter. That was her priority.

She eyed Maurice, clutching the rail for dear life. He wasn't exactly skinny, and it couldn't be easy, squatting on the wet wood in this weather. Lum, for his part, was faring worse. He was older, teetering on the rail.

"You've got to talk some damn sense into this guy," Maurice said.

"Stop him!" Lum said to Colleen, his voice breaking. "Please stop him!"

Colleen said to Maurice: "So you have no idea where Pamela Hayes is? You absolutely sure about that?"

"I'm telling you I didn't know shit about her," he gasped. "All I knew was that Eva had an ID that worked for the books. I knew it wasn't Eva's, sure, but I didn't even look at her application once I checked the date of birth on the driver's license. I actually felt sorry for her. That's it. I swear."

So Pam had taken off? That meant she was still alive.

Suddenly a blast of wet air blew and Lum's foot skidded sideways. He cried out, grabbing at the rail with curled fingers. He managed to grasp it, pulling himself back up.

"I can't hold on!" he gasped. "I can't hold on!"

"You don't have much time, Hayes," Moran said. "Ask Maurice about Grisset."

"Grisset?" she said. "The bad cop. What about him?"

Clinging to the rail, Maurice looked away.

"Tell her!" Moran shouted, turning the gun on Maurice.

Maurice hesitated. "He's looking for Laura Quinlan. And her kid ..."

A bolt of angry realization shot through Colleen.

"You had Grisset hunt down Laura Quinlan?" she said. "And Justine?"

"It was Lum's idea."

Colleen squinted at Lum. "Where is Grisset taking them, Lum?"

"You are not the police. You…"

"You don't want to argue with me," Colleen said, the pistol shaking in her hand as she pointed it at Lum. "*Where? Where* is Grisset taking Laura and Justine? Now!"

"He's taking them to Spider's house!" Lum gulped.

Images flashed through Colleen's mind. Crazy, mad images.

"It wasn't my idea," Maurice said. "Lum wanted you silenced."

"Maurice is lying!" Lum screamed. "He's lying!"

"No, he's not," Colleen said. She turned to Moran. "I need that shotgun."

"You're not going to Spider's," Moran said.

"Just give me that damn thing. I need it more than you do." Colleen waved the pistol. "We'll trade. There's at least one other gun inside the bar as well."

"Have it your way, Hayes," Moran said. They exchanged weapons. Lum shifted on the rail. Without his glasses, he was having difficulty seeing, maintaining his balance. Moran swung the Combat Elite on him.

The sudden motion caused Lum to start, and his fingers slipped off the wet wood. Lum scrambled to regain his grip but this time his fingertips slipped away. He tilted back, hung in the air for a split-second, as a silent scream crossed his face. Then he was gone. Into the fog.

There was a howl, followed by a splash, then the sound of water thrashing under the pier, Lum screaming for help.

Colleen narrowed her eyes at Maurice, still on the rail. Then Moran. "Maurice is your only living proof that

Grisset was involved with Lum. Don't kill him. I'm going to find Laura. And Justine."

"Do you really think you can do that alone, Hayes?"

"You just take care of Maurice."

"How are you planning to get up there? To Spider's?"

"I borrowed a bike from one of the Dead Boys. It's stashed near the roller coaster."

Moran took off his glasses, his eyes showing an unnerving steadiness. "You'll need more cartridges." He slipped his glasses back on, pushed them up his nose. "In my car. Under the seat. It's unlocked. And watch out for a gold Mercedes with a bullet hole in the trunk. It belongs to the Smoke Dragons. They'll be on the lookout for you."

"Thank you for all you've done."

"Don't leave me here alone with him!" Maurice screeched.

"He won't kill you," Colleen said. "He needs you alive."

Maybe.

CHAPTER 35

JUSTINE WONDERED why she hadn't heard the voice
for a while—the voice of the Bird Lady. She told herself it
was probably OK, it was just because she hadn't seen her.
Or maybe because Justine was at Irene's, the babysitter's.
And the Bird Lady wasn't next door anymore.

That's what Justine told herself.

But inside she sensed a different reason the Bird Lady
had stopped talking. One she didn't like.

Justine couldn't sleep.

From her bed—which was actually Irene the babysitter's bed—Justine heard Mom and Irene talking in the living
room. Mom had been crying at first, but Irene was making
her laugh now. They'd been up most of the night.

"You should get down on your knees and thank the lord
—whoever *she* is—that that butthole you married ran off
with that floozy," Irene said. "He set you free, girl."

Mom and Irene snickered. Irene was a big woman with
a big laugh.

"He's got rocks in his head," Irene said. "And most likely
a disease or two to go with them by now."

"*Shush*," Mom said, but she was giggling. Justine could hear a bottle clank against a glass. More wine was being poured.

"Watch the rug," Irene said.

Justine climbed out of bed, padded out to the living room, where Mom and Irene had their noses in wine glasses. Mom was on Irene's sofa with Irene, Irene in her big-ass muumuu. The jug of red wine was almost empty on the coffee table, and there was laughter coming out of the TV set. Justine had her six-legged spider under her arm.

"Justine," Mom said, coming up for air, slurry, her green eyes out of focus. "Back to bed. It's late-late, roommate."

"I can't sleep," Justine said.

"Why not?"

"I got scared." And the truth was, it was scary without the voice now when it had once been scary with it.

"Scared of what, Juss?"

"You know," Justine said, looking at the floor.

"I thought we weren't going to talk about *her* anymore."

"Shit, girl," Irene said to Mom: "Can't the poor child say what's on her mind? Way you lived over there next to that spook house, I'm surprised she *don't* be hearing things."

Mom drank a noisy sip of wine, eyes bleary. Metallic laughter barked from the TV.

Their laughter was broken by a knock at Irene's front door.

"Now who in the hell could that be, this late?" Irene said.

"I'll get it," Mom said, setting her glass down on the floor with a little red splash. She unfolded her white legs from under her. "Maybe it's Colleen. I gave her your address."

"You can't even stand, girl." Irene put her thick arms back on the sofa, pushed herself up. It was an effort. She ambled over to the door. At the door, she leaned over to it, said: "Who is it?"

"Police, ma'am."

"Police *who?*"

"Lieutenant Grisset. Santa Cruz PD."

Irene put the chain on the door, pulled it open as far as it would go.

"Better let me see a badge," Irene said.

"Sure," Justine heard the man say.

Irene peered through the crack. "And what's this all about?"

"A friend of yours—Laura Quinlan?"

"What about her?"

"Is she here?"

"Yes, she's here," Irene said.

"May I come in?"

Irene looked over at Mom. Mom shrugged.

Irene unchained the door, stood back.

A big man came in, wearing a jacket with a big tie and flared pants. His hair was blond and wavy, and his face was big and square.

He put his badge away and stared at Justine.

"Hey, cutie," he said with a pretend grin. "I could just eat you up with a big spoon."

That made her shiver.

"Don't talk to my daughter like that," Mom said, overlapping her words.

The man came into the room, eyed Mom.

"Mrs. Quinlan?"

"Yes."

"I'm going to have to ask you and your daughter to come with me."

"Is that so? Where?"

"Down to Center Street Station."

"Why?"

"It's about a neighbor of yours up on Delaveaga. You filed a report? She was the victim of domestic abuse?"

The Bird Lady.

"But it's the middle of the night," Mom slurred.

"It's actually morning," the policeman said.

"*Early* morning."

"It's an emergency."

"An emergency? It certainly wasn't the other two times we went down there to file reports." Mom pronounced the word *certainly* with a *shh* sound.

"I'm sorry about that, Mrs. Quinlan. But there have been developments in the case and I'm going to have to ask you and your daughter to accompany me down to the station to identify a man we have in custody."

"You let him out."

The Spider.

"Well, now he's back behind bars. And we need your daughter to identify him."

Mom shook her head. Her hair flipped about. "No one was interested in anything we had to say before. And I'm not driving my daughter all over creation at this hour."

"*I'll* drive, ma'am," the policeman said. "You've obviously been drinking."

"Then I'm not in the best shape to identify anyone, am I?" Mom said in a snippy tone. "You'll have to come back later."

"Ma'am, it's your daughter we really need. She was the witness to the event. Now, if you'll just cooperate ..."

"We're not going anywhere! And my daughter isn't going anywhere near that place again. She's had more than enough of this business. I'll come down sometime tomorrow —when it's convenient. Now leave."

The policeman put his hands in the pockets of his slacks. Change rattled.

"It's not really an option, I'm afraid."

"What in the *hell*?" Irene said to the policeman, hands on her big hips. She jutted her chin and boobs out. "Lady told you to leave, I reckon you best do as she says."

The man nodded, pulled his hands out of his pockets, flexed them.

"That's what you reckon, huh?"

"I sure as hell do. Now get out my damn ..."

The man punched Irene in her belly like his arm was a jackhammer. Justine jumped in shock as Irene doubled over, grabbing her stomach, started gulping, her mouth open like a fish, like she was about to throw up. Mom screamed, got up, wobbly as a deer, and Justine ran over to Irene, her heart throbbing, Irene woofing as she staggered about, holding herself.

"Maybe we should just start this conversation all over again, Mrs. Quinlan," the policeman said, reaching into his jacket, coming out with a square pistol. "I need you and your daughter to come with me."

CHAPTER 36

BY THE TIME Colleen kickstarted Spider's Harley back to life, her heart was racing right along with the motor. The sun was starting to claw its way through the fog curled across the Boardwalk. Smoke puffed from the tail pipes, swirling with wet vapor. She stuck Moran's Mossberg into a saddlebag, barrel first, and pulled the flap over as far as it would go, buckling it in loosely. The stock poked out. She couldn't ride around for long and not attract attention, not even in California. But it was not yet dawn and no one was out. She stomped the chopper into first, let the clattering clutch out, and twisted the throttle.

The burnt pipes roared down Ocean Street as the matte-black bike shot past a litany of cheap motels. She crossed the river at Highway 1, moving fast.

She'd head back to Spider's, praying he hadn't caught up to Laura and Justine yet.

Across the river, Highway 9 into the mountains. A mile past a BP station, the trees started to thicken.

Then Colleen thought she caught a glimpse of something in the handlebar mirror as she rounded the first sharp corner.

Seeing things. She'd been awake for hours.

No she wasn't.

Colleen leaned into another corner, faster, tires squealing, skidding just a little, and she came out of it.

Still there.

A car in the mirror.

Following.

A warm sickly prickle ran down her back.

Closer now; she could hear its engine. Not a cop. On the blurring road: a sedan, shadowy figures inside. A circular hood ornament poking up. Mercedes. The one she had seen earlier that morning. The one Moran had mentioned. Smoke Dragons.

The car whined up close behind her.

She shifted down and twisted the throttle, the Harley's slick rear tire sliding out in a squeal. The bike yanked her through another tight mountain curve.

But the Mercedes was right there again, engine bawling.

A Harley was a pig of a bike, and the curves wouldn't yield any distance. The Mercedes was close behind.

On a piece of straightway it pulled up alongside her.

She glanced left, caught a glimpse of the driver's face.

A young Asian guy. He grinned at her.

She popped the bike down into second, the engine shuddering, then screaming, then taking off. The woods broke and a ritzy neighborhood whipped by at seventy miles an hour.

Then it was back into trees again.

The air cracked behind her.

Guns. They were firing.

On a narrow strip of uphill curve, long enough to steer

the Harley with one hand, Colleen wrestled the Mossberg out of the saddlebag, eased the throttle, the chopper wobbling, unsteady.

A bank of trees loomed, the first turn after the straight-away. She eased into the middle of the road, riding the center white line, so they wouldn't be able to pass easily. She brought the shotgun up, resting it over her left forearm as she hung onto the handlebar with one hand. She shifted back up with her foot. She hoped they hadn't seen her maneuver the gun. Her blood was racing between her ears.

A pair of bright headlights up ahead blinded her. A van was coming straight for her. A face at the driver's wheel stared aghast. Colleen veered back to the side of the road, tried to hold the gun down.

Too late.

The van shot by, horn blaring, the whip of wind pulling her, throwing her back. *Hang onto the shotgun*, she told herself, fighting with the handlebar at the same time.

The air cracked behind her. More shots. Two? She shifted down, gears grinding, shedding miles per hour.

Let them pull up alongside her.

The Mercedes obliged, on her left now, engine wailing. Colleen looked over, saw the trees tearing behind the car alongside, the face grinning out the open window.

A large automatic rested on the sill.

She could see the kid's lips move. Then he smiled again, a nasty smirk.

Colleen hung onto the handlebar with her left hand and brought the Mossberg up with her right. The gun blew against her, and she righted it as the kid's mouth dropped into an O of surprise.

She squeezed the trigger.

Thunder.

The Mossberg kicked up, smacked her chin. Her head rang and her vision blurred. She fought to hold on. But the Mercedes squealed off to the left as the Harley veered off to the right. The shotgun fell away. Colleen grasped the handlebars with both hands, holding the bike steady, knowing if she didn't, she'd be a smear on the asphalt. She managed to straighten it out as the Mercedes hurtled straight ahead, bearing for a huge redwood tree standing guard at a curve.

Slowing the Harley down, she stopped, watched the Mercedes fly straight for the tree. The car plummeted off the road, bounced up, and into the trunk of the redwood.

A mighty crunch was followed by the sedan crumpling into a blossom of orange. Colleen placed her feet on the road to steady the rumbling bike, watched the flash engulf the car. Flames licked the trunk. Her heart rushed, blood filling her neck and head.

She spun a one-eighty and turned the Harley back to where the Mossberg lay askew in the middle of the road. She drove by in first gear, disengaged the clutch as she swooped down, wobbly, and picked up the gun with one fluid motion. Turning again, Colleen passed the burning car.

She could hear screaming inside.

Colleen shifted up into second, picking up speed, the fire behind her flickering in the rearview mirror.

Spider was next.

CHAPTER 37

THE BIG POLICEMAN slammed the trunk lid on them.

Everything went black. Mom held Justine close.

Justine couldn't remember the big man clearly, scared as she was; she couldn't recall anything very well in the dark trunk.

But she wouldn't ever forget him pulling a huge gun out of his jacket and making Mom and her leave the house. That's when Justine's heart started to thump in her ears. It hurt her chest, too, seeing Mom's face crumble.

The smell of oil and rubber shrouded them. Mom held Justine in the dark cold.

"Don't worry, Juss," she said. "It will be all right." But Mom's voice was wonky, and her skin was prickly and cold, like chicken skin.

They lay in his car trunk while the big man did something with Irene. Led her around to the back of the Irene's bungalow house. They could hear Irene calling him bad names as he took her away. Then there was a loud bang behind Irene's house. Mom let out a soft cry. And then they could hear him walking back to the car. No Irene, just the sound of his shoes crunching in the gravel, then him whistling.

Whistling.

"What was that, Mom?" Justine said in a shaky voice.

"Shush, Justine, please, honeybun, shush."

Mom held her tight. Mom was kissing the top of her head, stroking her.

They heard the Grisset man walk up to the trunk.

He stopped.

"You two make one sound," he said, "you'll get what she got."

Mom squeezed her harder and she could feel Mom wanting her not to cry.

Justine heard the car door opening. He got in and the car settled down on his side. Then the car started up; then they were rolling, bouncing.

"This is because of the Bird Lady," Justine whispered. "Isn't it?"

Mom's mouth pressed up into her ear and whispered. "Justine—honey—you've got to think about one thing and one thing only: when this is all going to be over things will be better. You've got to be strong. I love you so much."

"Will this be over, Mom?"

There was a pause. The car hit a bump and they were shaken.

"Yes, honey, this will be over." Mom was shaking. "Everything is only temporary."

The big car bobbed onto a road and made turns and went up outside of town and Justine could hear the trees out there in the wind, going by. She didn't want to say she was scared, because then Mom would think she wasn't being strong.

"Where is he taking us, Mom?"

Mom held her head under her arm and patted her silky hair.

"Close your eyes, Justine. Think about the time we went to play pee wee golf. Wasn't that fun?"

And Justine wasn't quite sure why, but she almost felt like she did go to sleep for a while. While she almost went to sleep, she had that dream again, only it was more than a dream. The Bird Lady was running down the hill, it was steep forest, it was dark, and she was running through the trees.

The tires underneath the trunk were whirring, making her almost more asleep.

Then the tires stopped humming. There was dirt, then more gravel, chomping under the tires.

The car lurched to a stop.

Justine could hear voices—men's voices—familiar ones, coming up to the car, talking fast, swearing.

Mom was hugging her tight, not talking, not crying anymore.

A key scratched into the trunk lock and opened the trunk with a squeal, letting gray light flood in, bright because it had been so dark in the trunk. The arms of a giant tree were spiraling over the car.

"Well, lookee here," the Spider said.

Leering in, his dirty hair pulled back behind his ears. Behind him was one other Bad Boy, with the Grisset man who had hurt Auntie Irene. The big one from next door, who had a problem—the one with the ball of fuzz hair—Fridge or Dredge, Justine didn't see him.

The Bird Lady wasn't there either.

And Justine knew why she hadn't heard the voice anymore.

The Bird Lady was gone.

Her chest hurt and her head spun.

The Spider leaned in and put his bony hand on Mom's leg.

"Howdy, neighbor," he said. "How about dinner and a movie?"

Mom flinched her leg away.

Justine saw he had a blood-soaked dishtowel tied around his thigh. He had been hurt.

The Grisset man said: "You cut that shit out, right now, Spider. I mean it. This is just to get Hayes to hold off."

"Fuck you, Grisset," the Spider said. "Where they're going, it don't make no difference if I buy her a beer or not."

The other Bad Boy laughed, grinning like a pirate.

"Please," Mom said, sitting up in the trunk. "Do what you want with me, but let my daughter go." Justine felt Mom squeeze her. "Just let her go. Let her go now."

Justine saw the pirate one lick his cracked lips. Justine was shivering, out of control, and could feel herself needing to pee.

"Bonus," the pirate muttered.

"Hell, neighbor," the Spider said to Mom. "You're not in much of a position to bargain. Besides, I think I might like you better if you put up a fight."

"Touch her and I'll kill you!"

They laughed. Justine was fighting the need to pee, and it was getting the better of her.

"You sick bastards knock that off," the Grisset man said, but Justine saw even he looked a little scared.

"Shut it, Grisset," the pirate one said, shoving him away from the car.

"Fucking lowlifes," the Grisset man said, but standing well back anyway.

There was a sound, a motorcycle growling up the road.

"The fuck is that?" the Spider said, cocking his ear up like a dog, pulling his hair back behind it with a bloody finger. "I thought you said no other cops, Grisset."

"That's not the heat," said the Grisset man, turning to look. "That's going to be your buddy: Colleen Hayes."

The Spider said: "Get the bitches into the house."

CHAPTER 38

COLLEEN KILLED the engine and dumped the Harley in the bushes at the end of the dirt road to Spider's house. She pulled the Mossberg from the saddlebag and crouched down.

The road sloped downhill, untrimmed buckthorn reaching in from either side, blocking the road from the right more than the left, to the wood shake house submerged under the twisting branches of an oak tree. It was still morning and the air hung with fog and the darkness of the overgrowth prevented any real daylight from breaking through. She felt wiry and exhausted at the same time; she'd been up all night, and the altercation with Lum and his people had frayed her nerves.

She angled her head and listened. Nothing but the trees speaking with the wind.

Colleen headed left into the bushes, snaking through undergrowth, down to where she could get a better view of the house. While she surveyed Spider's lair, she loaded the gun back up with shells. Other bikes were still parked out front, in addition to a large white LTD sedan.

The trunk was open.

She craned her neck and saw the telltale chrome spotlight poking out on the driver's side. An unmarked police car.

The open trunk didn't bode well.

Colleen's heart milled as she thought of Grisset, the rogue cop, bringing Laura and Justine here. She tried not to think of Spider and the Dead Boys and what they might be doing right now. Her emotions twisted into ugly thoughts, wild anger fused with fear and desperation, and her eyelids flickered as she fought for control. More than ever, she needed to keep things in check, not lose it the way she'd done that day ten years ago when she'd killed her husband.

Because everything seemed to return to that day. She couldn't make the same mistake twice. Justine and Laura might not survive it.

She wound through the rest of the growth until she emerged from the bushes behind the Ford and squatted behind the open trunk, the Mossberg ready. Peering around the car, she saw the house, dark and still. But not empty. The faint thumping of bass and drums and squealing guitars throbbed from within.

A shadow appeared at a barred window.

Then the window screeched open.

The shadow spoke. "Who the fuck is out there?"

Colleen raised the Mossberg, aimed at the shadow.

Fired.

The air shook. The window shattered into a spray of tinkling glass.

A burst of semi-automatic fire rocketed from the broken window, spitting holes in the sedan's windshield, punching through the upright trunk lid. Colleen dived back for the bushes, her blood pumping.

"Hey, bitch!" Spider yelled. "Any more of that shit and I'm gonna start on the girl. And I mean the little one. Yeah, we got 'em both here, both of them. Just think on that for a while."

Colleen took a deep breath, poked her head around the scrub. She could see the shattered living-room window, but no Spider. But it wasn't easy to see. The front of the house was dark under the sprawling branches.

"Justine's a sweet young thing," Spider shouted. "You know that?"

An acidic discharge flooded Colleen's stomach. She needed to get in that house. Somehow.

But she needed to stay cool.

"Mom's pretty nice, too," Spider said. "Damn. I might just have to give the dog a bone."

Colleen had already been on the roof once, back by the kitchen. But it was a good thirty-forty yards away.

"Spider!" Colleen yelled. "I'm the one you want—not them. Take me. Me for the woman and the girl. Even trade."

There was a pause.

"Now you're talking," Spider shouted back.

"So let 'em walk."

"You must think I'm slower'n steam off shit, Cowgirl. Now let me just tell you how it's going to be. You're gonna throw that big-ass gun down in the middle of the driveway, then you're gonna put your hands on your head, then you're gonna walk out here, nice and slow, where I can see you. *Then* we're gonna trade."

"And let you shoot me? Let them go first, Spider. When I see them, I'll come out, meet 'em halfway. Otherwise it doesn't work."

"Well, I agree it ain't much, Hayes, but it's about all the

deal you got. So you just come on down, or it's no deal at all. Cause I got the ladies. And you don't."

Colleen tried to make Spider out by the window. *There.* There he was.

Her brain was working overtime, but not getting much traction. She bit the inside of her lip.

"Then just let the girl go, Spider," Colleen said. "When she's safe, I'll come on out. You have my word."

"Words don't work, Cowgirl. I'll tell you what: You just take your time and think about things. In the meantime, we're gonna have a little party with Mom here on the workout bench. When you think you've had enough, you come on out."

"Colleen!" Laura screamed. "Don't do it!"

"Well, God damn," Spider yelled. "Bitch appears to like you, Hayes. She's a fine-looking specimen and all. Once you get these shorts off. Jesus, look at that! Now that ain't too bad at all. Hayes? Here, I don't want you to feel left out."

A pair of denim cutoffs flew out the broken window. "So you just take your time, decide what you're gonna do. We got plenty to keep us busy."

Someone turned the stereo up. Guitars, thudding bass and crashing drums filled the air.

Colleen's head spun. She had to blot it out, the fury, put it on hold long enough to think things through. She crept back up to the top of the road where she'd left the motorcycle.

Back here, Spider's house appeared smaller, but it didn't diminish what was happening to Laura and Justine, happening inside Colleen's head.

"You're lucky I like you, Hayes," a voice growled behind her.

Colleen spun with the Mossberg.

Moran came out from behind a bush, the Colt Combat Elite in his hand.

"Jesus," Colleen said, lowering the gun. "Am I glad to see you."

CHAPTER 39

COLLEEN BUTTONED up Moran's blue work shirt, while Moran put on her old brown leather jacket. With Moran's medium frame, the two of them were close enough in size to pull off the costume switch. From a distance.

"This will be the only chance we get," Colleen said. "Just don't get too close. And stay around the back of the car, where they can't get a good look at you. Where you can get some cover."

"I still think I should be the one to go up on the roof."

Colleen shook her head. "I know the house better than you do. And you're a better shot than I am." And the blunt truth was that Colleen was younger and more agile than Moran.

"Run through it one more time, Hayes."

"You pretend you're me, distract Spider and the others. I'll climb on the roof, back of the house. Start a fire over the kitchen. Drive them out through the front of the house. Once the place catches they'll be thinking about saving their own skins. You be ready with your pistol. When they exit, I'll drop through the kitchen, make sure Laura and Justine get out."

Moran pulled the 45 Ruger from under his arm, checked the clip, punched it back into the heel of the gun, reholstered it. He pushed his glasses up his nose.

"It's risky, Hayes."

"It's the only real option right now. Otherwise the worst can happen to Laura and Justine."

Colleen picked up the gallon gas can Moran had retrieved from the trunk of his car. She had filled it halfway with gas they'd siphoned from the Harley. She checked her pockets for matches. She had checked twice already. Her nerves were getting the better of her.

"Here," Moran said, handing Colleen his handkerchief. "You might need this."

Colleen took the handkerchief, stuffing it in her back pocket. Moran picked up the Mossberg.

"Let's go." Colleen snaked down through the bushes along the side of Spider's house, the Combat Elite in one hand, gas can sloshing in the other. A relentless punk dirge plodded away on the stereo. She was close enough to hear Laura scream from the front of the house.

"You bastards!"

Justine was crying out for the Dead Boys to leave her mom alone.

It was unbearable. Colleen fought not to do anything rash. Once again, an eyelid blinked uncontrollably. She pushed through bushes until she was behind the house, making a wide arc around the back to where the shack was, where they'd kept Eva. Colleen uncapped the gas can. The pungent odor of gasoline assailed her nose.

The stereo went down, from ten to five maybe.

"Hayes!" Spider shouted out the living room window out front. "What's the holdup?"

Moran was playing for as much time as he could get.

Spider yelled: "Throw the gun out, Hayes. Like I told you."

Colleen crept up to the hut, shoving the Combat Elite into her waistband. She splashed a couple of pallets leaning against the back of the house with gas, then doused the wall by the kitchen.

The music screeched on.

Colleen kicked off her shoes and climbed up the pallets, using the slats like a ladder, the gas can balanced in one hand.

"Hurry the fuck up!" Spider hollered. "Throw the gun out or we start on the little one."

Hefting the can of gas gingerly onto the roof, Colleen scrambled up after it.

Spider shouted: "Now put your hands up, Hayes, and come out from behind that car." Moran must have shown himself, as part of the ruse.

Colleen stood on the shake shingle roof. It was old, brittle, dry.

"All the way," Spider yelled out the front window. "Where I can see you."

Colleen stooped under the branches that sprawled over the house, trying to remember where the beams were.

"Get the fuck away from that car, Hayes," Spider bellowed.

Colleen poured the rest of the gas over the roof, soaking the shingles. They absorbed the fuel like dry sponges.

"Where I can fucking see you!" Spider yelled.

Colleen set the empty gas can down and pulled the

book of matches from her pocket. She lit one up, realized how much her hands were shaking.

A puff of wind blew the match out. She flinched.

"If you don't get out here in five seconds, I'm shooting the woman," Spider shrieked.

Frantically, Colleen pulled another paper match, scraped it against the striker, lit up the whole book. She cupped the burning torch in her hands, letting it catch.

"Last chance!" Spider yelled.

Colleen dropped the fiery torch on the glistening shingles.

Woof!

A giant blue flame leapt over the back of the roof, shooting down the rear of the house. The hut popped and caught fire, snapping like a giant pile of kindling. Colleen hopped to one side to dodge the approaching fire, grabbed the branch of the tree overhead and climbed up.

The roof crackled. Flames turned orange as they took hold.

"Don't move, Hayes!" Spider yelled to Moran.

The rapid *crack-crack-crack* of a weapon erupted from out front. Just as Colleen had suspected: Spider had planned to shoot her regardless. She prayed Spider hadn't hit Moran. But Moran knew the score and was ready, armed with the Ruger and the shotgun.

The top of the house began to burn, the branches of the oak starting to pop. Her head swam with fumes and smoke. The heat of the growing fire made her break out in a sweat. Colleen pulled the handkerchief from her back pocket and tied it around her face, covering her nose and mouth.

"This is the police," Moran shouted. "Give yourselves up. You're surrounded."

The roof was a blaze beneath her. Colleen wiped dripping sweat from her forehead with the back of her hand. The bottoms of her feet were hot, her socks starting to smolder. She pulled the Combat Elite from her waistband and got ready to jump down through the skylight she'd broken.

Below, in the house, footsteps thumped into the kitchen. They stopped right below her.

"Spider!" a man's voice screamed. "The fucking house is on fire!"

The back door squealed open and from her perch in the tree Colleen saw a biker with short white hair and a beard running past the shed, arms pumping. She hadn't expected them to run out the back. But that was fine.

The man's back was to her. Colleen lifted the Elite with both hands, squinted, aimed. She squeezed off two rounds, two shots muffled by the rumble of the fire.

The biker spun and dropped in a dead heap by the fifty-five-gallon drum.

That didn't bother her.

More shouting. From the living room now.

More shots. Moran was firing as someone fled from the front of the house.

Through the roaring flames, Colleen heard a voice screaming below, in the kitchen.

"Those bitches are gonna burn to death, Cowgirl!" Spider yelled. "Burn that pussy!"

Two shots went off, zinging through the roof and tree branches. Colleen's intestines tightened into a knot. She pointed the Elite down into the fiery roof and jerked off three rounds into the kitchen below.

"Missed, bitch! Burn, pussy, burn!"

Colleen heard the kitchen door swing open again. Spider. And some other guy in leathers, some old bald geezer. They ran in the direction of the shack, Spider limping to one side, favoring one leg, the other with bandana tied around it. Colleen fired at Spider's skinny frame. Missed! Even with the bum leg, he was moving fast, zigzagging from side to side. She aimed at the bald guy running, squeezed the trigger. He arched back, arms up and out like a starfish, fell forward to the ground, still.

Colleen dropped to the burning shingles. They were hotter than live coals on the soles of her feet.

The roof collapsed partway underneath her. She sank down to the rafters, up to her crotch, and that hurt. For a moment her legs hung loose through the ceiling into the kitchen. The burning roof scorched her thighs. She heaved herself up, hair smoldering and burnt, and stepped over to the broken skylight. Eyes closed, she jumped into the house, gun in hand.

She crashed down onto the kitchen floor, tumbling to absorb the impact of the fall. The kitchen meth lab was engulfed in smoke. It would go up any second. Scrabbled up off the floor, gun in hand. She noticed a pile of wax paper packets on the counter. Dope for sale. She grabbed a few, stuffed them in her jeans. Part of the ceiling collapsed in a deluge of burning wood. Colleen dashed into the living room, a shower of embers spluttering behind her. The whistling of the fire and black smoke overwhelmed her. Her eyes stung with smoky tears. She hunkered down close to the floor, blinking to see. The living room was crawling with thick white smoke.

There was Laura, face down on a workout bench in bra and panties, hands and feet bound to the black metal supports with duct tape. Justine was furiously tearing at the tape on her mother's hands, tears streaming down her cheeks.

Colleen jammed the pistol in her waistband, rushed

across the smoky room, ripping the impromptu mask from her face. "Justine!" she yelled. "Get out of here! Now!"

"Mom! Mom! Mom!"

"Just do as I say, Justine!" Colleen pulled Justine off her mother. Laura's green eyes were wild with fear.

Justine sprung back to the bench like a magnet. "Mom! Mom!"

"No!" Again Colleen heaved Justine off. "Out the front door! I'll be right behind you with your mom. Promise."

It was no use. Justine wouldn't leave, hanging onto Laura's leg. Flames skulked across the floor. Smoke filled the bottom of the room like a deadly fog.

Finally, Colleen managed to rip the tape off Laura's ankles. A fingernail tore in the process, followed by intense pain. Laura's bare legs kicked wildly as she shook them free. Smoke billowed into the living room from the kitchen. Colleen ripped the last of the duct tape from Laura's wrists.

"Run!" Colleen shouted. "The kitchen is going to blow."

Laura leapt up, scooped Justine up in her arms, ran for the open front door. She fled out the door into the driveway with Justine.

Colleen followed, the doorway belching smoke behind her.

Two shots rang out from the side of the house.

"Get down!" Moran yelled.

Staying low, the three of them crouch-ran to the bushes, where Colleen broke away.

Moran had a big guy in a suit on the ground at gunpoint. That would be Grisset, who must have run out the front of the house.

Colleen glimpsed the top of Laura's head. Laura had Justine. Good. But she was visible.

"Laura, stay down!"

"Hayes!" Moran roared.

Two more loud cracks followed. The Dead Boys. The gravel sputtered with dust and stone fragments. Grisset was hugging the ground. Moran was stuck guarding him.

"Don't make me shoot you, Grisset!" Moran snarled.

"I won't," Grisset said. "I won't!"

Colleen raised her head, peered over to the trees out back.

Off in the trees, she saw the top of Spider's head. He pulled his hair behind his ear with a finger, looking around.

Colleen darted away. She didn't need any gunfire coming their way where it might hit Laura and Justine.

Another shot thundered through the branches.

Colleen stooped, pulled the Elite, aimed at the skinny shadow. She squeezed the trigger.

The shot went wild. The gun's slide racked back and open.

Empty.

Another shot exploded in the stones near her feet.

Spider stood up and pointed a big pistol at her. She ducked down. She couldn't have come this far and end up dying now.

But there was no report.

He was out of ammo too.

Yes.

"Moran!" Colleen yelled. "Cover me!"

Tossing the pistol, Colleen turned and sped toward the trees leading down the side of the mountain facing the ocean, where Spider was. In her burnt socks, the rocky dirt gouged the bottoms of her feet. Her lungs were heaving, her eyes dripping with tears from the fire. Her legs ached, shaking with spent adrenaline.

She saw Spider's silhouette spin and cut through the trees, disappearing into fog coming in from the ocean.

She stopped, lungs bursting, sucking air that wouldn't come fast enough. The soles of her feet were on fire, and she knew they were bleeding. Colleen bent down, hands on her knees, bracing herself long enough to regain some control. She had to keep going. She was spent. Nauseous. She needed a second wind.

She pulled one of the small envelopes from her pocket. Ripped it open. White powder fluttered into the breeze. What was left she tapped onto the back of her hand.

And snorted it up noisily, the smell of her singed skin filling her nostril as the bitter speed bit deep into her system. Heart valves knocked like an overworked engine running dry, but her exhaustion and worry faded as the drug's power kicked in. As unnatural as it was, it eased her nerves by setting them alight. She shot upright like a flag-pole, heart hammering away. A dark power overwhelmed her. Drug-infused blood rushed between her ears like a flash flood. She broke into a loping run, one without pain.

"You're a dead man, Spider!" she howled.

Her legs moved faster, as if they belonged to someone else. Her lungs filled with air. She entered the fog sifting through the trees. She felt as if she could run a marathon.

Spider was up ahead, hobbling on his bad leg. She was gaining on him.

Spider reached the edge of the trees. The ocean was stark and flat beyond. Spider turned to look back desper-ately as he limped along, and he lost even more yards doing that.

Colleen kept running, smashing her feet on the rocks. It didn't matter. At the edge of the trees, she stood, drawing in air, which reeled in her brain like a drug.

Spider staggered down toward the cliff.

"Run, Spider!" Colleen shouted. "Run!"

She saw him climb down the side of the mountain over bald rocks, moving slowly on his injured leg. Colleen caught up quickly, standing at the top of a jagged bluff. The side of the mountain down to the water was rock face, broken by small clumps of vegetation.

Spider peeled off his leather jacket, tossed it. It flapped off the side of the cliff like a wounded bird as he grabbed at stones, trying to work his way down. His tattoos caught the pale light. His skinny chest surged and fell. He let himself drop to a ledge with nothing but rocky beach a hundred feet below. He staggered on his bad leg, caught his balance.

He looked up at Colleen.

"It's over," she said. "No escape."

"Fuck you," Spider gasped, raising his fists. "Come and get me, bitch."

Colleen spotted a melon-sized bolder. She hoisted it above her head as if it weighed nothing, hurled it down. Spider danced to one side on a stiff leg and the rock smacked off the edge and bounced off, sailing through the air.

"That all you got?" Spider said.

Colleen found a fist-sized rock, aimed, threw it like a fastball.

Nailed him in the shoulder straight on. Spider recoiled, yelled. "Fucking bitch!"

"That's right, Dead Boy. Bitch."

Spider scrambled on down.

Colleen heaved another grapefruit of a rock, hit him in the back, yielded a crack of bone.

"Fuck!" he yelped.

She pressed her way down the rocks.

"Are you scared, Spider? Scared like Eva was?"

Spider was trying to lower himself over the last ledge of rock before the ocean, clinging onto a small tree stump poking out.

"Are you scared, Spider? Scared of dying?"

Colleen landed deftly on the flat shelf of rock jutting out into space. Spider's head was a few feet away now, his bony hands curled around the stump level with her feet, shaking as he tried to hang on. There was nothing but rock beach below and gray horizon behind him.

Colleen walked over. Spider clung to the stump above the cliff, eyes white with anger and more than a trace of fear.

"Look like you ran out of mountain, Spider."

"Help me up!" he rasped.

Hands on her hips, Colleen looked down.

"I don't think so."

Then she pressed the heel of her bare foot, the bloody sock worn through, onto the remnant of branch Spider gripped onto.

His face tightened with rage.

"What do you think you're fucking doing?" Spider pulled himself up half a foot, balancing his weight on a knee positioned in a crag of vertical rock.

"Where's Pamela?"

"Who?"

She pressed her heel down. The stump creaked.

"Pamela," Colleen said. "Pamela Hayes—my daughter."

"I don't know. Now help me the fuck up. This thing is gonna come loose."

"You never heard of Pamela?"

"What did I just say? No! Now cut that shit out!"

"Why?" Colleen said, pushing her heel down. "Why should you live?"

Spider gave a nasty grin.

"You don't have what it takes," he said.

"Beg, Spider." She pushed her heel on the stump. It creaked. "Beg for a few more seconds of miserable life."

"What the fuck!" Spider's knee slipped off its purchase of the cliff, and he twisted to one side, hanging onto the loosening branch.

"This is for Eva," Colleen said. She waved goodbye.

Then she jammed her heel down.

The stump tore loose from its tenuous hold in the rock.

Spider fell away, screaming, the loose root branch flying from his hands. His arms widened as he tried to catch air.

Somersaulting, seemingly weightless, until he landed on his back on the rocky beach down below. A *snap* wafted up after him.

Colleen stared down.

Like a broken doll.

"My back!" he croaked.

Colleen stared.

"Get help!" It was a tortured attempt at a scream, raspy and weak.

She shook her head from side to side.

Please!

An ocean wave washed up on the rocks, brushing Spider's outstretched hand. It moved weakly.

Colleen cupped her hands around her mouth. "Tide's coming in." Her words echoed off the rocks.

Spider's lips moved but his words had no sound.

Behind Colleen, up above, inland, a huge explosion shook the air.

The meth lab in the kitchen had blown.

Colleen turned and worked her way back up the cliff, slowly and methodically, until she got back to the smoldering, steaming house. A fire engine was sending a long arc of water over the flaming tree into the crumbling structure.

She found Laura in the back of the Santa Cruz County rescue truck, wrapped in a blanket. Justine sat on her lap, staring at nothing. Laura stroked her daughter's stringy hair. A paramedic with thick black eyebrows had a medical kit out.

"We gave the woman and girl a sedative," he said. "They're both in shock."

Colleen went out, leaned against the truck, everything catching up to her at once. She folded over, vomiting onto the ground. Tears seared her face. She stood back up.

Up at the end of the driveway she saw two black-and-white cruisers, cops talking to Moran. Grisset was in cuffs. Moran's one arm was limp, but he gestured excitedly with the other as he spoke. Even from a distance she could make out the wild look on his face.

She plodded up the hill, her legs spent. The cops put Grisset into the back of a patrol car.

"Thanks to you, Laura and Justine are still alive," she said to Moran. She eyed the back of the patrol car, Grisset, staring blankly ahead. "You got Grisset. You can make your case now."

"Let's hope so," Moran said. "But this wouldn't have happened without you, Hayes."

"Who knows?"

"Spider—did you get him?"

"No." Colleen shook her head. She didn't need another murder charge. "He got away."

The police officers looked at Colleen curiously.

"Which way did he go?" one said.

Colleen pointed through the trees, south. "That way."

"Let's go," the one cop said to the other.

Colleen saw the paramedic come out of the ambulance down by the house, looking around, as if for her. She walked down to meet him.

"She won't talk," he said. "The girl. Not a word."

EPILOGUE

Colleen watched Justine, who'd grown almost an inch, but who was still short for a child her age, help Moran's wife, Daphne, set the table for dinner. The sun was going down, and through the open windows you could smell the sea coming in, the aroma of ocean salt thrown off the waves. Justine kept her head down as she placed the plates evenly, her hair silky and neat, pulled back in a tail with a pink twist.

Hiding her face from a world that spoke.

Colleen wondered what Justine was going through. Since the fire she hadn't uttered a word, hardly looked another human being in the eye. Colleen had heard of people who didn't speak for years after a traumatic event.

Some never.

Moran was exonerated. The trial against Grisset was scheduled, and any charges against Colleen were dropped.

She had saved lives, helped solve numerous murders, and been pivotal in breaking up a drug ring.

Moran was retired off with a full pension. He kept an eye out on Justine, and her mother.

Colleen, if she could just keep her nose clean, maybe things would change for her. There'd been no word of Pamela.

Moran poured fresh drinks out in the sunroom over-looking the ocean. He handed one to Colleen and took a long gulp from his. His brief departure from alcohol was just that—brief.

"You leave tomorrow?" he asked Colleen.

"Yes," she said. "Back to San Francisco. I need to find work." She'd been working here and there as a waitress, whatever she could get. But she needed to move on. Find Pam.

"Well," Moran said throatily. "We'll miss you."

"Me too," Colleen said, clinking her glass against his.

Justine was sitting on the sofa, next to Laura, who held her. Justine stared at the sea.

"Maybe she'll talk while you're gone," Moran said.

"I'd hate to miss that, but I'd love to hear that it happened." Colleen watched Moran take another long slug, half finishing his drink, the sun disappearing behind him. His work was done.

"I've got some news for you," Moran said. "About Pamela."

Colleen looked up. "Pamela?" She'd almost given up.

"I just found out. Yesterday." He gave a sigh. "How much bad news do you need in one year?"

Her heart sank. "All of it."

"Missing Persons finally tracked her down."

"Where?" Colleen said. "Where is she?"

"Up near Russian River. Some commune, whatever they call them." He shook his head, took a long drink, finished it.

▭

Colleen pulled the used Ford Torino she had bought up to a sign that said God loves all her children – but not visitors!

"Come on," she said, leaning over, zipping Justine's jacket up for her. "Let's go meet Pamela." Laura had to register for the next semester and had no one to babysit for Justine. But Colleen was more than pleased to have Justine to herself for a day. Despite the sign, she was hopeful about her reunion with Pam and Justine felt like good luck.

Justine looked up now, not smiling, asking Colleen a silent question. Colleen could almost read her by now. Better than her mother could, truth be told.

"Pamela's like a sister to the Bird Lady," Colleen said.

Justine nodded slowly and Colleen prayed she might say something. A word. But she didn't.

"In your own time," Colleen said, brushing Justine's cheek with a fingertip.

They got out of the car, the wind picking up, making strange noises over the open land facing the sea.

Colleen took Justine's hand, led her through the gate, pulled it shut, latched it.

The place looked like old farmland, grazing land, out by the ocean. They walked up the winding dirt road to the house. It was a big house, white slats and shutters, well maintained.

They didn't want Colleen there, the people in orange

robes who floated like ghosts through the house. The men had shaved heads.

But Colleen insisted. More than insisted. Threatened them with the police.

Colleen held Justine's hand while they waited in a white room. Eventually, the people in the robes came back with Pamela.

Colleen looked at her daughter for the first time in ... how many years?

Pamela wore no makeup, no jewelry, just a robe and sandals. She'd been chewing her fingernails.

She had put on weight. That was a good thing. But her hair, her gorgeous red hair had been chopped into a ragged, reckless crew-cut.

Once Colleen got over the shock she saw Pamela's blue eyes were clear. But distant.

Vacant.

Colleen got up, her hope tempered by the withdrawn coldness in her daughter's face.

She stood back.

"Keep it brief," a man said. "Pamela's been through a great deal."

"Can we have a moment alone, please?" Colleen said.

"A few minutes," he said firmly. He pulled the white door shut and left her in the room with Pamela, and Justine, who sat on a white rattan sofa, staring at the wood floor.

"It's so good to see you, Pamela." Colleen hugged her daughter—or tried to. It was like embracing a mannequin. Again she stood back, rebuffed.

"Mother," Pamela said in a monotone. "That sounds so odd, doesn't it?"

"Not to me."

"It does to me."

Words hurt.

"You look well," Colleen said.

"I am better now. I'm becoming unobstructed."

"If you only knew how long I spent looking for you. What I went through. What others went through."

"Why ever did you do that?"

"Why do you think, Pam? You sent me a postcard. Six months ago? From San Francisco. Right before I got out of prison ... Don't you remember?"

"Yes, that's right. You'd just gotten out of prison."

"I came looking for you," Colleen said, "I..."

"Why? You killed my father."

"Yes, but ..."

"You never loved me."

"Now that's not true. That's simply not true, Pamela. I went to prison for you. I ... your father ..."

"You killed him." Her eyes flashed with latent anger. "You *killed* him!"

"You think I don't *know* that?" Colleen had to control her voice, stop it from rising. "Why do you think I did what I did, Pam?"

"He was my father."

"I couldn't let him get away with what he was doing to you."

A fleeting trace of awareness crossed Pam's face. She gave a sad little shrug. "But you didn't care about *me*."

Colleen choked back tears. "That's not true. Please don't say that."

"I'm not coming with you. Don't think that."

Colleen sighed. "When did all *this* happen?"

"This?"

Colleen waved her arm around the white room. "This."

"About the time I sent the postcards," Pamela said. "I needed to purge my past. It's part of the process."

Colleen recalled the postcard. She'd read it so many times:

I've made so many mistakes in so few years. I've used up my quota. I've found an answer to my problems. One that is final. Please understand.

"I thought you were going to kill yourself," Colleen said.

"In a way, that's what we do. We kill our old selves."

They stared at each other, Colleen searching for a trace of a lost girl. Where was she?

"I wasted your time," Pamela said.

"No, you didn't waste my time. Put your hand out."

Pamela blinked, as if considering that, then put her hand out. It seemed a begrudged effort.

Colleen reached out. And dropped the silver magpie earrings into Pamela's.

Pamela stared down at the birds.

"What are these?" she said.

"You don't remember? I gave them to you on your thirteenth birthday. You were never going to take them off."

"Did I say that?" Pamela continued to gaze down at the earrings. "Oh, I remember now," she said. "I gave these away. To my roommate. In San Francisco. She wanted them. So I said 'Yes. I don't need them anymore.'"

"Eva Braun," Colleen said. "Your old roommate. On Divisadero."

"Yes," Pamela said listlessly. "Eva. I don't remember her real name. She was one of those people who led me astray. A drug addict. She needed an ID to get some job in a bar. So I gave her mine. I didn't need it. I was done with it."

"Eva's dead," Colleen said.

"She was on a bad path."

"What about Leon?" Colleen said.

"Who?" Pamela said.

Colleen shook her head. "Someone who knew your old roommate. He thought *you* were Eva."

"Oh," Pam said. "Him. Another one who abused himself. He never really knew who he was either. Isn't that funny?" She actually smiled. "No one really knows who they are."

"I think I know who you are, Pamela. Even now."

"Don't call me that."

"What *do* I call you?"

"We don't have names. We don't need them."

"Everyone needs a name."

"I don't. I shed myself of who I was. Eva wanted to be who I was. She even treasured those silly earrings. Can you imagine? But that was such a long time ago. I've been through a great deal since then. I've been on a journey."

Colleen stared at her daughter.

"One thing I don't understand," Colleen said. "That postcard you sent me—from that bar—the Hornet. Eva used your name to get the job. How did you send that postcard?"

"Eva had a stack of them. They gave them to her. To hand out. I used them. To write to people. To tell them I was going away. On my spiritual journey."

Colleen had thought the worst. Suicide. At least she had been wrong about that.

"This is Justine," she said. "She's the daughter of a friend. A woman who lived next door to where your friend Eva lived."

"Eva was not my friend."

"Well, she certainly was at one point. Enough for you to give her your earrings. Your name."

"That was in the past."

Colleen bit down on her growing anger. "Pamela: everything that happens becomes the past. That doesn't mean it doesn't matter."

Pamela stared at her, blinking again.

"I can't see you again," she said. She handed back the earrings.

Justine kicked her legs against the rattan sofa and watched. She could see that Colleen wanted the cold young woman to come with her. Justine could see that. But she also saw that the daughter would never come, and Justine wondered why Colleen would even want her to. She was cold, and she wasn't nice to Colleen. But there *was* something familiar about her.

She reminded Justine of someone Justine heard about, or someone she had dreamt about maybe. She looked like she'd had pretty red hair at one time, but now it was gone. All gone. She reminded Justine of a bird, a bird that wanted to fly away. But she would never fly, because someone had cut all her pretty red hair off and she could not fly away now.

When Justine thought of that, she thought of the place she would go to sometimes, the place in her memory. Where the mountains were dark with trees and a pretty redhead woman ran down them, running from shadows. Sometimes the woman would talk to Justine, inside of her.

Inside.

Colleen and Justine walked back to the Torino, Colleen holding Justine's hand.

"What a washout," Colleen said with a sigh as she buckled Justine back into the passenger seat. "I'm sorry, Justine." Her voice was cracking but she got hold of herself. "I was hoping you two would get along like sisters."

Colleen turned away, resting her arm on the steering wheel, so that Justine couldn't see her cry. She watched the empty gray clouds over the ocean, past the house where her daughter now lived, searching for something. Anything. But there was nothing. Nothing but dead grey clouds.

"Don't cry," she heard Justine say.

Colleen turned to Justine, her eyes wet but open wide in surprise.

"What did you say, Justine?"

"Please don't cry," Justine said.

---

south of the border...

"Hey, mister—wanna buy a beer?"

Dredge looked up from his drunken slumber.

Sun blazing down.

Morning.

On the beach.

Mexico.

Yeah, Mexico.

More than a slumber, as it turned out. He'd passed out again, last night, on the beach.

He propped himself up on an elbow.

Man, did his head *hurt*.

He looked over at the tequila bottle in the sand. Dry as a bone. Even the worm was gone.

Tecate cans everywhere. The entire case—empty.

He stabbed his eyes to focus, up and down the glistening sand. A Jeep was parked, right up to the water. College kids, down for Spring break. Sleeping bags in the sand. He remembered helping them push the Jeep out of the water.

"Mister?"

"Sure," Dredge said. *"Una jodida cerveza."* His Spanish was getting pretty good. He sat up in his red floral beach shorts and wild green aloha shirt. Pink raw flesh frazzled.

"Two dollars."

Two dollars. Steep. But the Mexican kid held a dripping can of salvation right in front of Dredge's face, like nectar.

Dredge peeled out two wrinkled dollars from his fast-disappearing wad, but it did not matter.

"See you tomorrow morning, mister." Kid lugging his Styrofoam case on down the beach, sinking in the sand under the weight of it.

Dredge drank deeply. He did have a fondness for the stuff. Maybe too much.

Waves came rumbling in, splashing on a girl's feet as she strolled along the shore. Yellow bikini. She waved at Dredge.

He thought of Eva, the sight of her running through the trees that night. Away from Spider. Eva.

He couldn't save her. He had fucked up. Pure and simple.

He waved back at the bikini girl while he drank.

Should have bought two beers.

I know what you did, you filthy little boy.

"Yes, yes," Dredge said, crumpling the empty can,

tossing it on the growing pile. Establishing a little turf here on this beach. His spot.

He climbed to his feet, the almighty power of a fresh hangover hammering the back of his skull like a pounding brick.

But in the big scheme of things it was nothing.

Try hanging onto the side of a wet mountain all night, wondering if Spider and those motherfuckers were going to find you.

Which they didn't.

Where were his flip flops?

I know what you did to me, you pathetic little boy.

"Shut up, Gramma."

"Who you talkin' to, Dredgie?"

Startled, Dredge spun around.

His new buds, the ones who had driven their Jeep too far into the sand last night, needed help to push them out. Spring breakers.

"No one," Dredge said, shielding his eyes from the already fierce sun.

"Sounded like you were talking to yourself, Dredge."

"You have the best conversations that way, they say," Dredge said.

The one kid, from Long Island, with the frizzy hair, laughed through his nose.

"We're heading into town, Dredgie. Going to suck some breakfast beers down at the cantina. And you're coming with us."

Dredge couldn't remember their names.

"I'll meet you there," Dredge said. "I need the walk. Besides, I think I might need to puke on the way."

"Ha ha," Long Island said with a toothy grin. "See you there, Dredge."

"See you there, Dredge," said the other kid.

Dredge waved, stumbled away, shirt flapping over his big burnt gut. Head swimming.

Peace. He needed peace. So hard to find.

On the edge of town he heard voices singing. Gentle, soothing. Coming from a small white church, white reflecting the sun so bright it made his eyes water. Even so he was drawn to it and he headed over. The brown doors were open, and the voices floated out. *Cantemos al Amor.* Beautiful. Like a salve on his tortured soul. He hadn't been inside a church since he was a boy.

Maybe it was time.

He went in through the doors. The church was cool, and the voices echoed.

ABOUT THE AUTHOR

Born in the wilds of San Francisco, with its rich literary history and public transport system teeming with characters suitable for crime novels, it was inevitable that Max Tomlinson would become an author of mysteries and thrillers.

In addition to the Colleen Hayes series, he has written several novels set in South America, two espionage thrillers, and a paranormal comedy under the name of Max Radin that unveils the vampirism rampant in the music industry. He spends much of his time in a dark room writing about people who never really existed, doing things that never really happened. He lives with his wife and a big, nervous dog by the name of Dexter in San Francisco.

Check out the rest of the Colleen Hayes series, set in '70s
California:
Vanishing in the Haight
Tie Die
Bad Scene
Line of Darkness
Night Candy
https://maxtomlinson.wordpress.com/

REVIEW?

If you enjoyed **Whereabouts Unknown**, please consider leaving a review on Amazon, Goodreads, or the book site of your choice. Reviews really help authors get their work noticed. They don't have to be book reports; a few words do just fine. To authors, reviews are like gold. Many thanks!